A LOT OF BULL

The vet was staring at Kate's hair and she had to control an urge to smooth it back and explain that she'd just come from the gym. Besides, it was a little like the pot calling the kettle black. She couldn't do a thing about the heat rising in her cheeks, however.

Nick Martins, her duty sergeant, grinned unabashedly at her.

"Someone stole my straws," said the vet.

Kate stared at him, aware of the weight of her tote bag on her shoulder, the smell of the Tim Hortons coffee wafting over from the counter, the less pleasant but hopefully fainter smell emanating from her body.

"Your straws," she repeated blankly.

Behind the veterinarian's back, Martins' grin widened.

"It was actually the whole tank," said Charlotte helpfully. Kate wasn't sure, but she thought she saw a suspicious gleam in her admin assistant's eye.

Kate turned back to the vet. "Your tank."

He nodded. "I got a flat tire," he said. Seeing no understanding on her face, he continued. "On Highway 34. My spare died last month and I haven't replaced it yet. I got a lift back to Mendenhall to get the flat fixed, but by the time I got back to the pickup, someone had broken into the back and taken the tank."

"A propane tank?" she asked.

It was the vet's turn to look at her blankly. "Why would I have a propane tank in the back of my work truck?"

She was pretty sure they were both speaking English.

Martins finally stepped in.

"Chief, the tank contains plastic straws of bull semen frozen in liquid nitrogen. They're used to artificially inseminate cows."

"They're worth about fifty thousand dollars," said the vet glumly.

NOVELS BY THE AUTHOR

Mendenhall Mysteries series:

The Shoeless Kid
The Tuxedoed Man
The Weeping Woman
The Untethered Woman
The Forsaken Man

Backli's Ford
Ghosts of Morocco
Jilimar
Kirwan's Son
Obeah
On Her Trail
Shelter

THE**FORSAKEN**MAN

by

MARCELLE DUBÉ

FALCON
RIDGE
PUBLISHING

THE FORSAKEN MAN
Copyright © 2017 by Marcelle Dubé

All rights reserved,
Published in 2017 by Falcon Ridge Publishing
www.falconridgepublishing.com

Falcon Ridge Publishing
Cover image copyright © ysbrand via Depositphotos
Cover copyright © 2017 Marcelle Dubé
and Falcon Ridge Publishing

ISBN: 978-1-987937-16-9

ACKNOWLEDGEMENT

*My deepest gratitude to
Dr. Marion Anderson DVM, MSc
Equine Science Instructor at Olds College,
for her patience and grace in answering
my questions. Any errors or infelicities
rest squarely at my door, not hers.*

THE**FORSAKEN**MAN

by

MARCELLE DUBÉ

CHAPTER 1

There was absolutely nothing attractive about a sweaty, red-faced, middle-aged woman puffing on a treadmill.

Kate Williams, Mendenhall Chief of Police, watched herself bob up and down in the wall-length mirror and cursed the idiot who had thought setting mirrors in front of treadmills was a good idea.

Also reflected in the mirror were half a dozen men and women lifting weights, doing biceps curls and leg lifts, and running on treadmills just like hers. They all looked better at it than she did. In her defense, she preferred running outdoors. At least there she didn't stay in one place long enough for people to notice how she looked.

No one spoke, but the small gym echoed with the whining of the treadmill engines and the clanging of weights as they were taken off the stand or replaced. Beneath those noises were the regular grunts of effort from a few of the men.

It was barely past six in the morning, thank goodness, or there'd be many more people working out in Stan's Gym. The more people, the smellier the gym.

Stan's was one of four gyms in Mendenhall, Manitoba, population 16,514. Apparently, the citizens of Mendenhall liked to stay fit. Stan's wasn't her regular gym. She usually went to Fit 'n Fast on Hayes Rd. It was bigger, newer, and had more modern equipment. And it had a nice locker room and showers.

Her gaze strayed to the reflection next to hers. Rob McKell, her deputy chief, usually worked out at Fit 'n Fast, too. She hadn't asked him why he had switched, but she could imagine.

He didn't want anyone from his regular gym to see him like this.

She'd had to switch for a week two months ago while Fit 'n Fast underwent rewiring, and she'd bumped into Rob early one morning at Stan's. She hadn't planned to stay—Stan's was an old-school gym, with barbells and rubber mats, not even a sit-up board. Besides, she could tell that her deputy chief was uncomfortable having her around. But within a few days, the gym owner, Stan Harvey, took her aside and told her that McKell worked harder when she was there.

So she stayed.

McKell wasn't running. He was walking at a slow, steady pace, his face red and sweaty and lined with exhaustion and determination. He was younger than her by a few years, but the accident and shooting last fall had aged him.

She watched his legs. They weren't as strong as they had been before he took the bullet to the chest that almost paralyzed him, but they were getting stronger every day. Every time she saw him working out, a little part of her sent heartfelt thanks out to the universe.

They had thought they'd lost him, at first. And then they had thought he would never walk again.

"It's rude to stare," said McKell matter-of-factly.

Kate's gaze slid up his thin body to find his reflection looking back at her.

"Just admiring your technique," she said. "Slow but effective."

"Go to hell," he replied mildly.

Kate grinned at him. His reflection refused to look at her, but there was a small smile on his face.

"Don't you think it's time you dropped by?" she asked. In the seven months since the shooting and subsequent car accident that had nearly taken his life, her deputy chief had stayed away from the detachment. She knew he didn't want to appear weak in front of the constables, but if he was strong enough to work out, then he should start thinking about reentering work life, even if only part-time.

Kate suspected the hurdle stopping him was more psychological than physical. She had encouraged Samantha Paterson, the acting deputy chief, to call him occasionally to seek his advice. Hopefully that would help keep him connected to police life. He would have to make it the rest of the way himself.

He shrugged. "Maybe I'll swing by later this week."

Kate stifled a sigh. He'd been saying that for a month. Well, she couldn't force him. The doctors had said he was lucky to have regained the use of his legs, but that full recovery would take a long time. His body seemed to be recovering just fine, but his spirit wasn't.

They worked for a few more minutes until Kate judged he'd had enough, then she slowed the treadmill to a walk and then to a stop. He never stopped before she did.

She stepped off the machine, bracing herself with the handle against the momentary disorientation, and grabbed the towel hanging there.

"Right, well, I'll be at the station if you need anything," she said, wiping her face with the towel.

Rob nodded, then wiped his own face.

She suddenly realized that he was studying her reflection.

"What?" she said.

"You're looking a little thin, Chief."

Kate's eyebrows rose and her heart skipped a beat. This was the first time Rob had noticed anything or anyone beyond himself since the shooting.

She smiled at him in the mirror. "I had it to lose."

"No, you didn't," he said flatly.

Kate focused on her red-cheeked reflection in the mirror. Maybe he was right: she was looking a little gaunt. At almost fifty-five, losing weight quickly just deepened her lines. She looked severe.

She sighed.

"See you tomorrow."

* * *

Most of the snow was gone, and the early April sun definitely had some heat to it, but the wind was still bloody cold. Kate shivered as she hurried to her SUV. She had bought the Ford Edge last September after McKell's accident destroyed her Ford Explorer, which she still mourned. What had decided it for her was the fact that the Edge was a standard, which had charmed her. She'd learned on a standard forty years ago and she still preferred it to an automatic transmission.

She clicked her key fob to unlock the door and slid into the driver's seat with a massive shiver. She hated walking out of the gym all sweaty, but she hated showering in that tiny metal coffin even more. Stan hadn't renovated that gym in twenty years. She'd taken to showering at the detachment.

Stan's Gym was on Archer Drive, in the industrial area of Mendenhall. It wasn't even seven o'clock, but trucks were already out and about and workers were already making their way to work for the early shift. Kate stopped at the entrance to the gym's parking lot to let a delivery van with panes of glass strapped to its sides drive in, then pulled out into traffic.

Aside from the glass factory, the industrial section of Mendenhall consisted of a recreational vehicle rental business with behemoths locked inside a chain link fence behind the storefront, a car wash, a micro-brewery that was starting to make a name for itself in the province, and a couple of garages, one of which specialized in tires. It didn't take long to drive through to the Mendenhall Shopping Mall, beyond which was the downtown core.

The dashboard clock read 6:53. She had time to pick up coffee at the Tim Hortons on Main Street, then she'd be at the station just after shift change. A quick shower, then she'd read the log book while drinking her coffee.

She glanced at the rearview mirror, automatically checking what was coming up behind her, then found herself staring at her reflection in the mirror. Her eyes were clear and untroubled, and she realized that she was smiling. After a moment, she dragged her attention back to the road.

It had been a while since she'd felt like smiling. Between Rob McKell's brush with death, the disruption to her detachment, and her breakup with Bert, she hadn't had much to smile about. She looked around as traffic slowly moved into the more commercial part of Mendenhall. The grass was turning green around the edges of buildings, and the trees, mostly maple trees on this street, were in bud. Despite the wind, the thermometer in the Edge read ten degrees Celsius.

She had started to think spring would never come.

"Look at that, Kate," she told her reflection in the rearview mirror. "You survived another one." Her second winter in Mendenhall hadn't been nearly as cold as last winter, or as long. It had only felt longer.

Twenty minutes later, feeling a little self-conscious about her bedraggled appearance, she parked in her allotted spot in front of the detachment. Two of the squad cars were out of their parking spots, which meant that the constables on duty were out patrolling. A white truck, a Chevy Silverado with mud splatters all along the bottom and dents in the front bumper, was parked in the visitor parking stall.

She walked into the low-slung, wood-sided, post-World War II building, her tote bag hanging over her shoulder and balancing a cardboard tray securing coffee for herself, Nick Martins, who was on the duty desk today, and Charlotte Hrebien, the detachment's only admin support.

As always, the smell of boot polish, burned coffee, and damp wood greeted her. She let the storm door catch her on the butt so as not to have it slam, then reached back with her free hand to latch it. She wiped her running shoes on the horsehair mat, then looked up at the sound of low male voices.

She recognized Martins' voice, but the second one, while vaguely familiar, remained elusive. She started to move toward the duty room, then hesitated, remembering that she didn't look her best. Then she shrugged. What the hell.

She strode past the opening to the duty desk, where the duty officer usually sat on the elevated platform, and through the doorway on its right, into the duty room proper.

Martins and Charlotte were standing in front of the four battered desks grouped in the middle of the room, listening to a man who had his back to Kate. Martins glanced over the man's shoulder and nodded slightly at her but didn't say anything. He had been expecting her, of course.

Charlotte was writing in a notepad. The girl's hair now brushed her shoulders, having grown out from the short style she'd favored over the past eight months. She had taken to placing clips in the glossy brown curls to keep them out of the way and it opened up her face in a becoming way. As the only civilian employee of the Mendenhall Police Department, Charlotte wore whatever she liked to work. Today she had on a pair of plaid pants in muted tones of green and brown, and a button-up sweater in the same shade of green as the pants. It brought out the green of her eyes.

She looked up as Kate entered.

"Good morning, Chief," she said seriously.

The man who had been talking turned to look at Kate and she recognized him as one of the veterinarians in town. Macdonald? Jamieson? Some Scottish name.

He had a shock of graying, sandy hair in dire need of a trim, and hazel eyes. Attractive, in an outdoorsy, weather-beaten kind of way.

"Chief Williams," he said politely.

Damn it. The man knew her name—of course he knew her name; everyone in town knew her name—but she was no closer to remembering his. Charlotte, bless her, recognized Kate's dilemma.

"Chief, have you met Dr. Kendrick?"

"I think so," said Kate, setting the tray of coffees on the end of the counter, next to the log book. "Veterinarian, right? What's the problem?"

The vet was staring at her hair and she had to control an urge to smooth it back and explain that she'd just come from the gym. Besides, it was a little like the pot calling the kettle black. She couldn't do a thing about the heat rising in her cheeks, however.

Nick Martins grinned unabashedly at her.

"Someone stole my straws," said Kendrick.

Kate stared at him, aware of the weight of her tote bag on her shoulder, the smell of the Tim Hortons coffee wafting over from the counter, the less pleasant but hopefully fainter smell emanating from her body.

"Your straws," she repeated blankly.

Behind the veterinarian's back, Martins' grin widened.

"It was actually the whole tank," said Charlotte helpfully. Kate wasn't sure, but she thought she saw a suspicious gleam in the girl's eye.

Kate turned back to the vet. "Your tank."

He nodded. "I got a flat tire," he said. Seeing no understanding on her face, he continued. "On Highway 34. My spare died last month and I haven't replaced it yet. I got a lift back to Mendenhall to get the flat fixed, but by the time I got back to the pickup, someone had broken into the back and taken the tank."

"A propane tank?" she asked.

It was the vet's turn to look at her blankly. "Why would I have a propane tank in the back of my work truck?"

She was pretty sure they were both speaking English.

Martins finally stepped in. While he wasn't a particularly tall man, his thin, wiry build made him look taller. He had crinkly auburn hair, light brown eyes, and an overabundance of freckles that usually made her smile.

"Ma'am, the tank contains plastic straws of bull semen frozen in liquid nitrogen. They're used to artificially inseminate cows."

"Good grief," Kate blurted out. "Why would someone want to steal that?"

One of Dr. Kendrick's eyebrows rose and a half-smile formed on his lips. Now she remembered where she'd met him. Charlotte's beau was a veterinarian, too, and worked with Kendrick on a freelance basis. Charlotte had hosted a summer barbecue last year and invited everyone from the detachment, as well as Kendrick. He'd been dressed in jeans then and a tee-shirt. Today, however, he wore brown Carhartts—the practically indestructible heavy cotton pants that seemed to be the uniform of the working man around here. In deference to the cool spring weather he was wearing a fleece-lined black denim jacket over his plaid shirt.

"Depending on the bull," he said, "it can be worth a small fortune. Anywhere from thirty dollars to five thousand dollars. A straw. And there can be up to five hundred straws in a tank."

Kate tried to calculate what five hundred straws at five thousand dollars a straw might come up to. Millions. She blinked at the veterinarian.

At that moment, the telephone at the duty desk rang and Martins excused himself to answer it.

"How many straws...?" she asked.

"Fifty straws," said Kendrick. "Worth around a thousand dollars each. So, fifty-thousand dollars."

Holy...

"Mendenhall Police," said Martins just as the main door opened and closed. They all looked at the opening in front of the duty desk. Samantha Paterson glanced in as she walked by and did a slight double take at seeing so many people staring back at her. Martins nodded at her and she came around the wall and through the door into the duty room.

"What's going on?" she asked. She was in a little earlier than usual.

Kate shook her head and grabbed her coffee from the tray. "Stolen bull semen. This is Doctor Kendrick. He'll tell you all about it."

And then she beat a strategic retreat to the locker room.

* * *

By the time she came out, showered and uniformed, her hair up in its customary bun, and mostly caffeinated, the vet was gone and so was Paterson.

Charlotte looked around from her desk, her eyebrows raised, but Kate just smiled and went into her office. Within moments, she heard the clicking of Charlotte's low heels on the linoleum tiles of the duty room and looked up just as the girl—not a girl, really; she'd just turned twenty-six, after all—appeared in her doorway.

"How's Rob?"

Charlotte was the only one in the detachment who called McKell by his given name. Well, sometimes Kate did, too, but usually she called him by his last name. It had taken them a long time to build a working relationship. When she first got to Mendenhall to take the job of chief of police, a job that should rightfully have been his, he had been less than happy. That was almost two years ago. That first year had been a sore trial for her, culminating with getting shot. Accidentally, yes, but shot nevertheless. Still, that had been the turning point. McKell had started out as her nemesis and now she couldn't imagine running the detachment without him. But she still mostly called him McKell and he never, ever, called her by her first name.

"Slow but steady," she finally said. "He's going to try to make it in this week."

Charlotte sighed. They had both heard that before.

* * *

"Should we post it on the website?" asked Martins.

Kate had finished reading her emails and answering them, and had retired to the break room with what was left of her coffee and the log book. The sun streamed through the window, unimpeded by the budding oak tree that would cast welcome shade come summer. She sat on the battered, red leather love seat that Paterson had donated to the detachment last month, and luxuriated in the warmth of the sunbeam that lay across her lap. Martins had followed her in.

"Post what?" she replied absently. The log book entries were sparse, typical for a Monday morning. Sunday nights weren't known for their rowdiness, unless there'd been a hockey game that night. She frowned when she got to the log entry that detailed yet another break-in at the condo construction site.

"The theft," said Martins, drawing her attention. She looked up at him, puzzled, until she remembered. She almost groaned but stopped herself in time.

"Let's see what Samantha finds out," she suggested mildly. "Then we can decide."

Martins opened his mouth, clearly about to argue, but closed it at the sight of her raised eyebrow.

"Yes, ma'am," he said, and retreated back to the duty desk.

Kate sighed softly. A website. For Pete's sake. It had been Martins' idea. At first, she'd said no, but he had made a good case for it during one of their irregular staff meetings and Kate had seen a number of heads nodding around the break room. As acting DC, Paterson had committed to looking into it. A week later, she came back to Kate and told her that it was a good idea.

"We can use it for outreach," she said. "Post photos of people we're looking for, let Mendenhall know about anything that will affect them, and…" She looked up from her notes. "The citizens of Mendenhall can connect with us by email through the site."

"It'll cost money I need for other things, like equipment or training," argued Kate. "And someone will have to keep an eye on the damned thing and answer the emails. And who's going to update it?" she asked, warming to her argument. She shook her head. "We'll have to have training—I don't know, Samantha."

Paterson had looked at her, a faint smile on her face. "We're the only police department in Manitoba without one."

And so Kate had taken the request to city council and to her alarm, they had approved it. Now the Mendenhall Police Department had its own site, but fortunately it was managed by City Hall. All Kate had to do was keep the bulletin page updated and deal with the email.

She still resented the time it took, but apparently their website was a success. According to Martins, who constantly checked, the number of visitors had been growing steadily in the past four months. Charlotte kept an eye on the emails and forwarded the trickier ones to Kate.

A time sink. She should never have agreed to it.

Still. Maybe the theft was something they *could* post to the bulletin page. Someone must have seen the vet's truck on the side of the highway. Whoever stole the straws had to have come by vehicle—Highway 34 was busy in the morning with commuters heading into Mendenhall from neighboring hamlets.

While not strictly in Mendenhall city limits, the feeder road was part of the wider catchment area that the Mendenhall Police Department served.

If the thief pulled in behind the vet's truck, maybe someone would recall the type of vehicle. Maybe someone had seen the thief break into the back of the truck.

It was worth a try.

The radio in the duty room crackled. She thought she recognized Olinchuk's voice but couldn't make out the words.

"Hi, Chief," said Charlotte, breezing in. "I forgot to ask if you had a good weekend." She headed for the coffee pot.

"Yes," said Kate automatically, although her weekends were mostly like her weekdays, except that she didn't wear her uniform when she came to the detachment. "How was yours?"

"Fine." Charlotte finished pouring herself a cup and replaced the coffee pot. She leaned a hip against the counter and studied Kate critically.

Kate braced herself for the now-familiar remonstrations by her staffer to take better care of herself. But the girl surprised her.

"We went to see *Balconville* at the MTC on Friday night," said Charlotte casually. "You know, by that playwright from Quebec?"

Kate had no idea, but she nodded politely. She'd never been to the Manitoba Theater Center.

"We saw Bert," continued Charlotte, looking at her coffee cup as if it held tea and she could read leaves. "He was with a woman."

Kate's heart dropped five stories and bounced. Charlotte glanced at her and frowned. Kate finally pulled herself together.

"Really?" she said lightly. "How's he doing?"

Charlotte's frown deepened. "He looks like hell, too," she said bluntly. "I wish you two would figure it out before it's too late."

With that, she strode out of the room, leaving Kate openmouthed behind her.

For Pete's sake.

CHAPTER 2

The best part of her office was the big window that let in lots of daylight. When she sat at her desk, she had a view of the tiled roof of the Church of the Nazarene across the street, and above it, blue sky. Standing in front of the window, she could see the detachment's parking lot, the street with cars heading into and out of the downtown core, and the church itself.

She rounded the desk to her ergonomic chair. She had bought it when she first came to Mendenhall, to save her aching back. She sat down and stared at her cell phone, which she had left on the desk. Might as well call Mom before the day really got started.

A moment later, she held the cell phone against her ear and listened to the ring tone. After six rings, Mom's voice mail recording came on.

"You've reached the voice mail for Hetty Williams," Mom's warm contralto said. "Leave me a message and I'll return your call as quickly as I can."

At the beep, Kate forced a smile on her face, knowing it would translate to her voice. "Hi Mom! Just calling to chat. I'll try you later."

After she hung up, she sat staring at her blank computer screen for a minute. It was a little past eight o'clock in Mendenhall, which meant it was a little past nine o'clock at Mom's in St. Lambert, on the south shore of Montreal. Where could she be? Visiting Madame Bernier, her oldest friend? Or was she with Fred, her beau?

Kate's mind shied away from the thought that her seventy-eight-year-old mother might have spent the night at Alfred Stilwell's condo, even though Kate liked the man. It still felt like a betrayal of Dad.

Who's been dead for over fifteen years.

Shaking her head at her own foolishness, she grabbed the mouse to reactivate the computer screen and settled back in her chair. First she would get the monthly reports ready for the mayor. Then she would have to figure out what to do about the vandalism and thefts at the new condo site.

* * *

Paterson returned to the detachment an hour later and downloaded the pictures she had taken to the common drive on the computer, printed them out, and posted them on the corkboard on the wall between Kate's office and the DC's.

Kate, Paterson, Martins, and Charlotte clustered around the photos and studied them.

"Big truck," said Kate. She had seen it in the parking lot, but somehow, seeing it in a picture made it seem that much bigger. It was white, with a king cab, and one of those magnetized signs on the driver's door that read: KENDRICK VETERINARY SERVICES, Mendenhall. Below that was the phone number.

"A Chevy Silverado," replied Paterson.

"A thirty-five-hundred HD," said Martins. "A lot of power."

"He has to get to some wicked places," said Charlotte. "In all kinds of weather. You want something you can depend on."

Kate slid a glance at her assistant and tried not to smile. Ever since she'd started seeing her young vet, Josh, she had made it her business to learn everything she could about *his* business.

Then the urge to smile faded. Charlotte really loved her vet, and Kate had seen the way Josh looked at Charlotte. It was only a matter of time before Kate lost Charlotte to Winnipeg, where Josh was based.

"He had fifty straws stored in a liquid nitrogen tank," said Paterson. "He was heading for a farm belonging to Ernst and Johann Mulvahill, just outside Minnedosa."

Kate consulted her mental map of the province. Minnedosa was closer to Brandon. Wouldn't it make more sense to work with a vet from Brandon? And then another thought popped into her head— when did you inseminate cows?

"Is the tank marked?" she asked.

Paterson looked stricken. "I didn't ask."

Kate smiled reassuringly. "We'll find out later. Where did he get the flat?"

Paterson turned on her heel and led the way out of the duty room into the hallway, where a four-by-six-foot laminated map of Manitoba filled the wall between the break room and the forensics lab/interview room. She grabbed the marker and placed an *X* on Highway 34, just north of Mendenhall.

"He was heading to the 16," said Paterson, "on his way to Minnedosa."

Kate nodded. "What about..." She stopped. She'd already forgotten the name. "Where he was going?" she finished lamely.

"The Mulvahill farm?" asked Paterson, a small smile on her face.

"Yes, the Mulvahill farm," said Kate.

Paterson was an attractive, but not pretty, woman. If Kate had to guess, she'd estimate Paterson's age at forty, forty-two. She had a creamy complexion with a smattering of freckles over the bridge of her nose, and lovely green eyes that seemed to change with the weather. Her glossy brown hair showed a few strands of gray and she kept it in a low bun, like Kate's, to accommodate her cap.

As near as Kate could figure out, that was the only thing they had in common. Where Kate was barely five feet three inches tall and usually round, Paterson was a long, lean five feet eight, with angles that suited her uniform. Kate's hair was blonde going gray and she had to wear glasses now for reading. Paterson was a marksman, though not as good as McKell.

And where McKell and the rest of the constables had eventually warmed up to Kate and come to accept her, Samantha Paterson never had.

Paterson shrugged. "I've sent Trepalli and Friesen to speak to them, but I doubt they know anything about the theft."

Kate's mouth tightened. She didn't regret assigning Paterson to be acting deputy chief in Rob McKell's absence, but there were a few things about Samantha Paterson's approach to police work that irritated her, one of them being her tendency to jump to conclusions long before all—and sometimes any—of the facts were in. Paterson was always willing to revise her assumptions when she learned differently but Kate suspected that assumptions narrowed Paterson's field of vision when it came to investigations. She would have to talk to Rob about it. Maybe he could steer Paterson in the right direction.

The woman certainly wouldn't take advice from Kate. Orders, yes. But not advice.

Charlotte's telephone rang and she went to answer it.

"All right," Kate said finally. "Keep me posted."

"Of course," said Paterson.

Kate headed back to the duty room and her office, stifling a sigh. She didn't know what she had ever done to Samantha Paterson, but the woman just didn't like her. Oh, she was a good cop, but when it came to Kate, she became stiff and bristly, as though resentful.

Kate had just about given up trying to find a way through Paterson's barrier when McKell's injuries forced her to assign his duties to someone else. She finally settled on Paterson because the woman was good at policing, and Kate wanted to know what kind of investigator and administrator she would make. It was a good opportunity for Paterson and she knew it, but Kate had to admit that her detachment was under a bit of a strain, and suspected much of that strain came from her relationship—or lack of a relationship—with Paterson.

Hopefully Rob would be back soon.

Her early morning good mood thoroughly evaporated, Kate reentered her office and closed the door behind her. It was a small office, but it had room enough for her battered oak desk and two mismatched visitors' chairs, a coat rack imitating the Leaning Tower of Pisa, and two filing cabinets against the far wall.

She sat down and turned to her computer. She had to finish the monthly report, look over training requests, and work out solid rationales for ordering a new squad car and a van, as well as new computers, before tomorrow's meeting.

She could just imagine Mayor Dabbs' eyebrows climbing to his perfectly groomed hairline when she presented the request.

Then there was the condo complex being built on River Road. For the last three nights, someone had vandalized the site and stolen supplies. As near as she could tell, Porter Security, the security company hired by the site owners, was doing a poor job of watching the site. It might be worth paying them a visit.

It was going on lunchtime and she'd just about decided to open the window to let in some fresh air when someone knocked at the door and, without waiting, opened it. Paterson stuck her head in.

"Trepalli and Friesen are back."

Kate nodded. "I'll be right out," she said, trying to keep the irritation out of her voice. Would it be so hard to wait for Kate to respond before opening her door?

Stop it, she told herself firmly. Just stop it.

It was cooler in the duty room. It would be late afternoon before the sun made it around to the windows on that side of the building.

The big room was empty except for Martins at the desk, talking on the phone and jotting notes down on a pad of yellow, lined paper. At that moment, Trepalli walked by the opening, large brown mug in hand. It steamed a little and he was paying attention to it, trying not to slosh the coffee over the rim.

As if sensing her attention, he looked up, saw her, and grinned.

"Hi, Chief," he said, just before disappearing behind the wall, only to reappear at the doorway to the duty room.

"Good morning, Constable," said Kate as he entered, his shiny, black work boots rapping firmly on the tiles.

She studied him as he walked over to one of the four common duty desks and set his mug down. At twenty-six, he was her youngest constable, and easily the handsomest. At six feet one, he cut a fine figure with his swimmer's body, that thick, black hair, and those navy blue eyes.

When she'd first come on board as chief, Trepalli had been a player. He'd had a different girlfriend every week, practically, and gave every indication of enjoying his bachelorhood.

Then he met Kate's niece, Amanda.

"Mornin', Chief," called Friesen from the hallway.

Kate looked around to find Trepalli's partner entering the duty room with his own mug of coffee.

"Good morning, Constable Friesen," she said with a smile. She was about to ask them what they had found out at the Mulvahill farm when Paterson came into the duty room from her office. Kate nodded at her, tacitly handing her the reins.

"What did you find out?" asked Paterson.

Trepalli looked over his shoulder at his partner, and Friesen nodded. Trepalli sat down and turned to Paterson.

"Ernst Mulvahill," he said. "He and his brother, Johann, own the farm. They do grain farming and have cows." He pulled his notebook out of his breast pocket and flipped to the right page. "About a hundred head of beef cattle and fifty head of purebred Angus cows. The Mulvahills contracted with Stoneway Breeders, a big outfit out of Calgary, to buy the semen and had it shipped to Dr. Kendrick's veterinary clinic three days ago. Ernst was expecting Dr. Kendrick this morning." He shrugged. "That's all he knows."

Paterson nodded as if the information confirmed her suspicion and Kate waited to see if she would follow up with more questions. When she didn't, Kate turned to Trepalli.

"Did Mulvahill tell anyone about the bull semen?" she asked. "Did anyone else know the vet was coming this morning?" She felt Paterson's gaze on her but didn't look at her.

Trepalli swung around in his chair to look at both of them. "He didn't make a specific point of telling anyone," he said with a shrug, "but he didn't keep it secret, either. The farm has a staff of three men working with the herd, and a housekeeper."

"We interviewed them all," added Friesen, wrapping both hands around his mug as if his hands were cold. He shrugged, too. "Nobody popped as suspicious. Nobody admitted to having told anyone." His blue eyes were bloodshot.

Kate nodded, and waited again. This time, Paterson didn't disappoint.

"What about the brother," asked Paterson. "Johann?"

Trepalli shook his head. "He's in Winnipeg for a couple of days for medical tests."

Martins had finished with his call and now swung around to face them. Kate caught the expectant look on his face and sighed.

"All right," she said. "Post it, but I want to see it before it goes live."

He nodded. "Will do."

* * *

By three o'clock, Kate had finished her report to the mayor and city council, met with Charlotte to go over the budget, and was just getting ready to go to the construction site when Martins popped his head into her office.

"I've got the info prepped," he said. "If you want to take a look?"

Kate nodded and grabbed her cap on the way out of the office. Charlotte was working at her desk by the entrance to the duty room. A shaft of sunlight hit the top of her computer monitor, highlighting all the dust in the air. The window on the storm door leading to the back compound was open, letting in fresh air.

Kate took a deep breath, enjoying the faint smell of manure riding the air. It meant farmers were getting ready to seed. She shook her head slightly, smiling. If anyone had told her two years ago that she would like the smell of manure, she would have laughed them out of the room.

She followed Martins onto the duty desk platform where he settled into the tall chair and turned the monitor a little so she could see it.

She squeezed in behind him, trying not to crowd him in the small space, and took a look. He had two photos of the vet's Silverado, one a side shot showing the sign on the driver's door, and the other of the back of the truck with the tailgate down and the back window up.

On the monitor, the inside of the truck was thick with shadows but she could just make out the corner of a tall, narrow wooden box. Probably kept his equipment in there.

Above the photos was a caption in bold, black capital letters:

DID YOU WITNESS SOMEONE STEALING FROM THIS TRUCK?

Between 07:00 and 08:00 hrs on Monday, April 16,

persons unknown stole a liquid nitrogen tank from
this truck, on Highway 34 between Mendenhall and
Gladstone.

If you were driving by at about that time, you may have
seen something to help identify the perpetrator or
perpetrators. Please call Mendenhall Police if you have
any information pertaining to this crime.

"What do you think?" asked Martins. His auburn hair smelled of
apples.

Before she could point out that "thief" would work just as well as
"perpetrator" and that maybe he should add their phone number and
email address, Amanda arrived.

She breezed into the detachment on a gust of grass-scented wind,
wearing red cotton slacks, striped canvas slip-on shoes, and a white,
long-sleeved, cropped top, and carrying a braided willow basket with a
checkered blue-and-white cloth over top.

"Hi, everyone," she said as she strode into the duty room. Kate
straightened and grinned at her niece.

"Hey, Amanda," said Martins, swiveling to follow Amanda's
progress into the duty room and almost knocking Kate off the platform
in the process. "Sorry, Chief," he said, grabbing her by the forearm
until she regained her balance.

"No worries, Constable Martins," said Kate drily. "My niece seems
to have that effect on my constables."

Martins grinned up at her, then scrambled out of his seat to
relieve Amanda of her basket.

"Let me," he said gallantly.

Charlotte, watching from her desk, rolled her eyes. "You're not
fooling anyone, Nick Martins." She grinned at Amanda. "Marco's on
patrol."

Amanda laughed. "That's okay. I came by to leave samplings of
my new menu and a reminder for Thursday night. It's my friends and
family night before the official opening."

The phone rang and Martins agonized for a moment before reluctantly setting the basket on the end of the duty counter by the log book. Kate shook her head. Pavlov's dogs. Amanda appeared, and they all started salivating.

Charlotte came over and lifted the cloth. Beneath were plastic containers filled with sample sizes of hors d'oeuvres and desserts—at least the ones that transported well. Amanda reached into the basket and pulled out a folded sheet of paper that had been tucked in between two containers. She unfolded it and showed it to Kate and Charlotte. It read:

To the wonderful officers (and Charlotte) of
the Mendenhall Police Department
PLEASE COME
to an evening of good food and good wine at
AMANDA'S FOLLY
351 Princess Drive
Thursday, April 19 at 7 p.m.
(significant others welcome)

"Congratulations!" said Charlotte. She hugged Amanda fiercely. "I didn't realize it was so close!"

Amanda nodded happily. "Opening night is Friday and I'm a wreck!"

Kate's eyebrows rose. The girl was tired, yes, and run off her feet, certainly, but a wreck? Kate had never seen anyone so organized and focused.

Charlotte picked up the basket. "Let's put this in the break room and you can tell me all about it."

Kate took that as her cue to escape. Placing her cap on her head, she flipped through the pages of the log book. Martins finished his call and turned to her.

"What are you looking for?" he asked.

She didn't need to look at him to know his light brown eyes would be alight with curiosity. It had been a tough call passing him over for the promotion to acting deputy chief. But she knew he'd make a good DC one day. Maybe even chief. He would have been a safe bet. Samantha Paterson was the one who needed a chance to prove herself.

"I'm going up to the construction site on River Road," said Kate. "Do you remember who the foreman... oh, never mind." Her finger stopped tracing down the page as she found what she was looking for. "Elijah Rudger."

"Security only comes on at night," Martins pointed out.

"I know. I'm just trying to get a sense of what's going on." There wouldn't be any work getting done on the complex anyway, since the judge had shut it down. She shrugged into her bomber jacket and zipped it up. With the sun beating into the duty room, it was warm, but the wind would still have a nip to it. "I have the phone."

"Right," said Martins, settling against the back of the stool. She thought she heard him sigh as she rounded the wall and walked down the hallway. She couldn't blame the guy. Desk duty had to be the most boring job in a police station. At the same time, it was key. Without a smart, capable person on the duty desk, effective policing just wouldn't happen. And when all hell broke loose, the duty officer was the one person who knew all the moving pieces and what was needed.

She glanced inside the break room as she walked by. Amanda and Charlotte were standing at the counter, opening containers and setting food on plates.

Kate shook her head. After a tumultuous summer last year, Amanda had left Mendenhall to go back home to St. Lambert, in Quebec. Rose, Amanda's mom and Kate's sister, had been delighted, only to be disappointed again when Marco followed Amanda to St. Lambert and swept her off her feet—while helping Kate find out who had run Mom over and why.

So now Amanda was back in Mendenhall and Rose was mad at both of them. Kate sighed. Lately, Rose was always mad at her.

Amanda had accepted Marco's proposal, but they hadn't set a date yet. In the meantime, they'd bought a house together. Rose had actually sputtered when she found out. Kate had had to hold the phone away from her ear as Rose explained—loudly—how wrong it was to join finances before being married.

Kate was staying out of it. Amanda and Marco seemed to have a good plan. They'd bought the house three months ago and had been spending all their free time renovating it. Amanda's plan was to turn the big living room into a dining room for paying diners. She planned to be open two nights a week—Fridays and Saturdays—and offer a fixed menu. Service would be by reservation only.

As soon as the rest of the house was finished, she and Marco would move in together. Until then, Amanda was living at Kate's.

It wasn't something Kate would ever have come up with, but she liked the outside-the-box thinking involved. There would be no overhead to Amanda's part-time restaurant and it would give people a chance to see what she could do as a chef. The rest of the week, she planned to continue the catering she had started when she first moved here, a little over a year ago.

The wedding would come later, when the business was up and running. It made sense to Kate.

She pushed open the storm door and stepped out onto the cement stoop, letting the door close behind her. There were no squad cars in the front parking lot. Everyone was out.

She automatically glanced at McKell's parking spot. It was empty, as usual. Except for her red Edge and Amanda's green Tercel, the parking lot was empty.

Charlotte walked to work. Samantha Paterson and her husband only had one car, so her husband took the Caravan to work. Whoever was on duty would swing by and pick Samantha up when she called. Sometimes she walked the two miles from her house but not often. It wasn't easy getting two kids out of the house in the morning. Her husband, Theo, handled the afternoon shift.

It all seemed like an awful lot of work.

The sun warmed Kate's face but the breeze nipped at her ears, reminding her she had work to do. With a sigh, she pulled her car keys out of her jacket pocket.

Ten minutes later, she was out of the downtown core and driving along Mendenhall Drive past older homes with stone foundations and pastel stucco for siding. The farther she got from downtown, the grander the homes got.

She had mistimed her departure from the detachment and now found herself stuck behind a school bus as it brought kids home from school. She waited patiently as the bus stopped every three blocks to let kids off. Finally, she turned off on Thompson Drive, heading for the river.

The Riverview was a new condominium development, only three years old. Unlike the apartment building or townhouse format, these condo units were small, separate houses. The only thing differentiating one from another was the color of the siding, which came in green, brown, blue, and brick red. She'd visited the condo website. There were two basic models. One with two bedrooms and a loft that looked down on the living room, and one with three bedrooms and no loft.

She'd liked the design of the units—they were much larger than they appeared from the outside—but she wasn't tempted. She had decided to buy her own little single-family home the moment she saw the view from the backyard.

The Riverview development was quite attractive, too, especially now that the landscaping was done. Rose bushes lined the sidewalks, Manitoba maple trees had been planted throughout, and low juniper bushes grew along the front of each house. Almost every unit had a view of the river, which ensured high resale values.

But over the past month, the builder had started construction on a long, three-story building that not only towered over the shorter, two-story buildings in the development, but also blocked the view of the river for a number of the homes.

She'd been following the controversy as it blew up in the news and at City Council meetings. As near as she could tell, the builder had taken advantage of a fuzzy bylaw and the inexperience of the condo board. But the board had decided to hire a lawyer and now there was a stop-work order on the building.

She drove into the condo development and saw the building looming over the smaller single units. No wonder the residents were furious. The building stuck out like a strip mall on a golf course. It completely blocked the view for at least a quarter of the homes.

She was surprised no one had torched the place.

Half a dozen children carrying backpacks were on the sidewalks.

They'd probably just gotten off a school bus, because Henrietta Blum Elementary School was almost two miles away.

Kate pulled up to the construction site and got out. The building was clad in plywood, with openings for windows staring back at her like blind eyes. Some of the windows were covered in milky white plastic, but most of the plastic had been slashed into strips, allowing the elements—and cats, dogs, mice, raccoons, and gophers—in. Bright red graffiti covered the plywood up to the height that a short person could reach. It consisted mostly of freeform designs and obscenities. Not exactly something a tagger would come up with.

A blue metal mesh fence surrounded the site, enclosing stacks of plastic-wrapped lumber, rebar, a backhoe, and what looked like sacks of cement but might be something else. She couldn't tell if anything had been stolen or not.

Her feet sank a little into the damp earth as she began to walk around the perimeter, looking for where the vandals were getting in. To her right, the single-family homes perched on manicured grass.

The sun warmed the back of her head while the wind nipped at her fingers and the tip of her nose. She took a deep breath, enjoying the smell of sawdust, damp earth, and river weeds.

"About time you showed up."

Kate turned around, a practiced smile on her face. She didn't often have to face disgruntled citizens, but it happened often enough that she was always prepared.

There was no one behind her. She automatically looked up. A stern, lined face with a day's growth of white beard was looking down at her from the balcony of one of the condo units. The shock of white hair on the man looked like it should have been trimmed a few months ago.

"Good afternoon," she said pleasantly.

The old man nodded. "Afternoon," he said gruffly. "When are you going to make them tear down that monstrosity?"

It really *was* a monstrosity. It was easily the length of three of the single-family homes, and now that she was close to the end of the fence, she could see another foundation had been dug next to the building to accommodate another building.

Good grief. No wonder the owners were up in arms.

"I hear there's been some vandalism," she said mildly, shading her eyes against the glare to look up at him.

The old man stood up and leaned on the railing. He wore a faded, blue and gray plaid shirt tucked into a pair of jeans. He looked out at the building and shrugged.

"I'm just surprised nobody's set fire to it," he said grimly.

Kate eyed him speculatively. "You know if there's a suspicious fire, I'm coming to see you first."

The man looked startled, then grinned down at her.

"Fill your boots, Chief Williams," he said, "but I'm long past my glory days."

Kate allowed one eyebrow to rise.

"I'm not so sure," she said. "You look like you've still got a bit of vinegar left."

At that he laughed, clearly delighted.

"Well, my name is Fergus McClusky if you need to look me up," he said.

"Nice to meet you, Mr. McClusky," said Kate formally. "You know anything about the break-ins and vandalism on the site?" Her neck was getting sore from looking up at him and she finally removed her cap when it threatened to fall off. Immediately her head felt colder.

"Nope," said McClusky firmly, "and I probably wouldn't tell you if I did."

She stared up at him while he looked down at her, a challenge in his brown eyes. After a moment, she shrugged.

"Well, at least you're honest."

He sat back down and was immediately obscured by the balcony railing. His voice floated down, punctuated by the sound of children laughing nearby. "Nice to meet you, Chief Williams."

Dismissed, Kate resumed her walk around the perimeter fence, avoiding clumps of earth and loose stones. She didn't find a break in the fence, but it ended at the edge of the bluff. The builder hadn't bothered closing in the fence on that side, probably reasoning that no one would climb the bluff.

To one side of the fence was a metal container, like the kind that went on ships, only smaller. It was blue and closed with a bar, secured by a lock.

She held on to the fence and leaned over. The bluff was steep and seemed composed mostly of loose soil and young trees growing out of clumps of soil. She straightened and shook her head, wondering how stable the bluff was. It looked like a good rain would sweep it all away in a landslide right down to the river at the bottom.

She turned back and walked around to the other side of the building. Mr. McClusky was still on his balcony but she couldn't see his face. When she got to where the fence turned to follow the side of the new construction, she finally saw the break in the fence. Someone had taken snippers to the links that connected two fence panels and shoved one of the panels away to make an opening.

Crouching, she pushed her way through the opening and stood up. So. Anyone could have gone through. It wasn't necessarily kids. There was no gate, which meant the fence had been thrown up after the stop-work order was issued. Fat lot of good it had done.

She walked around the shell of the building, trying to peer into the window openings, but there was a ditch between her and the building, and the only door opening had been boarded over. Clearly, whoever was vandalizing the property came prepared with a ladder or a board to breach the gap.

Finally, she made her way back through the fence and headed for her car. As she got into the sun-warmed interior, she tossed her cap onto the passenger seat, frustrated that she'd found nothing to help with her case. Then she found herself wondering how Paterson was doing with the Case of the Stolen Semen.

She was laughing as she drove out of the condo development.

CHAPTER 3

I t's a numbered company," said Charlotte, her voice metallic on Kate's cell phone. "Based out of Toronto."

Kate automatically glanced at her watch. Almost four thirty, which made it five thirty in Toronto.

The sun streamed through the windshield of the Edge, warming the interior a little too much. She cracked open the window. She had parked on the street just past the condo development to call the station. She wanted to speak to Elijah Rudger, the foreman on the construction site, but she didn't have a number for him.

"The company may be based out of Toronto," she said, "but Rudger would be a local hire. Probably out of Winnipeg." There weren't any construction companies based out of Mendenhall.

"I'll call you back," said Charlotte, and hung up.

Kate stared at her dark screen and sighed. "Fine. Call me back."

She set the phone on its dash holder and pulled out into the street. It was getting perilously close to day's end, and she wanted to speak to whoever was in charge at Porter Security before the office closed down for the day.

The wind ruffled her hair as she drove and she finally had to close the window. It still wasn't that warm outside.

She encountered what passed for traffic on her way back downtown as people headed home at the end of the day. She could do the same, just go home and pick this up in the morning. She could get Stan Albertson, who was coming on shift at seven o'clock, to assign regular patrols of the condo development. There was no need to pursue it right this very minute.

But there had been vandalism and thefts at the construction site three nights in a row.

Besides, Amanda wouldn't be home. She was spending every spare minute at the new place, getting it ready for the grand opening on the weekend. The thought of a whole evening stretching in front of her with nothing to do... she might as well do something productive with her time.

Porter Security was in the industrial area of Mendenhall alongside half a dozen other businesses in a small, one-story strip mall. She found a parking spot in front of the Prairie U-Brew and walked over to the glass door of Porter Security, snugging her cap over her head.

The door was locked, but she could see a young woman inside the reception area, putting things away in a desk. Kate knocked on the door and the woman looked up. She shook her head and pointed at a clock on the wall, clearly indicating that the office was closed.

Kate knocked again, more firmly.

The woman ignored Kate completely.

Really?

Tamping down a spike of irritation, Kate pulled her identification wallet out, opened it, and knocked the badge several times against the glass door.

The woman jumped, then looked at Kate. Only then did she seem to realize who was at the door.

If this was the caliber of employee at Porter Security, no wonder there were problems at the construction site.

The woman hurried over to the door and unlocked it, opening it a crack so she could talk to Kate.

"Hi," she said nervously. "We're closed for the day."

Kate smiled thinly. "Clearly." She pulled on the door handle and the woman actually took a step forward before reluctantly letting go of the handle.

She had blunt-cut, chin-length, straight black hair with bangs that highlighted her huge brown eyes. In her black yoga pants, which seemed to be a standard uniform for young women these days, and a tight, vee-necked green sweater, she looked like she should be in high school.

Kate stepped inside and closed the door behind her.

"I'm looking for your boss," she said. Because this Sweet Young Thing wasn't in charge of anything.

"Mr. Theriault isn't here," said the young woman. "He's in Winnipeg."

Kate blinked at her, trying to decipher what the young woman was saying.

"Do you mean he works out of Winnipeg?"

The young woman shook her head. "No, he's just there today. He'll be back tomorrow morning."

Kate nodded and pulled out a business card from her pocket.

"Could you ask him to give me a call when he gets in?"

The young woman took the card and studied it, as if memorizing the information on it. She was even shorter than Kate's five feet three inches, but she looked taller thanks to her long, slim legs. A pretty little thing.

Kate took a moment to look around. The only truly nice thing about the Porter Security office was the big window in the front, letting in light. Unfortunately, the light highlighted the cheap laminated floor, the old brown desk that looked like it had been salvaged from a bankruptcy, and the mismatched shabby chairs in front of it. An empty coat stand listed next to the door.

The whole place looked like it had been furnished at a yard sale. At the back of the small reception area were a couple of closed doors. Theriault's office and a bathroom, presumably.

"Can I tell him what this is about?" asked the young woman.

Kate turned her attention back to the receptionist.

"What's your name?" she asked.

The young woman tilted her head slightly. "Adrienne Ostashek."

"I'm Chief Williams," said Kate unnecessarily. "I'm investigating the thefts at the Riverview site."

Adrienne nodded as if she understood, but her face turned red.

"Who is scheduled to work tonight?" asked Kate. If she couldn't speak to Theriault, then maybe she could interview whoever was patrolling the site.

"That would be Jason," said Adrienne. "He only comes on around seven o'clock tonight."

That wasn't the name recorded in the log book.

"What's Jason's last name? And do you have contact information for him?"

"Of course," said Adrienne, turning to her desk. To Kate's amusement, the receptionist pulled out an old-fashioned plastic card holder from the top drawer and searched through it for the right card. She jotted the information down on a yellow sticky note and handed it to Kate, who placed it on the inside back cover of her notebook so as not to lose it.

"Thank you," said Kate. "Who was on for the last three nights?"

Without hesitating, Adrienne said, "Mark Pinkley. He's off now for four nights." At Kate's look, she turned back to her card holder and jotted down Pinkley's information on another yellow sticky note.

Kate placed the sticky note on top of the other one and flipped the notebook closed before heading for the front door.

"Thank you, Adrienne," she said. "I'm sorry I delayed you."

"No worries, Chief Williams. I hope you find whoever is doing this."

Kate smiled at her and went outside.

Adrienne had seemed completely unaware of the irony of wishing the police well in finding the person responsible for stealing from the site her company had been hired to guard.

Kate's phone rang as she was getting into the car. She glanced at the screen. Charlotte. The girl was going home later these days. Whenever Josh wasn't in town, she put in more hours.

"Hey, Charlotte," she said. "What do you have for me?"

"Elijah Rudger has a permanent address in Winnipeg," said Charlotte. "But he rents a room in Mendenhall. Want the address?"

Kate pulled her notebook out of the pocket of her bomber jacket and pulled the pen out of her breast pocket.

"Go ahead," she said, wedging the phone between her ear and shoulder in preparation for writing. Adrienne Ostashek came out of

Porter Security and locked the door behind her before turning away and heading for the far side of the small mall. Maybe that was where employee parking was. She never noticed Kate still parked in front of the Prairie U-Brew.

Charlotte rattled off the address and Kate wrote it down.

"Did you get a phone number for him?" she asked.

"Yes," said Charlotte. "His mother gave it to me."

"His mother?" He lived with his mother?

"There were only a few Rudgers in the Winnipeg phone book," explained Charlotte. "Usually it's the older folk who still have land lines."

Kate considered the fact that she still had a land line and decided not to pursue the point. She jotted down the number, all the while kicking herself. She should have thought to ask Adrienne. The security company was bound to have a way to contact the foreman. He would likely be their first call if something went wrong.

It wasn't like her to forget something basic like that.

"Everything okay?" asked Charlotte, and Kate realized she must have sighed out loud.

"Yes," said Kate. "Did his mother say where Rudger is?"

"She said he's still in Mendenhall," said Charlotte promptly. "Because of the vandalism and thefts, he wants to be close by."

Kate considered what she had seen at the condo site. Slashed plastic covering the window openings and spray paint. The cut fence.

"Is Paterson back?" she asked. For the life of her, she could never bring herself to refer to Samantha Paterson as Deputy Chief, or even DC. That was McKell's title.

"She got back about an hour ago," said Charlotte. "Did you want to talk to her?"

This time Kate swallowed her sigh. For Pete's sake. Why hadn't Samantha reported in to her?

She glanced at her dashboard. Just past five. Samantha would be around until about six o'clock. Kate decided to talk to Elijah Rudger first.

"No," she finally said. "I'll talk to her after I see Rudger. You'll be gone by the time I get back, I expect."

"I will," said Charlotte. "Josh is in town today."

Well, so much for that theory.

The happy note in Charlotte's voice only served to remind Kate that she was on the verge of losing her. She'd seen the way Josh looked at Charlotte. It was only a question of time before he asked her marry him or to move in with him in Winnipeg. And Kate had seen the way Charlotte looked at the guy. She'd say yes.

"Right, then," Kate said with forced cheerfulness. "I'll see you tomorrow."

They hung up and Kate sat in the Edge for a few moments, feeling sorry for herself. Finally, she took a deep breath and pulled away from the curb.

Life was change, right?

* * *

The house on Ortona where Elijah Rudger was staying in Mendenhall belonged to friends with a spare room, Beth and Henry Charlie. Like its peers on Ortona, the house dated from the fifties and looked like it had been built by the military for their married personnel. While the houses had kept their original small footprint, most of them, like this one, had been renovated.

Beth Charlie answered Kate's knock at the front door.

"Hello," said Kate, smiling. By the smell of roasted chicken wafting through the doorway, she was interrupting these folks at dinner. Early dinner.

"Chief Williams," said Beth Charlie in surprise. "How can I help you?" She was in her fifties, like Kate, and kept her gray hair in a neat French braid. She wore a straight black skirt with a matching jacket and a pale pink silk blouse. Kate expected a pair of high heels to match the suit, but to her surprise, Beth Charlie wore a pair of beaded moccasins.

"Sorry to interrupt," said Kate. "I was hoping to talk to Elijah Rudger. Is he here?"

"Yes, please come in," said Beth. She opened the door wider and stepped back to make room for Kate in the small entrance.

"Eli?" called Beth up the stairs. "It's for you."

Elijah Rudger came around the corner and stood at the top of the stairway, allowing Beth to come up before he went down. Clearly, he saw space problems in the entrance, too.

He came down the stairs but stayed on the last step so as not to crowd Kate.

Even without the step, Elijah Rudger towered over Kate by almost a foot. If he'd been hollow, she would have fit inside him with room to spare. Big as he was, however, she didn't think there was any fat on him. Hard work had seen to that. He wore jeans and a gray wool shirt tucked into them, and a pair of runners.

"Sorry to interrupt your dinner," she said. "I was hoping to talk to you about the condo development at the Riverview site."

He nodded and stepped down.

"Let's talk outside," he said, reaching past Kate to open the door. She barely controlled an impulse to plaster herself against the wall. How did this man find clothes to fit him? She caught a whiff of a pleasant, musky aftershave as he leaned close to her.

She followed him around the back to a patio protected from the wind by the bulk of the house. White metal mesh chairs with cushions were arrayed around a glass table. This household was clearly anxious for summer to arrive.

A tall cedar fence surrounded the substantial yard. At the back, huge terracotta pots contained miniature trees—fir trees? She was never sure—and Kate could see where the garden beds awaited the first warm days for planting.

"Have a seat," said Rudger. He waited for her to sit down before taking a chair across from her.

He was in his fifties, judging by the crow's feet and the deep lines bracketing his mouth. Maybe younger. He clearly spent a lot of time outside, hence the tan on his face. His pale hair was more silver than blond, and he kept it in a buzz cut.

He leaned back in his chair and studied Kate. Brown eyes, Kate realized. She would have expected blue.

"What do you need?" he asked.

Kate pulled her notebook out, more to have something to do than because she needed it. She didn't think she'd learn anything new from this interview, but something about the Riverview affair bothered her and she was having trouble pinpointing it.

"I'd like to go over the facts of the thefts and vandalism," she said.

"I've already made a report," Eli pointed out mildly.

Kate nodded. "I know. In your statement, you said the first theft occurred three nights ago. So, Friday night?"

"That's right." He laced his fingers over his flat belly.

"What was taken that first night?"

He looked up, as if the information was in the air above his head. "They broke into our storage unit." He looked down at her. "It's next to the site and has a heavy-duty lock on it. They cut it off."

Kate nodded but didn't say anything. She'd seen the storage container. A breeze ruffled the short hairs escaping from her bun at the base of her neck and she contained a shiver. The sun was beginning to go down and shadows crept across the patio, dragging the cold in with them. The cold didn't seem to bother Rudger at all.

"They took some of our power tools," continued Rudger, apparently oblivious to her discomfort. "Routers, nailers, saws, a generator... all portable. The company's insured, of course, but it takes time to replace them."

"Maybe that's the point," said Kate.

He nodded. "That's what I'm thinking, too." He shrugged. "There hasn't been anyone on site for a week," he continued, "ever since the judge put the stop-work order on the company."

Kate studied him, pen forgotten. "Doesn't seem to bother you particularly," she pointed out.

He shrugged again. "Did you see that thing?" he asked. "Ugly as sin. It didn't fit in at all with the rest of the units. And I heard that the company rep railroaded the condo board into agreeing to allow the building. It took a while but the condo board finally got itself a lawyer and put a stop to it."

That pretty much tallied with what Kate had read in the papers.

"What about Saturday?" she asked.

He leaned forward, resting his forearms on his knees and letting his clasped hands dangle between them.

"They slashed all the plastic window coverings," he said sourly. "That lets the wind and rain in. If moisture gets in before we can repair the damage, it'll cost a lot more than just replacing the plastic. We won't even talk about the graffiti."

"You've hired a security company, haven't you?" asked Kate.

Rudger straightened and his expression shifted to one of contempt.

"Not me," he said shortly. "I would never have hired Porter Security. Waste of company money if you ask me."

Kate couldn't help but agree.

"So why did the company hire them?"

Rudger shook his head. "Cheaper, I guess. I mean, they're the only security company in town. To hire someone else would mean bringing them in from Winnipeg, or maybe Brandon. Maybe provide accommodation."

"Did Porter Security report the break-in? The damage?"

He shook his head in frustration. "I did. On Saturday morning and Sunday morning. And this morning. If those guys were patrolling the condo grounds, they were doing it asleep."

Yes, indeed. She'd be curious to talk to them, Mark Pinkley in particular. He was the one who'd been on duty each time the theft and vandalism occurred.

"Did you notice anything odd leading up to the theft or the vandalism?" she asked. "Anyone paying particular attention to the site?"

He laughed. "If looks could kill, we'd all be dead many times over." At her look, he continued. "We aren't exactly popular with the condo residents. There've been small disruptions, like parking right in front of the storage unit so we couldn't access our tools, or filling holes that we'd dug during the day. Small stuff."

He gave her a crooked smile. "Frankly, I'm surprised no one's torched the place yet."

Kate nodded. "Is that when the company hired Porter Security?"

He snorted. "They only hired security because their insurance company forced them." He shook his head in disgust. "I've never worked for an outfit like this before."

"Why stay?" she asked. "And why are you still here, even when the job's shut down?"

He shrugged. It seemed to be his favorite means of communicating.

"I'm contracted to the end of the project," he said. "As for staying here instead of going back home…" He looked around the yard. "I sublet my apartment in Winnipeg for the duration of the project. Figured it would be cheaper than going back and forth all the time."

He sighed again, clearly wishing he hadn't.

CHAPTER 4

By the time Kate returned to the detachment, it was almost six o'clock and she was starving. The smell that greeted her when she opened the door drew her into the break room like a cartoon character following a trail of aroma.

"What *is* that?" she asked Trepalli, who was standing in front of the microwave as if staring at it would make it work faster. He had taken his uniform jacket off. With his sleeves pushed up over his muscular forearms and a lock of dark hair falling over one eyebrow, he looked like he belonged on the cover of a romance novel.

Once again, Kate wondered what his and Amanda's children would look like. Selfishly, she hoped they decided to have children right away. Once Rose had grandchildren, she would surely stop calling Kate for updates on whether or not "that man" was treating Amanda right.

He turned to her with a grin. "Leftover beef stew," he said smugly. "Amanda made it."

Kate raised an eyebrow and her gaze dropped to his waist. Amanda had been keeping Marco Trepalli in lunches since her return to Mendenhall. How long would he keep that figure?

His grin faltered and he looked down at his belt, clearly wondering what she was looking at. She grinned and left the break room, but not before noticing that most of the food Amanda had left behind was gone.

"Hi, Chief," said Martins, looking up from the duty log. He was typing it into the electronic record, adding search tags. It was the duty officer's job to update the log on the common drive at the end of every shift.

"Nick," she said, nodding. "Is Samantha still here?"

Nick Martins nodded at the DC's door. "I think she's on the phone."

Now that she was closer, Kate could hear the low murmur of Samantha's voice coming from behind the door.

"Did you learn anything new?" asked Martins, swiveling on his stool to look at her.

Kate shook her head. "Not really, except never to hire Porter Security."

He nodded. "Yeah, I gather they did a poor job on the Riverview security."

Poor wasn't the word she would have used.

"Can you see what you can find out about them?" she asked, heading into her office. "Charlotte's got some information, so between the two of you, tomorrow?" Charlotte had left for the day. "And maybe you can talk to Albertson and get him to assign patrols to the Riverview property tonight?"

Martins nodded and she walked into her office, only to step out again. "And can you ask Samantha to see me before she leaves for the day?"

He nodded again and Kate finally went into her office. She shrugged out of the bomber jacket, noting that the smell of Marco's stew had made it all the way to the back of the building. She had leftover stew, too, but at home.

There was a definite advantage to living with a chef.

She only planned to check her emails before heading home. A quick bite and then she'd go over to Amanda's and Marco's new house to help with the final push to opening day.

She'd been going for a couple of hours every other night, helping the kids out. Most of the constables had donated time, too, at one point or another. Amanda had become friendly with some of their wives, and even Samantha Paterson seemed to like her.

Kate dropped her cap on top of the filing cabinet and sat down in front of the computer. As she began to scan through her emails, she wondered if there had been any responses to their request for information about the theft of the bull semen. Probably not. Martins would have been itching to tell her if there had been.

A rap on the door frame startled her and she looked up to find Samantha Paterson staring back at her.

"You wanted to see me?"

"Come in," said Kate. Rob McKell would have automatically come in and sat down, knowing they had to debrief.

Oh, stop it, she told herself. Different people, different styles.

Samantha came in and sat down in one of the two wooden chairs Kate kept. They crowded the office a little, but she couldn't just have people standing in front of her desk.

"Anything on the theft?" asked Kate.

Samantha shook her head. "I drove back to Highway 34," she said. "The spot where Doc Kendrick broke down is inside a curve. There's a screen of trees on either side of the road. He managed to pull over onto an access road, which put him even farther behind the trees. He couldn't have picked a more secluded spot if he'd tried."

"Tracks?" asked Kate hopefully.

But Samantha shook her head again. "Gravel. No tracks, no evidence." Her shoulders slumped a little. "I think we need to interview Ernst Mulvahill and his staff, and the doc and his staff again. I don't believe that someone just happened along and helped themselves to a tank of frozen semen."

Kate agreed. If it had been a crime of opportunity, they would have stolen the doc's equipment, too. What were the chances that someone who knew about frozen semen would happen to come along in the hour the vet had left his truck alone?

Was it an hour?

"How long was his truck unattended?" she asked.

"About ninety minutes," said Samantha promptly.

"Mendenhall is about twenty minutes away from where he broke down. Why did it take him so long?"

"He called one of his staff to pick him up, but then they had to wait for the service station to open, get the tire repaired, and then drive back to the truck."

Kate nodded. She'd been on the bad side of a flat tire a time or two.

"All right," she said. "So that's your next step? Re-interviewing everyone?"

Samantha nodded. "Unless you can think of anything else?" There was a coolness to her tone that Kate suspected masked defensiveness. Samantha Paterson was a good cop, but she wasn't too sure of her skills as an investigator.

"No," said Kate promptly. "I think that's the right course of action. You need to interview Johann Mulvahill, too."

Samantha frowned. "He wasn't even home," she pointed out. "He was in Winnipeg, getting medical tests."

Kate just looked at her, waiting. A fine blush crept up the woman's cheeks and she grudgingly nodded.

"They could have been lying," she agreed. "We'll check it out." She made as if to get up, then sat back down. "Nick says you were investigating the Riverview theft?"

This time Kate did sigh. She was pretty sure one of the local residents was responsible, though it would be hard to prove it. That old man—McClusky?... If he'd been a few years younger, she might have suspected him, but she had trouble imagining him hauling equipment out of the storage trailer, let alone hauling a plank across the ditch to crawl into the half-finished building.

She told Samantha about the site visit and her visit to Porter Security.

"Do you know the owner?" Kate broke off her report to ask.

Samantha shook her head. "They're out of Toronto," she said, "according to Charlotte. Even the manager is from Toronto, although I think he lives here now."

Kate nodded. "He was out of town when I got there. I did speak to Elijah Rudger. The foreman," she added at Samantha's puzzled look. "He's living here for now, too, in a room at a friend's house on Ortona." She gave Samantha the gist of the conversation.

"So, everyone seems to agree that Porter Security is doing a poor job," said Samantha.

"That's why I'm asking Albertson to assign regular patrols of the Riverview tonight," said Kate. "This is becoming irritating."

Samantha nodded her agreement and rose to leave, barely stifling a yawn. Kate stood up, too.

"I'm leaving," she said carefully. "I can give you a ride home, if you like."

But Samantha was already shaking her head. "No, thanks, Chief," she said politely. "I've already got one." She smiled and left.

Kate shook her head and sat back down again. Of course, Samantha had a ride.

CHAPTER 5

Gus Theriault, the manager of Porter Security, looked closer to thirty than forty, with a pleasant, open face and bright brown eyes under thick eyebrows. He reminded Kate of a young Beau Bridges.

"Have a seat, Mr. Theriault." She waved him to one of the chairs in front of her desk and then resumed her own seat. He wore a sports jacket, a white shirt, and jeans, an outfit she had come to think of as business casual in Mendenhall.

She'd waited until ten o'clock, and when he didn't call her, she called him and asked him to join her at the detachment. She made it clear she wasn't impressed.

"My secretary tells me you came by yesterday," said Theriault, unbuttoning his jacket and trying on a winning smile. It faltered when Kate just stared at him.

"I'm investigating the thefts and vandalism at the Riverview site," she said.

He nodded. "Yes, we've been quite concerned."

Kate allowed one eyebrow to rise and he had the grace to blush.

"I expect you would be," she said tartly, "seeing as you are contracted to keep the place secure."

The blush deepened and he sat back in his chair and crossed his arms over his chest.

"That's not quite correct," he said, each word clipped and tight. "We are contracted to patrol the site once a night, between nine p.m. and six a.m."

This time both of Kate's eyebrows rose. "How is that supposed to help?" Once a night? That was ridiculous. All the vandal had to do was wait until the security guard had done his or her sweep and then they'd know the rest of the night was open.

"Exactly," said Theriault. He ran a hand through his hair in frustration. "I pointed out that one sweep wouldn't be enough but that's all they wanted. My guess is their insurance requires them to have security, but isn't too specific about how much."

His irritation was clear, and Kate found herself stepping down her own. It wasn't this guy's fault that the condo developer was a cheapskate.

Maybe she'd been a little too quick to rush to judgment. Usually she had more patience, but her sleep had been interrupted by nightmares of Bert falling off the cliff behind the construction site. She'd slept right through her alarm and missed her workout, the first time in months.

She knew why, too. She'd driven to Amanda and Marco's place last night to see if they needed help. Instead, she'd turned around and driven home like a coward when she spotted Bert's Honda CRV parked in front of the house.

Still, it wasn't Theriault's fault.

"I get the guys to sweep it more often."

Kate blinked. The sun peered through a gap in the cloud cover, highlighting the fact that her window hadn't been washed since last fall.

"What do you mean?" she asked.

Theriault shrugged. "Whenever there's time in their patrols, I get them to swing by the site. Even a slow drive-by might be enough to make someone think twice."

Kate nodded her agreement. Visibility was a key ingredient to security.

It bothered her that the developer hadn't arranged for more security. There was a lot of money tied up on the site. Just the equipment stolen from the storage container would run into the thousands of dollars, not to mention the damage to the shell of the building. Surely additional security would be cheaper?

"Did they contract with you directly?" she asked as the thought occurred to her. "Or did they go through your head office?"

"They went through Toronto," said Theriault, leaning forward. "About the time the stop-work order went through."

"Do you know who the owners are?" she asked. "All we have right now is a number, as in a numbered company." She could find out, of course, but it would take time. If Theriault had the information...

He shook his head. "No, sorry. I never spoke to anyone from the company." He thought for a moment. "I do have a copy of the contract they signed with head office," he said. "There'll be a name and address on that. I can get it to you as soon as I get back to the office."

"Thank you," said Kate. "That would be helpful."

She escorted him out of the detachment and returned to the duty room, where Martins stood at Charlotte's desk, pointing at something on her computer screen. So far, no one had responded to the alert on their website about the theft of the semen straws, much to his disappointment.

As she headed back to her office, she glanced inside Paterson's office. Samantha had responded to a call earlier that morning with Mike Olinchuk, her usual partner. With Samantha taking on the DC's duties, that left Olinchuk patrolling alone most of the time, although Trepalli and Friesen took turns patrolling with him, too.

But when there was a call-out to what might be a dicey situation, Samantha went with Olinchuk. Mike Olinchuk was a fine officer, but Kate was of the better-safe-than-sorry school of thought.

"Any news from Paterson and Olinchuk?" she asked out loud.

Martins straightened and shook his head. "No, ma'am. But it would take a while to interview them all."

Kate nodded. The call had come in maybe half an hour ago. A white panel van had cruised around Henrietta Blum Elementary School a few times, alarming the administration. Paterson would probably handle the interviews while Olinchuk patrolled the streets around the school. It was probably completely innocent—these incidents usually were—but no one wanted to take a chance.

She took another couple of steps and stopped.

"Mr. Theriault will probably call in with information on that numbered company," she told both Martins and Charlotte.

"Do you want us to keep digging?" asked Charlotte, leaning back in her chair to look at Kate. Today she wore black slacks—real ones, not those yoga things the receptionist at Porter Security had been wearing—and a long-sleeved tunic top with a muted paisley pattern in greens and blues. It brought out the green in her eyes.

"Yes," said Kate. "He only has their address. I'd like to know who they are."

She walked into her office and flicked on the overhead lights. The day had grown overcast and dark, and although it was too cold to be muggy, the air felt heavy, as though she had to push through it when she walked. Rain would be good, she told herself firmly. It would wash away the winter grit on the roads and the snow mold leftover on the lawns.

The thought did little to cheer her. That damned dream had done a number on her.

With a sigh she sat down and pulled a pad of yellow lined paper toward her and picked up her pen, only to sit there twiddling it while she stared at the blank paper.

The investigation into the theft of frozen semen wasn't moving at all. It didn't help that she was short-staffed and that Samantha had to pitch in when Olinchuk needed help. That didn't advance the investigation, and the longer they took, the harder it would be to find the culprit.

And she was getting nowhere with her own investigation. The vandal or thief could be anyone. Someone who saw an opportunity and grabbed it—maybe. It could be someone connected to the condo development, even if they didn't live there. Maybe a family member upset at what was happening to their parent or sibling.

She wondered if Mr. McClusky, the feisty senior she'd spoken to at the Riverview site, had any family in the area. Maybe a hot-headed grandson? Or granddaughter?

She pulled her keyboard tray out and clicked on the shortcut for the Canadian Police Information Center, CPIC. After logging in, she typed in Fergus McClusky's name and address into the search parameters, but came up with nothing.

Either Mr. McClusky was a criminal genius who always managed to avoid police interest, or his bark was worse than his bite.

Turning back to her pad of paper, she wrote "Riverview" on the left side of the page, and "Straws" on the right, and divided the columns with a vertical line. Under each heading, she jotted down everything they knew about each case, which wasn't much. Then she drew a horizontal line under both columns and started jotting down the questions she wanted answered in both cases.

The screen door slammed shut as someone entered. She listened for the murmur of voices that would indicate a visitor, but heard Samantha's voice instead. She glanced at her watch. Almost eleven o'clock. That hadn't taken long. She waited for the sound of Samantha's boots on the linoleum but there was nothing.

Finally, she pushed away from her desk and emerged into the duty room.

Martins had resumed his seat at the duty desk, and Charlotte was murmuring into the telephone tucked between her ear and her shoulder, writing on a notepad.

"Was that Samantha?" asked Kate.

Martins looked up from the screen.

"Yes. She's in the break room."

Kate nodded and headed for the break room. She hadn't had enough coffee this morning, anyway.

Samantha Paterson was standing in front of the coffee machine, head bowed, absently stirring the coffee in her cup. She didn't look up until Kate was within a few feet, and then she jumped.

"Sorry," said Kate, examining the other woman carefully. She had dark circles under her eyes and the lines on either side of her mouth looked a little deeper. "Everything all right?"

Samantha placed the spoon in the sink and picked up her cup.

"Of course," she said. "I'll be in my office."

Kate's eyebrows rose.

"Hang on," she said. "What about the panel van?"

Samantha blinked a couple of times and then seemed to focus on Kate.

"False alarm," she said. "It was a service van from Winnipeg. Driver couldn't find an address." A yawn caught her by surprise and she clamped a hand over her mouth. "Sorry."

Kate put her hand on Samantha's free elbow and guided her to the couch.

"Sit," she said and waited until the woman sat down. "Now," she continued, "what's going on? You look asleep on your feet."

Samantha's face turned red and she looked down at the mug of coffee resting on her lap.

"I'm fine," she said stiffly.

Kate waited. And waited. Finally, the other woman looked up. "Bad night," she finally admitted. "Adam's got the flu."

Adam... oh yes, her boy. Her daughter's name was Amy.

"Theo stayed home?" asked Kate.

Samantha nodded. Kate examined her acting deputy chief and sighed.

"Looks to me like you should have stayed home, too."

Samantha immediately shook her head. "No, ma'am," she said. "Too much to do. We're understaffed."

Well, Kate couldn't argue with that.

"Tell me what's on your plate," she said. "We'll see if we can redistribute."

Samantha took a deep breath. "Everything would be manageable except that I need to go to Winnipeg to interview Johann Mulvahill."

Kate sat down next to Samantha, trying not to jostle the cup on the other woman's lap. "I thought he was just there for tests. When's he due back?"

Samantha shook her head. "They don't know. Apparently, the initial tests found something and now they want to run more in-depth ones."

Well, that didn't bode well for the man.

Samantha sipped her coffee and pulled out the notebook from her breast pocket. She flipped it open one-handed and used her thumb to get to the right page.

Sign of an experienced police officer, thought Kate.

"I also want to re-interview everybody at the Mulvahill farm," continued Samantha. "I can send Trepalli and Friesen to interview the gas station attendant and the vet's assistant, but..."

"I know," said Kate. She couldn't send Trepalli and Friesen to the Mulvahill farm since they had done the initial interviews. Besides, that would leave only Olinchuk free to respond to any calls.

There was no help for it. Kate would have to go to Winnipeg and interview the Mulvahill brother. Which meant putting her own investigation on hold.

At least there hadn't been any incidents overnight. The extra patrols must have deterred the vandals.

"I'll go," she said, getting up. "If I leave now, I can probably be back here before five."

Samantha stood up, too. Her hand was wrapped around the mug as if she was cold.

"Actually, Chief," she said slowly, "I have an idea."

Kate nodded. "Okay—what is it?"

Samantha Paterson was at least five inches taller than Kate, and built lean so that she looked even taller. Kate figured she couldn't weigh more than a hundred and thirty pounds, but she might be wrong. That lean build hid a lot of muscle.

Samantha stared down at Kate as if trying to decide whether or not to tell her. Kate tried to keep her eyebrows under control and her face open. Finally, Samantha spoke.

"I was wondering if we could ask DC McKell to do the interview."

Kate blinked up at her acting deputy chief, her mind a complete blank. As the silence stretched on, Samantha's face grew redder.

"Never mind," she finally said, turning away. "It was a dumb idea."

For the second time, Kate stopped Samantha with a hand on her arm. Samantha turned a stiff, questioning face to Kate but Kate was still working through the angles.

Would asking Rob McKell to drive to Winnipeg hurt his recovery? No, of course not. The man had to go once a week to meet with the neurologist, among other specialists. Interviewing someone wasn't taxing, especially as nobody expected Johann Mulvahill to know anything of value. It would be something they could cross off their list, and it would break McKell's stasis. He would finally have a way back into police work, all in the guise of helping out his short-staffed detachment.

Holy cow. Samantha Paterson's idea was brilliant.

"Chief?" asked Samantha uncertainly.

Kate looked up at her, absently admiring the woman's eyes—although they were bloodshot today.

"Samantha," she said slowly, "that's absolutely brilliant. On so many levels." She grinned at her acting deputy chief and patted her on the arm in approval.

Samantha's face was still red, but she was smiling.

"Will you call him, then?"

Kate thought about it for a moment. She let go Samantha's arm and wandered over to the coffee machine. She opened the cupboard and pulled down a mug with the city's coat of arms on it—a clutch of sunflowers on a shield with blue sky above and cows below.

Like Samantha earlier, she stood staring down at the mug for a few moments, thinking it through. Finally, she looked around.

"No," she said. "If I ask him, he'll think it's a trick. If you ask him, he'll think you need the help."

Even as she said it, her heart sank. Samantha Paterson would bristle at the suggestion that she needed help, even though she did.

To Kate's surprise, Samantha broke into a slow grin, turning her usually stern face beautiful.

"That's pretty sneaky," she said admiringly.

Kate found herself absurdly grateful at the woman's praise. She raised an eyebrow. "Said the pot to the kettle."

Samantha laughed out loud, then quickly stopped as if the sound had surprised her. "Whatever works," she said. And with that she turned and walked out of the break room.

CHAPTER 6

Like Kate, McKell had a land line. When he didn't answer it, Samantha tried his smart phone, but to no one's surprise, he didn't answer that one, either. Kate didn't think he'd had it turned on in the last seven months.

She stood at her window, leaning on the window sill, and looked out at the day. The sun tried valiantly to pierce through the wall of clouds and she felt a sudden, fierce longing for the long hot days of summer, where she could work in her backyard in shorts and a tee-shirt.

Across Mendenhall Drive, the Church of the Nazarene looked empty. Someone had been working on the flower beds lining the driveway, however, as the soil looked freshly turned and watered.

Cars drove by, heading to and from the downtown core. Mendenhall Drive was one of the main thoroughfares in town. Just down the street from the detachment was city hall, and beyond that, at the intersection of Mendenhall Drive and Main Street, the fire hall.

Was McKell avoiding Samantha's call, or was he out? Kate knew he was capable of going to the grocery store, of driving himself to the doctor, of going to the barbershop. He wasn't as capable as he had been seven months ago, but he was on his way back.

If he could only get it through his thick skull that he *needed* to come back.

She toyed briefly with the idea of calling his brother Sam in Ontario, if only to suss out what he thought the problem was. Finally, she decided against it. It felt like an incredible invasion of Rob's privacy.

But she had to do something. This reluctance of his was becoming unhealthy.

Her desk phone rang, startling her, and she stretched to pick up the receiver.

"Chief Williams," she said.

"Hi, honey," came Mom's warm contralto. "Am I interrupting you?"

A tiny bit of tension she hadn't even realized she was carrying floated off Kate's shoulders.

"Hi, Mom," said Kate cheerfully. "No, you're not interrupting. How are you?" Since the hit-and-run last year, Kate always worried about her mother. She tried to call a few times a week, even if only to say hello.

"I'm fine, dear," said Hetty, a hint of impatience in her voice.

Maybe she was calling a little too often.

"I see you tried calling me yesterday," continued Hetty. "I only just got home today. Alfred and I decided to spend a few days in Quebec City. Did you know the daffodils are out there? And the tulips are starting."

Kate's eyebrows rose. Mom and Alfred Stilwell had gone away for a few days? On a romantic getaway?

"That's nice," said Kate cautiously. "How are things at home?"

"Dear," said Hetty, "Alfred and I are moving in together."

Kate swiveled her chair and sat down in it. She stared out the window at the gray sky.

"Katie?"

"Yes, Mom?"

"Did you hear me, dear?"

"Yes, Mom."

There was a long pause. Finally, Hetty laughed.

"I've never known you to be at a loss for words."

Kate swallowed, then cleared her throat.

"Well," she tried. She cleared her throat again. "I've just had a shock," she said. "It may take me a moment."

Hetty laughed again, and Kate smiled, in spite of herself. She hadn't heard Mom laugh like that in years.

"We're always together," said Hetty. "It just makes sense to find a place where we can *be* together. Neither one of us is getting any younger."

Kate worked at tamping down her objections. Mom was entitled to her happiness. She'd been a widow for many years and it wasn't being disloyal to Dad. Kate should be grateful that Mom had found someone she liked enough to want to live with. And Mom was right—at seventy-eight, who knew how much time she would have with her new-found love?

She took a deep breath.

"I'm happy for you both," she said. "Alfred is a fine man and he's lucky to have you."

"Thank you, sweetheart," said Hetty, and Kate thought she heard the thickness of tears in her voice.

"But why doesn't Alfred just move in with you?" Kate asked quickly, not wanting to deal with emotions. "Lord knows, the house is big enough."

"No," said Hetty immediately and Kate could almost see her shaking her head. "That was mine and your dad's home. It could never be mine and Alfred's."

Well, that made sense. And it was a relief. Kate knew herself—she would have hated the thought of another man living in her father's house.

"Have you told Rose?" she asked.

"This morning," said Hetty with a sigh.

"Let me guess," said Kate. "She didn't take it well."

"Your sister doesn't deal well with change."

Kate laughed out loud. "Now there's an understatement if ever I heard one."

A soft knock at the door caused her to turn around. Samantha stood in the doorway, an expectant look on her face.

"Mom," said Kate, "I have to go. I'll call you later in the week, okay?"

"No need, sweetheart," said Hetty hurriedly. "I'll call you if anything changes."

Kate hung up and turned back to her acting DC.

"Got hold of the DC," said Samantha with a little smile. "It took a little convincing, but he said he'd interview the brother this afternoon."

Kate grinned in satisfaction.

* * *

"Well," said Martins around a mouthful of ham sandwich, "there's nothing special about the Mulvahills." He swallowed and took a drink from his thermos.

Standing behind Charlotte, Kate nodded and Martins continued.

"They've got a mixed farm. They grow some grain and some beef, but they also breed purebred Angus cows. Apparently a bull is all they need for the commercial beef, but there's real money in Angus cows, depending on the lineage."

Hence the bull semen.

"No flags on the brothers," added Martins. "Nothing on their staff, either, except for a few driving violations and parking tickets."

"Maybe Samantha will find something in the interviews," said Charlotte. She kept her gaze on the screen as she flipped the mouse around. Kate kept looking away to keep from getting dizzy. Samantha had left right after lunch to do follow-up interviews at the Mulvahill farm.

Charlotte was digging through the public information available on the Government of Ontario website to figure out who was 128444, Inc., the company that had hired Porter Security to patrol their construction site.

Kate took a deep breath. They wouldn't be wasting their time on the damned internet search if Gus Theriault would just send the information he had promised to send. She glanced over at the fax machine, under the corkboard with the various photos of the veterinarian's vehicle and printouts of what the semen tanks would look like. The machine sat empty.

There was no point watching over Charlotte's shoulder. The girl would let her know what she found. Instead, Kate should be interviewing Mark Pinkley, the security guard who'd been on duty all three nights when there had been thefts and vandalism at the construction site. And maybe she could track down Jason Cromarty, too, the security guard who had been on last night.

She had postponed a meeting scheduled for right after lunch with the city's new chief financial officer. The mayor hadn't responded to her request for an additional squad car, van, and computers. His CFO had, calling Charlotte to set up a meeting with Kate.

She could hardly refuse. But she planned on taking Charlotte, her secret weapon, with her. Charlotte had worked with Kate on the numbers and knew more about spreadsheets and accounting than Kate ever would.

If she could, she would have sent Charlotte *instead* of her, but she didn't have the nerve.

She was just about to ask Martins to call Gus Theriault when the telephone rang.

"Mendenhall Police," said Martins into the phone. He waited a moment, then swiveled on his stool to look at Kate. "Yes, Mr. Theriault. Thank you for calling. I'm ready."

He spent the next little while writing information down on a pad of paper, then hung up.

"Mr. Theriault apologizes for taking so long to get back to us," said Martins, clearly trying not to grin. "Apparently, the contract had been misfiled."

Kate tried not to roll her eyes, but it hurt. She took the piece of paper from Martins and looked down at it. Martins' loopy scrawl was barely legible.

D. A. Landry
Chief Executive Officer
128444, Inc.

There was no phone number, but there was a Toronto address, which she didn't need right now. Still, the name might get them somewhere.

"Let's see," said Charlotte, coming over.

Kate handed her the piece of paper.

"All right," murmured Charlotte, looking down at it. "At least we have a starting point."

"Let me know what you find out," said Kate. "I'm going to go find Mark Pinkley and Jason Cromarty, the two Porter Security guards." She glanced over her shoulder at Martins. "Their addresses should be in the log book."

CHAPTER 7

A battered, ten-year-old Ram pickup truck was backing into Mark Pinkley's driveway when Kate pulled up to his address. The truck was tan and blue, with a few rust patches at the bottom of the passenger door. It looked like it had been in a couple of fender-benders, too, and no one had bothered fixing it up.

In the sky, clouds piled into each other, layer upon layer, each one pregnant with rain. A little rain would be good, thought Kate again before getting out of her vehicle, plucking her cap off the dashboard as she straightened. She placed the cap on her head and took a moment to study the house.

Pinkley lived in a small cottage in the older part of Mendenhall that was still technically downtown. Although a few small businesses had set up among the houses—a knife sharpener for one, she noted with interest—the neighborhood still clung stubbornly to its residential roots.

Pinkley's house couldn't possibly have more than two bedrooms, and they would be small. The house was well kept, however, judging by the exterior. The pale gray paint job was recent and the white front door and shutters were new. The bushes in the front garden were still protected with burlap bags.

The driver's side door of the pickup opened and a balding black man got out, letting the door slam behind him. He walked around to the back of the pickup and let the tailgate down.

As Kate approached, she saw that the bed of the pickup was full of plastic bags of soil and grass seed. The man looked up as she approached, pushing the bag he had been pulling off the truck bed back onto the tailgate.

"Afternoon," said Kate pleasantly. She nodded at the supplies in the back of the truck. "Getting a little gardening in?"

The man shrugged and glanced at the sky before returning his gaze to Kate.

"I'll be glad if I can get these into the shed before it starts to rain. You're here about the Riverview thefts?"

"I take it you're Mark Pinkley?" asked Kate, just to be sure.

He grinned and his naturally serious face lit up. He was a handsome man, maybe forty or forty-two, with a lean build and good shoulders. He towered over her five-feet-three-inch frame by at almost nine inches.

"Sorry, Chief Williams," he said. He wiped his right hand on his jeans and stuck it out. "Mark Pinkley. Adrienne told me you'd be checking in with me."

"Adrienne?" asked Kate, shaking his hand. Who the heck was Adrienne?

"Receptionist?" said Pinkley. "At Porter Security? You spoke with her yesterday."

Oh, yes. The girl who really hadn't wanted to talk with her.

Kate nodded. "Do you have a minute?"

He glanced at the sky again, as if calculating, then shrugged again.

"Sure. Do you want to come in?" He waved at the house.

Kate shook her head. "This won't take long," she assured him. "And then you can finish up."

He hiked a hip onto the tailgate, which brought him down a few inches. "What do you want to know?"

Kate pulled out her notebook and a pen and flipped to an empty page. The wind picked up a little, swirling the dust and grit into dust devils in the middle of the street. Except for a car parked in front of the knife sharpening shop—which seemed to be located in the basement of a house similar to Pinkley's—the street looked deserted. It was the middle of the afternoon. Kids were at school and parents at work.

"Tell me about your routine," she started. "And at what times you patrolled the Riverview condos."

For the next few minutes, Pinkley told her about his assigned duties, his patrols, the locations he just drove around and those where he got out and checked doors. He told her about his last three nights at work.

"Are you the only one on duty at night?" she asked.

He nodded. "Lately. Most of our work is daytime work, believe it or not. Sometimes we've had too many night security patrols for one person to handle, but this last month or so, we've only needed one guard at night."

That seemed about right to her. Mendenhall was a small town, with fewer than twenty thousand people. She couldn't imagine there would be that much work for a security company.

"What kind of work do you do in the daytime?" she asked, out of curiosity.

"We provide security for the mall and a variety of small businesses," he said. "We also monitor home alarms, including medical and panic alarms. Someone is always on call, usually out of the office, but sometimes from home." He waved at the house again. "Mr. Theriault handles most of the walk-in clients, but we have to do a lot of on-site assessments to figure out placement of alarms and cameras—that kind of thing."

"What are your shifts?" asked Kate.

"Four nights on, four off. Twelve-hour shifts."

Huh. Similar to the detachment's shifts.

"I worked Thursday night through Sunday night," he continued. "Seven at night to seven in the morning."

"So, you saw nothing out of the ordinary on your shifts?"

He shook his head.

"I varied the times I patrolled the condos," he said. "And I tried to do it at least twice—three times a night if I had time—at Mr. Theriault's direction. Never at regular times. I never saw anyone or anything suspicious." His lips tightened and he looked down at his gravel driveway. "Every time, I only heard about the theft or the vandalism the next day, when Mr. Theriault would call me."

He's embarrassed, thought Kate. Of course, he was embarrassed.

"They were watching for you."

He nodded and looked at her. "That's what I figure, too. They've been watching. What I don't know is how they knew I wasn't coming back. Sometimes I didn't know whether or not I'd be able to squeeze an extra patrol in until the last minute. I think we should place motion-activated cameras at the site."

Kate raised an eyebrow. "The owners won't pay for more than one patrol a night. I doubt they'll spring for cameras."

Pinkley sighed and stood up. "I know. They're tying our hands behind our backs."

Kate closed her notebook and tucked it into her jacket pocket.

"We're looking into it," she assured the man. "And we're patrolling the development, too. Maybe that'll deter them."

"Yeah," said Pinkley. "But I'd still like to catch the bastards."

* * *

She drove off before she remembered to check Jason Cromarty's address and had to pull over again. She was just fishing her notebook out of her pocket when her phone rang.

She glanced at the display. Samantha. That was probably the first time Samantha had ever called her.

"Hi Samantha," she said. "Are you back at the detachment?"

"Chief," said Samantha, her voice so clear she might have been sitting in the Edge. "I'm just leaving the farm. Ernst Mulvahill just got a call from Grace Hospital. Johann Mulvahill is dead."

CHAPTER 8

Martins was on the phone and Trepalli and Friesen were back at the detachment by the time Kate returned. They were seated at the common desks in the middle of the duty room, typing up their notes from the interviews they had done with the gas station attendant and the vet's assistant. Both constables looked up as Kate walked in and Martins, on the phone, nodded a greeting at her.

"Chief," said Friesen. His dark blond hair was freshly cut and his uniform looked neatly pressed, even after eight hours. Even his boots looked spit-polished. "Heard about Mulvahill. Do we know what happened?"

"Not yet," said Kate, removing her cap and slapping it against her leg to shake the raindrops off the bill. The promised rain had finally arrived. "Paterson should be back shortly. Hopefully she knows more."

"Do we think there's something suspicious in his death?" asked Trepalli, voicing Kate's own question.

"We'll know more when Samantha gets here," she repeated. She glanced around. "Where's Charlotte?"

"Supply run," said Martins, hanging up the phone.

"Any luck with our numbered company?"

He shrugged. "I was on the phone when she left, but she'll be back soon."

Kate nodded and retreated to her office. It was starting to feel like her whole world was on hold.

The news of Johann Mulvahill's death had hit her hard and she wasn't sure why. The man had gone to Winnipeg to undergo medical tests, so clearly there had been some concern about his health. He hadn't even been home when the semen tank was stolen from the vet's truck.

Surely there wouldn't be a connection between his death and the theft of the semen. What connection could there possibly *be*?

Still... from undergoing tests to suddenly dying seemed like quite the leap. She sat staring blindly at her screen until she heard the murmur of voices in the duty room that announced Charlotte's return.

Pushing back from her desk, she made her way to the duty room. Her boots felt heavy and she seemed to be making a lot of noise on the linoleum floor. She was tired.

Trepalli and Friesen were still plunking away on their respective keyboards. They didn't look up as she walked by.

"Hi, Chief," said Charlotte, shrugging out of her pale blue wool car coat. She hung it up on the coat stand by the rain-splattered window next to her desk and swiped her hands over her brown curls, flicking rainwater off. A white plastic bag dripped on her desk and bulged with office supplies. A box of staples perched on top of a box of purple hanging files.

"Did you have any luck with identifying the numbered company?" asked Kate.

As she spoke, Martins walked out of the break room with a mug of coffee in his hand and flipped on the light switch as he walked into the duty room. The room flooded with light and Marco looked up from his typing.

"Thanks."

Martins nodded and returned to his stool.

"The registered CEO is Dwayne Albert Landry," said Charlotte, sitting down at her desk. She grabbed the mouse and started moving it around, activating her screen. "His address is the same one Porter Security provided, out of Toronto. I was just waiting for—ah, there it is," she said with satisfaction.

Kate waited as patiently as she could while Charlotte read something on her screen. Finally, Charlotte sat back.

"I spoke with someone at Service Ontario," she said. "They were able to get me the name of the principal right away, but it was going to take some digging to find the names of the other officers in the company." She looked up at Kate. "The woman I spoke to said I probably wouldn't get the information until tomorrow morning, seeing as it was almost closing time there. I guess it was easier to find than she thought." She hit a button and the printer under her desk whirred to life. A moment later, her eyebrows rose and she handed Kate a sheet of paper that read:

Dwayne Albert Landry, Chief Executive Officer
Celia Anderson-Capaz, Chief Operating Officer
Holman Rehayem, Chief Financial Officer
Leonard Hodgson, Director
Stephanie Huenaerts, Director

All of them had Toronto addresses except for Leonard Hodgson, who lived in Winnipeg.

"Well, well, well," murmured Kate, glancing up at Charlotte.

"What?" asked Martins, just as the outside door opened. They all turned in time to see Samantha Paterson walk past the opening, followed by Rob McKell.

"Rob!" Charlotte jumped up from her chair and rushed over to the DC, flinging her arms around him and almost bowling him over.

"Whoa!" he protested, staggering back and laughing.

Kate glanced past his shoulder at Samantha, who shrugged self-deprecatingly.

"The DC was on his way back to Mendenhall," she said. "It made sense to meet here so he could brief everyone at the same time."

Kate nodded solemnly, trying desperately not to smile. Samantha Paterson had *skills*.

Friesen and Marco joined the little group at the entrance to the duty room, shaking McKell's hand and slapping his back. Then Martins shouldered his way past the two constables to pump McKell's hand.

"About time you came by," said Martins gruffly. "Place isn't the same without you."

Well, wasn't that the truth.

A tightness she hadn't even known was in her chest suddenly released, and Kate took a deep breath for the first time in seven months.

He looked good, in spite of being thin. His color was strong. He was freshly shaven and his hair looked freshly cut in his favorite buzz cut. He wore jeans that actually fit and a green sweater under a leather jacket.

If someone met him today, they would never know he had almost died last year.

The hubbub died down enough for Kate to be heard.

"Hey, Rob," she said with a smile. "Thanks for coming in."

He nodded and the smile faded from his face. As if on cue, everyone stepped away from him. He took a deep breath and Kate controlled a sudden urge to offer him a seat. He would hate it that she saw him as weak.

Still, she wanted him to sit down. She glanced at the clock. Just shy of five thirty. Too early to expect the night shift.

"Before you brief us," she said, "let's get Olinchuk in, too. We can all be briefed at the same time." She didn't like having no one at all on patrol, but it was dinnertime on Tuesday, quiet time. And it was bad enough Olinchuk ended up patrolling alone too much of the time. She didn't want to exclude him on this.

Martins nodded and returned to the duty desk to call Olinchuk in.

"Coffee?" Kate asked McKell, nodding toward the break room.

Martins put his hand over the mouthpiece of the phone. "I just put a fresh pot on."

"Sure," said McKell.

Paterson turned and led the way to the break room. She pulled open the cupboard and took down three mugs.

She glanced at McKell and Kate over her shoulder. "Sit," she said casually. "I'll pour."

Good girl, thought Kate. She sat down next to McKell on the love seat and waited for Paterson to bring the mugs over. To Kate's surprise, Samantha Paterson had added a bit of sugar to her coffee, just the way she liked it.

"Thanks," said McKell, accepting his mug.

The rain pattered against the lone window in the break room. It was a cold rain, the kind that snuck down the collar and trickled down the spine like an icy finger. Kate took a sip to warm herself.

Paterson added cream and sugar to her own mug, then sat sideways on one of the wobbly kitchen chairs tucked under the ancient wooden table that sat across from the love seat. She smiled at McKell.

"You look pretty good for a guy who took a bullet and then rolled his boss's car."

Kate just about choked on her coffee and McKell laughed, though she couldn't tell if it was at her spluttering or Paterson's words. In any case, it was good to hear him laugh again. For a while, Kate had thought McKell was done with enjoying life.

She had finally worked her way out of the morass of guilt in which she'd landed when the bullet that had been meant for her almost killed Rob. She knew it wasn't her fault, but seeing Rob in that hospital bed, with tubes and wires coming out of him... and seeing how long it was taking him to make his way back... even now, guilt threatened to swamp her.

"So, Amanda's opening is this weekend," said McKell, changing the subject. "Will you be going on Thursday?" he asked Kate.

Kate's eyebrows rose. "Of course, I'll be going," she said. "Everyone will." She glanced at Paterson, who nodded.

"Everyone who isn't working is going," amended Paterson. "And those who are working will take turns. We've all worked on this opening. It's our baby, too."

Kate grinned and took another sip. Amanda and Trepalli certainly commanded loyalty. Of course, it helped that Amanda bribed everyone with food.

"You'll be coming, too, won't you?" asked Paterson of McKell.

He shrugged. "Maybe. Although I've pretty much already tasted everything she's going to serve."

Both women looked at him, puzzled. In the duty room, the phone rang and Martins' low voice answered. Charlotte laughed at something unintelligible one of the constables said.

"What do you mean?" Kate asked.

McKell looked at her. "She's been bringing food over for months," he said. "She says I'm her guinea pig, but I think she's heard about my cooking." He smiled crookedly.

Kate felt tears pricking her eyes and looked away.

Amanda had been bringing McKell food. If that wasn't the sweetest...

They'd all brought the DC food, once he got out of hospital and the rehab center. Charlotte had organized the delivery chart and for the first two months he was home, he never had to go shopping or cook. Then he insisted they stop, that he was well enough to look after himself.

Apparently, that was when Amanda stepped in.

Well, Rose, you and John raised yourselves some good kids.

She would have to remember to call her sister and tell her so.

The crunch of tires on gravel announced the arrival of a car, and Paterson twisted in her chair to look out the window.

"It's Mike," she said.

They heard a car door slam shut and the sound of boots on gravel, then the door opened.

"We're in here, Mike," Paterson called out as Mike Olinchuk pushed his way past the screen door. He nodded and took his cap off, shaking the rain from it, before coming into the break room.

"Hey," he said when he spotted McKell. "Good to see you, DC."

"Thanks," said McKell. "But Samantha's the DC now."

Samantha shook her head. "*Acting* DC."

Kate rolled her eyes. "Let's go into the duty room, so Martins doesn't have to run back and forth."

Mike Olinchuk nodded and went back into the hallway. He was a big guy, with massive shoulders that made him look shorter than he was. His face looked like it had been sculpted out of clay with a trowel, but his bright brown eyes spoke of intelligence and kindness. He was one of the gentlest men Kate had ever met. He had brought his wife Janine with him from Ontario and now they had a child, although Kate couldn't remember if it was a boy or a girl.

They followed him into the duty room. Trepalli was half sitting, half leaning on the desk he had been using, arms crossed, listening to Friesen and Charlotte argue about forms. He looked up when they walked in, and nodded at Olinchuk.

Martins hung up and swiveled on his stool to face them. "All right, then," he said. "Let's hear it."

McKell pulled out a chair from one of the desks in the middle of the room and sat down. Kate did the same, just to keep him company and give Samantha the floor. She nodded at her acting DC.

"I had just finished talking with one of the staff in the barn when Ernst Mulvahill came out of the main house. He was white and shaking, and was holding a cell phone. He'd just gotten the call that his brother was dead." She sighed and took a sip from her mug. "Well, clearly there wasn't going to be any more interviewing today, so I returned to my vehicle. That's when I saw that DC McKell had left me a voice mail."

"You're the DC," murmured McKell, looking down at his mug.

"*Acting* DC," corrected Paterson again, firmly. She cleared her throat. "He was already on his way back to Mendenhall, so I asked him to meet me here. Over to you, DC McKell."

McKell gave her a sardonic look, then turned to Kate.

"Not much to add, really," he said. "I was actually at the hospital when he died. I was in the hallway outside his room, waiting for a nurse to finish with him. After a moment, a doctor and another nurse came rushing in with a crash cart, so I knew something was up. I went in—one nurse was doing CPR on him while the doctor and the other nurse set up their equipment. They tried shocking him, but he was gone."

Kate nodded, hoping he had more.

"When they noticed me," he continued, "they shooed me out of the room. I waited until the doctor came out and told her who I was and why I was there." He set his mug on the desk and laced his fingers together.

"Turns out Mulvahill was getting tested for prostate cancer, and the doctor had no idea why he had died. She said that they had seen no indications that he was in danger, and that they would have to do an autopsy to find out why."

"Isn't—wasn't Ernst Mulvahill in his seventies?" asked Trepalli.

As if that was as old as anyone could expect to get.

"Seventy-one," said McKell. "And except for his prostate, he was in good shape. I mean, the guy had been a farmer all his life and he was used to hard work."

"Still..." said Trepalli doubtfully.

"So, you're saying that my best years are behind me?" asked Kate sweetly.

Trepalli turned beet red and everyone laughed at him. Kate turned back to McKell.

"What did the doctor think caused his death?"

McKell shook his head. "She didn't know and didn't want to guess, but I could see she was upset. She promised to send me a copy of the autopsy when she got it... but that might be a few weeks from now."

Olinchuk was standing by the counter, near the log book. Now he uncrossed his arms and leaned an elbow on the counter.

"Everything about this case is weird," he said.

Paterson looked at him. "In what way?"

"Too many coincidences," he said with a shrug.

That's it exactly, thought Kate. She stood up and walked around the desks to stretch her legs.

"You're right," she said. "The fact that the vet's truck had a flat just as he was transporting the semen," she said, unfolding a finger. "The fact that someone just happened to come by when his truck was unattended." She unfolded a second finger. "The fact that Johann Mulvahill just happened to be away on the day the semen was to arrive." A third finger. "The fact that Mulvahill died just when we're about to question him." A fourth finger. "And..."

"And," said McKell quietly, "if the semen was so valuable, why did the vet leave it in the back of his truck?"

They all turned to look at him.

Kate felt like a proper fool. Why hadn't she thought of that?

Trepalli held up a finger. "His assistant came to get him," he said. He flipped through the pages of his notebook. "She drives a Smart car."

Tin can on wheels, thought Kate. There was no room for more than a couple of bags of groceries. Or a tire.

Still, McKell had put his finger on an important point that should have occurred to Kate yesterday. It should have occurred to Paterson, too.

And it brought up an important point. The tank was portable and easily transported. And it held fifty thousand dollars' worth of bull semen. Even if James Kendrick couldn't take it with him, wouldn't it have been more prudent to stay with the truck and guard the tank? He could have sent the flat tire to the service station with his assistant.

Another thing to add to her mental list of things she wanted to check. Kate glanced at the clock. Almost six o'clock.

"All right," she said. "We'll pick this up again in the morning. Sergeant Martins, you and Charlotte dig up information on insurance on the semen—whether Kendrick had any, whether the Mulvahills had any."

"And we should do background checks on the Mulvahills and their workers," added McKell.

Kate nodded, noting his use of "we." They had already done a cursory check on Mulvahill and his workers, but it would be worthwhile to go deeper. She wondered when they were going to find time to do all this research.

"And I need to finish interviewing them," said Paterson.

"And there's the question of the board of directors," said Charlotte.

They all turned to look at her and Kate almost groaned. She had forgotten—briefly—about the condo development and its troubles. Yes, they needed to follow up on Mr.—oh, Lord, she had already forgotten his name—the director who lived in Winnipeg.

"The Mulvahills have a board of directors?" asked McKell, clearly confused.

Kate shook her head. "Different case." She swallowed a sigh and looked at Charlotte. "I'll interview him." In Winnipeg. That would be the better part of a day gone.

"Him who?" asked Martins.

"Leonard Hodgson," said Charlotte promptly. "He's on the board of directors of..." she glanced at her computer screen. "...128444, Inc."

She looked up at Martins. "Unlike all the other directors who live in Toronto, he lives in Winnipeg."

Martins' eyebrows rose, but Kate warned herself not to read too much into the fact that Hodgson lived in Manitoba. It could just be that the company decided to invest in condos in Mendenhall because one of their directors lived nearby and could keep an eye on things.

But so far, nothing about this company had felt right. She just didn't have the time or resources—

"I can help."

Silence fell on the room. Kate looked up from the linoleum she had been studying. McKell was staring at her. He shrugged.

"I can sit here as well as at home," he said casually. He put up a hand as Paterson opened her mouth to speak. "I'll sit at one of the common desks," he said firmly.

Paterson closed her mouth and nodded her agreement.

"All right," said Kate finally. "I'm going back to the Riverview development. It's suppertime—I can probably catch some of the owners at home. Maybe somebody saw or heard something that will help."

Paterson turned to Trepalli. "Constable, why don't you help her out with the interviews? Ben and Mike can patrol together for what's left of the shift."

McKell slid a glance at Kate.

Yes, indeed, Samantha Paterson was learning to take charge.

* * *

Kate and Trepalli were just getting into Kate's Edge when Dr. Kendrick pulled up in his white Silverado. He parked in the visitor spot and, leaving the engine running, got out and jogged over to Kate's window. She opened the window, letting in the cool, damp air, and he leaned over, one arm resting on the door jamb above his head.

"Evening, Chief Williams." He smiled down at her, his faintly grizzled round face creasing and his eyes crinkling. He had slightly crooked teeth, which only served to emphasize what a nice smile he had. His hair was still a mess but now there was a faint mist of droplets on it. But really, it was his hazel eyes that were his best feature. His lined black denim jacket gaped open, revealing a gray and red plaid shirt.

He smelled a little like Old Spice and a little like horse.

"Good evening, Dr. Kendrick," said Kate, smiling. "How can I help you?"

He shrugged one shoulder. "I was on my way back from a job and I thought I'd swing by to see if there's anything new on the theft."

Kate shook her head.

"We're still investigating," she assured him. "As soon as we know anything, we'll let you know."

She could feel Trepalli tensing up next to her and knew he was wondering if she would ask him about leaving the tank unattended in his truck. After all, they'd just been talking about it. But experience decided her against it. She would rather already know the answer before she asked him the question.

She looked into the man's smiling eyes and hesitated, but only briefly. She never liked sharing bad news.

"I'm afraid I do have other, very sad, news," she began, and saw the smile fade from his face. "Johann Mulvahill died in the hospital this afternoon."

The smile left Kendrick's face as if someone had erased it. He moved back a few inches as if he wanted to distance himself from the news. Then he took a shaky breath.

"Jesus. What happened? I thought he was only going for tests."

Kate nodded. The cool air had invaded the car and she had to control a shiver. It would be rude to turn the heat on while he was hanging in her open window.

"We don't know yet," she said with a shrug. "Did you work closely with him?"

He nodded and slowly straightened, his gaze on a spot somewhere above her car.

"Yes. I've known him for over twenty years. He kept me on after I moved from Brandon to Mendenhall, fifteen years ago. A good man."

"I'm sorry for your loss," murmured Kate. And it did seem like a loss for Kendrick. In the deepening twilight, his face looked drawn, older. Sadder.

"Thank you," he said automatically. He looked back down at her suddenly. "I won't keep you any longer, Chief," he said quietly. "Thank you for telling me." He tapped the roof of the Edge and turned away.

As he walked back to his truck, Kate closed the window and turned the heat up. The rain had begun again.

Next to her, Trepalli stirred.

"Well," he said.

Kate thought he was going to ask her why she had told the vet about Johann's death or why she hadn't asked about the tank. Instead he turned to her, a look of speculation on his face.

"I might as well have been on Mars for all the notice he took of me," he pointed out. "The good doc only had eyes for you."

Oh, for Pete's sake. Kate drove out of the parking lot as her face slowly turned red.

CHAPTER 9

They drove in silence toward Riverview, the Ford's tires hissing against the wet pavement as the day galloped toward evening, stealing the light as it went.

"I'm sure Bert would help if you asked him," said Trepalli from the passenger seat.

Kate turned to look at him. He faced forward, staring out the windshield, his cap resting on his knee.

They hadn't spoken at all on the drive to the condo development. That was one of the reasons she enjoyed his company—he never felt the need to fill a silence.

In the almost two years she had known the young constable, she had grown very fond of him and thought he and Amanda were a good match. Kate had yet to work up the courage to ask Amanda how she had come to terms with Trepalli's risky job.

Her own risky job.

When McKell had been mistaken for Kate last year and almost killed... Well, that had been the last straw for Bert. Yes, she could have been killed on the highway, but there was nothing she could do about it. This was her *job*. She had a responsibility to the constables under her command. McKell could step in and take over, but she wasn't nearly ready to give it up.

She was old enough to know she would survive the heartbreak

of losing Bert, but she resented him for it. Resented the unspoken request that she give it all up for him. And when he changed his mind and asked her to marry him, she hadn't been able to get past the bitterness.

And now Trepalli wanted her to reach out to Bert.

"We don't need Bert's help," she said calmly.

The windshield wipers swished regularly, keeping up with the rain. She felt sorry for the people they drove past, waiting at the bus stops.

"He could arrange to have someone interview that fellow in Winnipeg," Trepalli pointed out. "You wouldn't have to drive there."

Kate swallowed her irritation. He was trying to help. She turned into the Riverview development and slowed down.

"First of all," she said, "we don't know if Mr. Hodgson is even in town. If he is, I want to speak with him myself. I don't want someone not involved in the case to interview him and provide a secondhand report."

Trepalli nodded and kept silent, but Kate was frustrated. What was the point of that suggestion, she wondered. Did he feel she wasn't doing her job right or was he—in his own clumsy way—trying to get her back together with Bert?

That ship had sailed. Bert had moved on and so had she.

She pulled up to the side of Mr. McClusky's house. Across the road, the shell of the apartment building looked bedraggled and forlorn, like a cardboard box left out in the rain.

"What an eyesore," murmured Trepalli, placing his cap on his head.

"Yep," said Kate. "That's why there's a stop-work order on the site. The board is challenging the builder's right to build an apartment building."

He leaned forward to better see the plywood-clad building with its open-eyed windows. "I'm surprised no one's set fire to it."

Kate smiled. "That's probably on the menu if we don't find out who's doing the damage and stealing the company's tools." She pointed to her left. "I'll take the units on this side. Why don't you take the ones behind us? I wouldn't bother with Mr. McClusky's unit," she hooked a thumb toward the old man's house. "I've already spoken with him."

"All right," said Trepalli. Taking a deep breath, he opened the passenger door and stepped out into the rain.

Right. Kate sighed and opened her own door. Nobody ever said police work was glamorous. Or dry.

The first unit she went to, the one closest to the construction site, had a small sign screwed to the wall by the door.

Mrs. Adeline Fromme

Music Teacher

Kate rang the doorbell and heard the chimes over the muffled sound of someone haltingly playing a piano.

The door opened and a small woman in black slacks, a white shirt with frills down the front, and an intricate gray lace shawl over her shoulders opened the door.

"May I help you?" said the woman politely when she saw Kate standing on her small porch. An overhang kept the worst of the rain off Kate, but she could feel her backside getting damp.

"Sorry for interrupting," said Kate. "I'm Chief Williams of the Mendenhall Police. We're investigating the thefts and vandalism that have been occurring here." She nodded toward the construction site.

"Keep practicing, Audrey," called the woman over her shoulder when the piano fell silent. The sound picked up again. "Yes," she said to Kate. "I'm Adeline Fromme. I'm afraid I haven't seen or heard anything that might be of use."

Kate studied the woman's face. She had pale skin and hair more white than brown. It was cut in a short, no-nonsense bob. Her brown eyes were lively and interested, and she looked directly at Kate.

"Perhaps you've seen something that you discounted as unimportant?" Kate suggested. "Someone walking by late at night? Or a strange car driving by?"

The woman took a moment to consider but finally shook her head. "I'm sorry," she said. "My attention is divided right now. If you leave me your card, I'll call you if I think of anything."

Kate nodded and fished out a business card. "Does anyone else live with you?" she asked.

The old woman shook her head. "No."

"All right," said Kate pleasantly, though her backside was getting unpleasantly cold and the background plunking on the piano was getting on her nerves. "I expect neither you nor your neighbors are very happy about the building going up."

"We are *not*," said Mrs. Fromme sharply, and two roses suddenly bloomed on her cheeks. "That builder said he canvassed us and obtained our permission before building but that's a lie!"

Kate's eyebrows rose at the sudden vehemence.

"Does everyone feel like you?" she asked mildly.

"I should say so," said the woman. "The condo board convened a meeting and we all made it clear that we wanted to put a stop to it."

"Was anyone in particular more... upset?" asked Kate.

Mrs. Fromme's sharp brown eyes narrowed. "We were all upset, Chief Williams," she said stiffly.

Knowing she wasn't going to get anything more out of the woman, Kate thanked her and moved on to the next house. She could see Trepalli talking to someone across the road, but the person was hidden behind the door.

No one was home at the next place she tried. At the third house, a teenage boy opened the door. They stood staring at each other for a moment. He was tall and thin, wearing jeans and a white tee-shirt that said QUESTION AUTHORITY in big, black letters. His hair was shaved on either side with a mop of jet black hair flopping down the middle of his head like a fallen Mohawk.

The boy blinked and Kate shook herself out of her surprise.

"Hi," she said. "I'm Chief Kate Williams of the Mendenhall Police. Do you live here?"

The boy tilted his head slightly as if trying to figure out what she was saying. There was a faint shadow under his lip. "Let's see some identification," he said.

Kate controlled an impulse to roll her eyes. He was perfectly within his rights to ask. Although she would have thought the uniform and police car might have been clues.

She fished out her identification and showed it to him, resisting when he went to take it from her. He leaned in to examine it, then nodded. She replaced the identification in her jacket pocket.

"What's your name?" she asked pleasantly.

"Why do you need to know that?"

She sighed and looked at him quizzically. "Because I gave you my name, and it's polite to reciprocate."

"You sound like my mom," he said.

She wasn't sure but she thought she saw his lip twitch. How old was he? Fifteen? Sixteen? She tried not to let his age influence her, but experience had taught her that most vandalism was perpetrated by teens. And this one was not intimidated by authority, apparently.

"Is that good or bad?" she asked.

This time a grin broke through the truculent teenage mask.

"Depends on the day," he admitted. "I'm Eric Brian. What do you want?"

Well, at least he was direct.

"Do you live here?" she asked again. "Or are you visiting?" Beyond him she caught a glimpse of a kitchen with books and papers on the table.

He shrugged. "I live here until I'm old enough to leave."

For Pete's sake. Kate grabbed on to her patience and held on grimly.

"Are your parents home?"

He shrugged again. "Not yet. Why?"

She pulled out her notebook and clicked on her pen. "What are their names, please."

He hesitated for a moment, then said, "Armand Brian and Helen Stooke. Why do you need to know?"

She nodded toward the construction site.

"We're investigating the vandalism and thefts that have been taking place. Have you seen anything suspicious around the construction site?"

"Isn't this a little below your pay grade?" he asked with a smirk. She could see goosebumps on his arms but he slouched nonchalantly in the doorway as if he had all the time in the world.

She cocked an eyebrow at him. How did his parents stand it?

"Are you saying I *shouldn't* be interested in destruction of property and theft?"

He looked suddenly unsure and she pressed her advantage.

"Do you know anything about the vandalism and thefts?" she repeated.

He shook his head, but his glance slid away.

Hmm. "You haven't seen strangers around the site?"

He shook his head again, this time looking directly at her.

"What about people you know?" she asked softly.

His gaze dropped again, and after a moment, shook his head.

So. He had seen someone he knew around the site. Or maybe he had been there himself. Did that mean he was involved in the vandalism and theft, or that he had snooped around the site, something all kids did?

Either way, he wasn't prepared to tell her. Fine.

She fished a business card out of her pocket and handed it to him.

"Please ask your parents to call me," she said. "I'd like to talk to them, too."

He looked up at her uncertainly, clearly wondering if she was going to complain to his parents about him.

"And if you think of anything that might help us with the investigation," she continued, "please call."

"Okay," he said.

As he closed the door, she noticed that he was barefoot. Kid must have been freezing.

She stayed on the small porch for a few minutes and wrote down the information from his interview and the one from Mrs. Fromme. Then she slipped the notebook back in her pocket and went to the next house.

Half an hour later, she and Trepalli met back in the car and sat shivering with the heater on full.

None of her interviews had been particularly informative. Of the five Trepalli had done, only one had yielded any kind of useful information.

"A Mr. Henry was up in the middle of the night on Saturday," said Trepalli, reading from his notes. He took off his cap and set it on the dashboard. It had gotten dark enough that they'd had to turn on the dome light.

"He said he happened to be looking out his kitchen window when he saw someone cycling by."

Cycling. It hadn't occurred to her that the perpetrators might be using bicycles for transportation. It would explain why no one had heard any vehicles. A bicycle was silent and could easily be hidden.

"Did he see...?"

"No," said Trepalli. "He couldn't tell who it was and he wouldn't be able to identify the bicycle again except to say it was a mountain bike." He closed his notebook. The shoulders of his uniform jacket were dark from the rain.

If he felt anything like Kate did, he would want to go home and change. Or maybe take a hot bath.

"All right," she said with a sigh. "We'll call it a day."

He nodded. "Ben and I can carry on with the interviews tomorrow," he said. "Someone saw something or knows something. If we shake the tree enough, something will fall out."

* * *

She dropped Trepalli off at his apartment. Apparently, there would be no working at the house tonight. Tomorrow night would be the last push before the friends and family night on Thursday, and he and Amanda wanted a night to themselves.

As she drove through downtown and back to her place, Kate wondered selfishly if Amanda had any leftovers in the fridge. The house was dark when she arrived, but was redolent of butter and chicken. She snooped through the plastic containers in the fridge, and to her delight, found one with a yellow sticky note with "Aunt Kate" written on it in Amanda's handwriting. She opened it and found a chicken breast smothered in some kind of cream sauce and carrot slices and broccoli nestled next to it.

Yum. Her mouth watered at the thought but first she wanted to take a hot bath. While the water ran in the tub, she took off her damp uniform, hung it up to dry, and wrapped her chilled body in her polar fleece housecoat—the best Christmas gift Rose had ever given her.

Then she went back to the kitchen and rummaged in the junk drawer for a small pad of paper—when had she ever stayed at the Vancouver Fairmont?—and a pen. As an afterthought, she poured herself a glass of Pinot Grigio and grabbed the cordless phone before going back to the bathroom. She might need to call Albertson.

The water was deliciously hot as she sank into it and she groaned, half in pain, half in bliss, sliding down until her shoulders were covered in lilac-scented bubbles and her knees stuck out like two pink islands.

Life was full of little pleasures.

After a while, she pulled the notepad closer to her along the rim of the tub and grabbed the pen.

Again, she drew a vertical line down the length of the page and wrote RIVERVIEW and BULL SEMEN on either side of the line.

She should really leave Samantha to work out what needed doing on the theft of the semen, but she just didn't know if Samantha was fully up to it. The woman had occasional bursts of brilliance, but police work was more about plodding thoroughness than flashes of insight. Most of the time, anyway. Then again, Rob was going to be there tomorrow and Kate knew Samantha would turn to him for help.

Still, it wouldn't hurt to take notes. On the bull semen side of the sheet she wrote:

Check insurance for vet
Check insurance for farm
Why didn't vet stay with the truck?
Johann Mulvahill—suspicious death?
Finish interviews with Ernst and farm workers

On the Riverview side of the sheet, she wrote:

Continue interviews
Talk to other security guard—Cromarty?
Set up interview with Leonard Hodgson
Charlotte and Martin to dig into 128444, Inc.
Who's insuring the place?

She sipped her wine and set the glass down as she tried to think of anything else she could do regarding the thefts and vandalism at the condo site, but nothing came to her. Both lists were pretty skimpy.

The phone rang and she jumped, knocking her wine glass onto the bath mat. She cursed and went to grab it only to switch midway and grab the phone when it threatened to vibrate itself into the tub.

"Hello?" she said sharply. She couldn't help the irritation in her voice.

"Kate?"

The adrenalin spiked again, making her hands shake. Bert. Why was he calling her?

"Hello, Bert," she said as calmly as she could.

"Is this a bad time?" he asked. He sounded so close he might have been in the same room. She glanced down at her wet, naked body and felt the heat rise to her cheeks.

"As good a time as any." The words just about strangled her, and for a moment, a bubble of hysterical laughter threatened to undo her. "What's up?" she managed to get out.

"One of my detectives just finished talking with a Dr. Elaine Strickland. She wants us to investigate a suspicious death. Her patient died this afternoon at Grace Hospital, and she thinks that he was murdered."

The water sloshed around Kate as she sat up straighter in the bathtub. "Let me guess," she said. "The patient is Johann Mulvahill."

She could almost see Bert nodding at the other end of the line.

"How did you know...?" she asked.

"Dr. Strickland told us that she had spoken to McKell this afternoon."

The water was growing tepid. It was time to get out and dry herself off.

"What did McKell want to talk to Mulvahill about?" asked Bert.

She sketched out the theft of the bull semen and the Mulvahill brothers' connection to the theft. He was silent for a moment, mulling over the new information.

"Why does she think his death is suspicious?" asked Kate.

"She says there was no reason for him to die. In spite of having prostate cancer, he was in no danger. At least, no immediate danger. And she says one of the nurses on the floor reported seeing someone coming out of his room before they found him dead."

Good reasons.

"We're investigating," continued Bert, "and I'll let you know what we find out. It might be nothing."

But they both knew it was more than "nothing." There were too many coincidences.

"All right," she said finally. "Maybe you should hold off on telling Ernst Mulvahill about the doctor's suspicions until we know more."

Bert was silent for a moment. Then, "Do you suspect the brother?"

Kate shrugged. "Right now, I suspect everyone. Thanks for letting me know, Bert."

"You're welcome. Kate?"

"Yes?" she said cautiously.

"Are you in the bathtub?"

"Of course not," she said and hung up.

CHAPTER 10

McKell was already at Stan's Gym when Kate pulled into the parking lot the next morning. Only a few other cars were in the lot and she parked next to his car.

The sun had yet to crest the horizon but the eastern sky was full of pink promise as she pushed open the glass door into the gym. There were only five other people there, none of whom looked up as she crossed to the change room. McKell was nowhere in sight. He was probably in the men's changing room.

A few minutes later, dressed in her sweat pants and a plain white tee-shirt, she emerged from the change room to find McKell skipping rope in the far corner. He spotted her and she nodded at him on her way to the weights station. It was only twenty minutes later, when they both ended up at their regular treadmills that they actually spoke.

"You missed yesterday," said McKell. His pace wasn't fast, but it was steady and he was breathing regularly. He wore his usual mid-thigh, loose cotton shorts and a black tee-shirt that said in washed out white letters: "Cop Games, Mendenhall, Manitoba, 2010."

His skin color looked good.

"Slept in," said Kate. "Did you miss me?"

He slid a glance at her but didn't dignify her with an answer.

"Got a call from Bert last night," said Kate. She picked up her pace to a slow jog.

McKell looked at her in the mirror, eyebrows raised, a small smile on his lips.

Oh, for Pete's sake.

"Dr. Strickland, from Grace Hospital, contacted Winnipeg Police about a possible homicide."

The smile left McKell's lips. "Johann Mulvahill."

Kate nodded. "She has no proof, but clearly it bothered her enough to want to bring the police in."

McKell kept walking, thinking it through. Kate increased her speed again and concentrated on her movements. The outside door opened and an older man walked in, gym bag in hand. He headed for the change rooms. A young man was at the weights station, sitting on the bench and doing biceps curls. On the mats, one man was doing sit-ups as if the fate of the world depended on him, while another man knelt in front of him, bracing his feet, and counting out the sit-ups. At the back of the gym by the change rooms, Stan sat in his tiny office, his head bent over paperwork.

It had taken her a while to fall asleep last night, despite having slept poorly the night before. She kept wracking her brains, trying to figure out why anyone would want to kill Mulvahill. She finally gave up when she concluded she just didn't have enough information yet. That was when Bert invaded her thoughts and it was a long time before she could sleep.

"There's a chance Mulvahill's death and the theft of the semen aren't connected," said McKell finally.

They looked at each other in the mirror and Kate shrugged. Yes, there was that chance. If so, it would be a *heck* of a coincidence. She wasn't as dogmatic as some other investigators she had met who firmly believed there was no such thing as a coincidence, but still. It was highly unlikely.

"The semen is worth about fifty thousand dollars," said Kate. A week ago, she would never have thought those words would cross her lips. "Is that reason enough to kill a man?" A man who wasn't even in town at the time of the theft?

"We both know people are murdered for much less," said McKell, his mouth turning down. "What I want to know is who would have enough motive to want to kill him?"

"We need more information," said Kate. "Are you still going to the detachment?"

He nodded at her in the mirror.

"Good," she said on a sigh. "We need all the help we can get."

* * *

Martins looked up from the computer keyboard when Kate walked into the detachment, uniform over one arm, tray of coffee cups in hand, and her bag hanging off her shoulder.

"Morning, Chief," he said cheerfully. His crinkly auburn hair looked as if he had made an unsuccessful attempt to tame it.

"Good morning, Sergeant Martins," said Kate. She entered the duty room and placed the tray of coffee cups on the counter. "Everything all right?"

"Good morning, Chief," said Charlotte from her desk. She was in early—it was barely seven thirty. That must mean Josh was going to be in town and she wanted to get off early.

"Morning, Charlotte," said Kate with a smile. Today Charlotte wore black pants and a fitted, white, long-sleeved shirt, with a lovely, flowered scarf arranged artfully around her neck. Kate always admired people who knew what to do with scarves. Then Kate's glance landed on Charlotte's bare feet in skimpy little sandals.

"Oh, my," she murmured. "I admire your optimism."

Charlotte grinned. "It's going to be warm today, you just wait and see."

Kate turned to Martins and raised an eyebrow. He shook his head.

"These crazy kids," he said with a grin. "And yes, everything's fine. It was a quiet night, according to Stan."

"Good," said Kate. "The constables are already out on patrol?"

Martins nodded. "Yes. Friesen and Olinchuk are patrolling together today. That'll leave Trepalli free to continue interviews if you need him."

Kate nodded and turned toward the shower room, then stopped.

"DC Langdon called me last night," she started.

"Really?" said Charlotte with interest.

Kate took a deep breath.

"He told me that Johann Mulvahill's doctor came to them with suspicions that he had been murdered."

"That poor man," murmured Charlotte.

Martins blinked but waited for Kate to finish.

"They're investigating. They'll let us know what they find."

Martins nodded slowly. "So, this theft may have turned into murder."

Kate sighed. "I'm going to take a shower. Leave me a coffee."

* * *

Kate was putting her boots on when Martins knocked at the door.

"Come in," she called, straightening up as he walked in.

"Elijah Rudger is on the line for you."

Elijah Rudger. She stared at Martins for a few seconds before the name finally clicked into place. "The foreman at the condo site."

Martins nodded. "He sounds upset."

Well, that didn't sound good. "All right," she said. "I'll be right there." She finished tying her laces and headed for her office just as Martins transferred the call to her line.

"Hello, Mr. Rudger," she said. "What can I do for you?"

"Someone drove the cat off the cliff," he said without preamble.

Kate stared blankly at the filing cabinet, trying to decode his words. Finally, she realized that he meant the Cat—the Caterpillar. She tried to remember it from the construction site but all she could bring up was a generic yellow machine with a shovel at one end.

"The Cat," she said, trying to give herself time.

"Yes. It's a backhoe. I have the only set of keys, so they must have jury-rigged the starter. They just drove it off the cliff!"

She could hear wind whistling in the background. He must be at the site.

"That must have made a lot of noise," said Kate.

"Exactly! No one reported it?" Frustration laced his voice and she couldn't blame him for being mad. Starting the Cat up would have made a racket, especially in the middle of the night. The machine somersaulting over the edge of the cliff would have made even more noise. Someone would have heard. The fact that no one reported the noise spoke volumes about how much the residents detested that building.

"Now we have to figure out a way of getting it out of there before it falls all the way into the river and we get cited for environmental contamination," continued Rudger angrily. "Isn't there something you can do?"

Kate bit the inside of her mouth to keep from blurting out that there wouldn't have been an issue if the company had chosen to store its equipment securely and hire an on-site security guard. Instead, they may as well have left a neon sign with an arrow pointing at the site, flashing "STEAL ME! STEAL ME!"

"Who do you report to, Mr. Rudger?" she asked. Yet another thing she had forgotten to ask. What was the matter with her?

"Local guy," said Rudger after a moment. "One of the directors of the company lives in Winnipeg. His name is Leonard Hodgson."

Huh. Well, it probably made sense to have Rudger report to the local guy. But goosebumps chased each other on her forearms.

"Thanks for letting us know," she said. "Please call the detachment when you figure out how to raise the backhoe and we'll send some constables to control traffic."

"And provide protection," said Rudger grumpily. "I'm starting to wonder if those people are all in on it."

* * *

It was still only a few minutes past eight o'clock by the time Kate arrived at the Riverview complex and parked behind Trepalli's patrol car. She had instructed him to park on the main road of the condo complex and to be very visible.

She got out and met him by the patrol car. The sky was clear, promising warmth later in the day, but for now, the wind was on the cold side of fresh. She could feel her cheeks pinking up.

"What's up?" asked Trepalli as she approached.

"Follow me," said Kate. She led the way past the individual units and thought she saw a curtain twitch in Mr. McClusky's window. They rounded his house and crossed to the construction site. Kate's hands felt cold but she didn't want to tuck them in her pockets.

Elijah Rudger was on the far side of the half-built building, staring down the cliff. He turned when he heard them coming and only then did she see he was on the phone. He raised a hand in greeting but kept talking.

He was dressed in jeans and work boots, with a down vest over a blue and gray checked shirt. His pale hair gleamed in the morning light.

"Who's that?" asked Trepalli in a low voice.

Kate turned to him and was suddenly struck by the difference in the two men. Elijah Rudger was a big man, broad and tall, with the heft of a man still in his prime and who had worked hard physically all his life. Trepalli was just as tall as Rudger, but he was all lean muscle and long legs. Rudger was built for strength, and Trepalli for speed.

"His name is Elijah Rudger," said Kate. "He's the foreman. He called me this morning to tell me that someone sent the Cat over the cliff."

Trepalli blinked at her, long lashes sweeping down to hide those gorgeous blue eyes before revealing them again. Without a word, he headed for the cliff.

Kate followed him, nodding at Rudger as they passed him. They followed the construction fence to where someone had pulled the last segment out, leaving it to lean crookedly. She and Trepalli edged closer and peered over.

There, dangling drunkenly from a small tree halfway down the cliff, was the bright yellow backhoe. It looked as if it was hanging on for dear life. If the tree gave way, the backhoe would tumble the rest of the way to the river bank, and maybe into the river itself.

"Holy..." murmured Trepalli. "That wasn't very smart."

"No, it wasn't," said Kate. She realized suddenly that she was angry. Pissed off. This was past the point of protest, past the point of "sticking it to the man." This was willful destruction of property and damage to the environment. She'd had enough of these people.

"See what I mean," said Elijah Rudger, coming up behind them. "It's going to cost a small fortune to haul it back up the cliff—if it can even be done." He looked down at Kate, his brown eyes angry. "I thought you people were investigating the thefts and damage."

"Why don't you worry about securing your company's equipment properly and let us worry about the investigation?" she said sharply.

She caught a glimpse of his offended expression before she turned on her heel and headed toward Eric Brian's house. She heard Trepalli's boots on the pavement behind her.

"Come with me," she said grimly. "Just stand next to me and look stern."

"Yes, ma'am," he said smartly.

A strapping young constable at her back would reinforce how serious this was.

She reached the door and rapped sharply on it. A moment later, it opened to reveal a slim woman in her mid-thirties dressed in a nurse's pale blue scrubs. Her fair hair was cut short and slicked back like a helmet, as if she'd applied gel and let it dry like that. She had pretty hazel eyes filled with curiosity.

"Hello," she said. "Can I help you?" There was a sprinkling of freckles on her cheeks and on the bridge of her nose.

"Ms. Stooke?" At the woman's nod, Kate continued. "I'm Chief Kate Williams of the Mendenhall Police Department. This is Constable Trepalli. Are you aware of the vandalism and thefts that have been taking place at the construction site?"

Helen Stooke's eyebrows rose. "Chief Williams, everybody in the development is aware of it."

Kate nodded and glanced over the woman's shoulder into the kitchen. A man stood in the middle of the room, in his stocking feet and wearing jeans and an untucked pale yellow shirt. He held a mug in one hand and a piece of toast in the other.

"I spoke with your son about our investigation yesterday."

"You spoke to our son?" said the man sharply. He walked up to his wife and stood behind her. He had thinning brown hair that needed combing.

It was Kate's turn to raise her eyebrows.

"I gave him my card to give to you," she said. "I asked that you call me."

The man, presumably Armand Brian, turned his head and bellowed, "Eric!"

"Yeah?" came a voice from the recesses of the house.

"Get your butt down here!"

"Armand," said Helen Stooke warningly.

There was a clatter of shoes on uncarpeted stairs and Eric Brian came into the kitchen, his face a cloud of resentment. Then he caught sight of Kate and Trepalli standing behind her, and he swallowed.

"Hello, Eric," said Kate sweetly. "Nice to see you again."

His face flushed and he glanced quickly at his parents. "I forgot to tell you."

Liar, liar.

Before the boy's father could explode—seemingly a regular occurrence—Kate turned back to his mother.

"Last night, someone tipped a backhoe belonging to the construction site over the edge of the cliff." She glanced swiftly from face to face and allowed her anger to show. "Do any of you know anything about that?"

Helen Stooke shook her head. "No," she said firmly. "I just got home from working a night shift. Armand?"

He shook his head, too. "No. I was in bed by eleven. We both were." He nodded to his son.

"A backhoe makes a lot of noise starting up," said Trepalli gravely.

Kate glanced at him and saw that he had crossed his arms over his chest. She had to control a sudden urge to smile.

"Did you hear anything, Eric?" she asked the boy. Both his parents turned to look at him and he actually took a step back.

"No," he said.

"Because we've gone past willful damage to private property," she continued. "Now we're talking environmental damage if the backhoe ends up in the river. Even now, the oil and coolants could be leaking out of the machine and making their way into the water."

"Dear Lord," blurted the mother.

Kate nodded. "Yes, and if remediation needs to take place, that could be very expensive. I don't know if the condo corporation can afford it. I doubt any single homeowner can."

"Hang on there," protested the father, suddenly shifting from angry father to aggrieved homeowner. "Why should the condo corporation be held responsible for the actions of some hooligans?"

Kate shrugged. "That'll be up to your insurance companies to work out," she said crisply. "My job is to find out who did it and arrest them."

Her words dropped into the kitchen like mini bombs. All three of them jerked back. Then Helen Stooke and her husband turned as one to look at their son.

He stared at them openmouthed, then waved his hands in front of him.

"It wasn't me!" He glanced from one parent to the other. "Honest!"

Helen Stooke turned back to Kate. "Do you have reason to believe our son is involved?" she asked stiffly.

Kate smiled. "No more than anyone else who lives here and wants to see that building gone." Then she stopped smiling. "Of course, your son did seem delighted at the vandalism and theft when I spoke to him yesterday."

The woman took a deep breath. "Don't read too much into it," she said. "That seems to be a natural condition of the teenage boy."

Kate fished a card out of her pocket. Again.

"If you think of anything that could help with our investigation, please call. If you hear any rumors about what happened, please call. If you have any suspicions at all, please call."

Helen Stooke nodded and took the card. "We will," she said, looking at Kate. "Good luck."

Kate turned away and Trepalli followed her down the stairs. She heard the door close behind them.

"Do you think it was the kid?" asked Trepalli when they were far enough from the house.

Kate shrugged. She hated to be one of those people who automatically blamed young people, but they weren't known for having great impulse control, were they?

"Doesn't it seem weird, though?" asked Trepalli thoughtfully, stopping in the middle of the road and looking at the half-built building. Someone had spray painted crude genitalia onto the plywood in bright red.

"What?" she asked.

"Well, I can see kids spray painting the building," he nodded toward the house they had just left. "But the thefts? Where would a kid hide something like a generator? They'd need a pickup to haul it away. And where would they sell it? No." He shook his head. "It feels all wrong. And pushing the backhoe off the cliff? That's incredibly risky, don't you think?" He swept a hand out, taking in the condo units. "I mean, this isn't exactly the mean streets of Winnipeg."

What if he was right? That would mean more than one person was involved in what was happening here. Just how likely was that?

She examined the graffiti again. Exactly the sort of thing a teenager would think was funny. But the thefts? The backhoe? Maybe Trepalli was right.

"Are we going to talk to anyone else?" asked Trepalli as a woman holding two children by the hand walked past them. The kids looked like they were around six or seven and had backpacks on. Walking them to the bus.

Even as they watched her go by, a car drove past. Someone heading to work, no doubt. They were quickly losing their window of opportunity.

Kate looked over at Fergus McClusky's house. "Only one more," she said. She briefed Trepalli on her first encounter with the old man as they walked over to his door. She had decided against re-interviewing him yesterday, since she'd already spoken to him the day before. But things had changed since then.

"Still want me to be the tough guy?" asked Trepalli when they stopped by McClusky's door.

In spite of herself, Kate smiled. "That won't work with this one," she cautioned, and knocked on the door.

The door opened suddenly, as if McClusky had been waiting on the other side. He was wearing a worn pair of Carhartts and suspenders over a red shirt with a gray undershirt peeking above the top. He hadn't shaved and his white whiskers gave him a grizzled look, especially as his hair was tousled and pushed up on one side as if he'd just scrambled out of bed.

"Mr. McClusky," said Kate. "Nice to see you again. This is Constable Trepalli."

Next to her, Trepalli nodded politely. "Sir."

McClusky grunted something in response, then looked at Kate

again. "I suppose you want to come in."

"Why thank you," said Kate sweetly, stepping into the house and forcing McClusky to step back. She waited for Trepalli to come in and then closed the door behind them. They both removed their caps.

"We'll just stay on your rug," she said, pointing down at the braided rug beneath her boots. It looked of the same vintage as McClusky himself. She wondered if there was a Mrs. McClusky in the picture. "We're not interrupting your breakfast, are we?"

They were in the kitchen where an electric kettle, toaster, and microwave stood on the counter, polished and waiting. No dirty dishes in the sink, no crumbs on the counter. The terra-cotta tile floor was swept and clean. A small square pine table with two matching pine chairs stood in one corner of the small kitchen. The only thing on it was a plant with pink and white flowers. Kate had no idea what it could be.

McClusky raised an eyebrow. "I had breakfast two hours ago."

Kate studied the man's hair. If that was true, then clearly Mr. McClusky had forgotten to comb his hair.

"Is there a Mrs. McClusky?" she asked.

Pain swept over the old man's face and disappeared again.

"Adeline died ten years ago," he said gruffly. "It's just me now."

Kate felt like an ass. "I'm sorry," she said.

"Long time ago," he said, waving away her sympathy. "Now, what do you want?"

Now that she could see him up close, she figured he was probably around seventy, seventy-one, with deep lines in his forehead and bracketing his mouth. His face and neck were brown, as if he spent a lot of time outdoors. His teeth seemed to be all his and were the color of old ivory. And while he was thin, he was more wiry than skinny.

"Someone started up the backhoe that was on the construction site and drove it over the edge of the cliff," said Kate.

Both of his eyebrows rose this time and he stood blinking at her for a few seconds. Finally, he stuck his hands in his pockets.

"Did it go into the river?"

"No, sir," said Trepalli suddenly, almost startling Kate. "At least, not yet. It's caught up about halfway down."

"Jesus," said the old man, looking down at his stockinged feet and shaking his head. "If that isn't the stupidest thing."

"We're going to try to raise it," said Kate, "or at least the company is. But there's no guarantee it'll work. In the meantime, all kinds of toxic waste could be seeping out of the machine."

McClusky was nodding, as if he knew what she was talking about.

"Sir, did you hear anything last night?" asked Trepalli.

"No," said McClusky on a sigh. "No windows upstairs on that side of the house. And my bedroom is on the far side." He glanced up at Kate suddenly, then looked away.

"Mr. McClusky?" said Kate gently.

"What?" he replied, looking out the window as if something outside the house was vitally important.

Trepalli cleared his throat, attracting the old man's attention. "Sir, any information you can give us could help us stop this escalation. Before nearby homes get damaged, or someone gets hurt."

McClusky faced Trepalli, his brown eyes narrowed as if he were considering the constable's words. Finally, he sighed.

"I don't sleep so good anymore," he said. "Sometimes I get up in the middle of the night and go for a smoke on the balcony." He looked pointedly at Kate. "You saw me there the other day."

Kate nodded.

"I was on the balcony last night when someone went by on a bicycle."

Trepalli glanced down at her, then back at McClusky.

"Why is that unusual?" he asked.

McClusky shrugged. "It was about two thirty in the morning," he said. "And damned cold. I could see my breath."

"What direction was the cyclist going?" asked Trepalli.

McClusky pointed at his door, as if there was no wall between them and the outside. "East to west," he said, "heading toward the construction site."

"Could you see who it was?" asked Kate.

He shook his head. "Whoever it was, he was wearing a dark jacket with a hood."

"Why do you say *he*?" probed Kate. Hadn't Trepalli interviewed somebody yesterday who said they had seen a bicyclist in the middle of the night? Not likely to be a coincidence, but unless McClusky gave them something to go on, his information was useless.

"He was big," said McClusky. "Wide shoulders. Long legs. And the bike was one of those heavy-duty mountain bikes with the fat tires."

"Did you see where he went?" asked Trepalli. He had taken his notebook out and was taking notes.

McClusky shook his head. "Once he turned the corner of the house, I lost sight of him."

Kate sighed. It wasn't much.

"Sorry," grumbled McClusky. "But that's all I saw."

"It's more than we had, Mr. McClusky. Thank you." She hesitated a moment, then asked, "Why not smoke inside?"

McClusky shrugged. "Adeline never let me smoke inside."

Kate nodded. Then she grabbed one of her business cards from her pocket and handed it to him. "If you see or hear anything else, please call me, day or night. My cell phone number is on there, too."

He took the card without agreeing to anything and Kate and Trepalli made their way back to the patrol car.

"Didn't someone you interviewed yesterday...?" asked Kate as they walked.

"Yes," said Trepalli, his heels thumping on the asphalt. "Mr. Henry, two doors down from Mr. McClusky." They reached the patrol car and he unlocked it. "He couldn't provide a description, either. He did say he thought it was a man."

There were fewer cars parked in front of the homes as more and more people left for work. A teenage girl hurried past them, one eye on the road and one eye on the smart phone she held in her hand.

"I'm not sure what we gained by all of that," said Trepalli glumly, nodding in the direction of the construction site. "Want me to go talk to Rudger if he's still here?"

Kate considered a moment, then nodded.

"Find out when the crane will get here, or whatever Rudger's going to use to haul the backhoe out. You can check in with Martins about providing traffic control here. In the meantime, I need to figure out where Mr. Hodgson is."

"Hodgson?" asked Trepalli blankly. He stood behind the open car door, one elbow leaning on the window frame, one foot up on the car's frame.

"The director of 123-whatever Incorporated who lives in Winnipeg."

"Right," said Trepalli.

Kate swallowed a sigh and headed for her own car. She was *not* calling Bert on this.

CHAPTER 11

Kate decided to check in with the detachment before heading to Winnipeg. Paterson was planning to head for the Mulvahill farm from home, and Kate felt uncomfortable leaving the detachment without either a chief or deputy chief around. If things were too busy, she'd wait until Paterson returned before heading for Winnipeg.

It was still clear and cold by the time she walked into the detachment, shortly past nine. Charlotte was right—it was going to be warm by the afternoon. In the meantime, however, Kate was glad she kept an extra pair of gloves in the Edge.

"Morning, Chief," said Martins around a huge yawn. His eyes were bloodshot.

"Bad night?" asked Kate as she walked into the duty room. McKell looked up from one of the common desks and nodded at her before returning his attention to the screen. Charlotte flashed her a smile from her desk.

"Ellie's got the flu," said Martins, referring to his ten-year-old daughter. Smart kid. Unabashedly red hair. "I'm pretty sure she got it from Samantha's boy." He looked around at Kate. "They're falling like flies at the school."

Oh, great. The kids were bringing the flu home, which meant the parents would soon be getting sick, which meant her constables would be coming down with it soon.

"Wash your hands, wash your hands, wash your hands," she muttered, pointing her cap at him. "What did you find out about Hodgson?"

Martins yawned again and took a drink from his coffee cup before pulling a pad of paper toward him.

"Hodgson owns a small construction company in Winnipeg," he said. "Small stuff. Individual houses. Renovations. Decks. That sort of stuff. Nothing on the scale of Numbers, Incorporated."

Kate just stared at him and he shrugged.

"I can never remember the numbers."

"Is he around?" asked Kate with a smile. There was no point driving to Winnipeg if the man was in Toronto.

"According to his wife, who runs the office out of their home, he's on a job site in Winnipeg. She gave me the address." He scribbled something down and ripped off the paper from the pad, handing it to her.

"Thanks," said Kate, stuffing the paper into her pocket. "Trepalli call?"

"Yes, ma'am," said Martins. "I told him to stay there, since the tow truck will be there any minute."

"I thought they were bringing in a crane," said Kate.

"Not available until tomorrow," said Martins. "So they're going to try the tow truck first. It's a heavy duty one that they use for big rigs."

Kate pictured the backhoe and its precarious position on the cliff. She was pretty sure the backhoe weighed less than most cars, so that wasn't the issue. Getting the tow truck close enough to the edge without risking it falling over, and then having someone scramble down to the backhoe to hook it to the tow truck—that was going to be a problem.

Well, there was nothing she could do about it. Trepalli was on-site. He'd call if there was a problem.

"What about here?" she asked.

Martins nodded toward the office closest to his desk. "Samantha's at the Mulvahill farm," he said. "Finishing up the interviews. She called in a few minutes ago with Mulvahill's insurance information."

"And I spoke with Dr. Kendrick a little while back," said Charlotte, still typing away at her keyboard. "I have his insurance information, too." She glanced at Kate. "I'm waiting to hear back from both insurance companies."

"Good," said Kate. She looked at McKell. "How's it going, Rob?"

He lifted a to-go cup of Tim Hortons coffee in a salute. "Doing deep background checks on Kendrick, his staff, and the Mulvahills and their staff."

All right. "What about Friesen and Olinchuk?" she asked Martins.

"They're almost finished dealing with a small accident," he reported. "One person sent to hospital to get checked out but no serious injuries." He cocked his head at her. "Everything's fine, Chief. Just go."

Kate could feel McKell's grin. She ignored him.

"Fine," she said. "I'm going. Please call Chief Stendel and let him know I'll be in his bailiwick." It was only common courtesy to let the chief of police of Winnipeg know that an officer from another jurisdiction would be conducting business in his stomping grounds. In the past, she would have called Bert.

"Will do," said Martins.

All right, then. Time to go. She placed her cap on her head and turned toward the doorway. Then she stopped.

"Still no cause of death on Johann Mulvahill?" she asked Martins.

He shook his head.

"Let me know if you hear," she said. "Let me know if anything changes."

"Will do," he said again. "Now, go."

She nodded. "Can you check with Elijah Rudger about the insurance company for Numbers?" she asked.

Might as well be thorough.

* * *

She stopped at the Tim Hortons before taking the highway to Winnipeg. Normally she didn't mind the hour-long drive. It gave her a chance to sort through whatever case she was working on. But today she was going to need more coffee.

It was almost nine thirty and there were only a few people in the line-up. She took off her cap and went to stand behind a heavy-set young man doing something with his phone. She was trying to figure out exactly what he was doing when a hand on her elbow startled her. She looked around.

James Kendrick smiled down at her. He really did have very nice eyes.

"Dr. Kendrick," she said, smiling back. "Great minds?"

He laughed, and even the young girl behind the counter looked up and smiled at the sound. He must have been a bit of a heartbreaker when he was young. She wondered if he was married, but didn't think so. No wedding band. No married "vibe."

"I'm on my way to my next patient," he said. "Figured I should get reinforcements first." He leaned in conspiratorially. "Sour cream glazed donuts," he confided. "They're my weakness."

Kate dropped her voice.

"Your secret is safe with me," she assured him.

"Thank you, Chief," he said solemnly, "but I think the secret is out." And he patted the slight bulge of his stomach as if to prove it.

She liked a man who could laugh at himself.

Then it was her turn and she moved up to the counter to order her coffee. When she had it in hand, she smiled a goodbye to the vet and headed out.

At some point, she was going to have to ask that man a few questions about the theft, but the line-up at Tim Hortons wasn't the place.

It was Wednesday morning and there was very little traffic to demand her attention. The sun shone in a cloudless sky and the fields on either side of the highway were starting to green up, the short stalks all bending toward the north as if a giant hand had ruffled them. The air coming through the vents had a faint tinge of sweet hay—a scent that never really went away, even in winter. She thought of it as the underlying smell of Manitoba.

Well, that and manure.

She took a sip of the coffee and replaced the cup in the holder. Maybe when she was in Winnipeg she could pick up a gift certificate for Amanda and Marco, for the opening of Amanda's Folly. She had no clue what the girl needed for her new venture but she'd been talking to Jerry Wolsynuk over the weekend. Her old friend had retired from the Royal Canadian Mounted Police a few months earlier and moved to cottage country in Ontario. Jerry had suggested a gift certificate to a restaurant supply company. That way, Amanda and Trepalli could pick out exactly what they needed.

Kate thought that was a great idea. Not fancy, maybe, but certainly practical. Now all she had to do was find one.

First, she had to speak to Leonard Hodgson. She had studied a map before leaving Mendenhall—a paper map, not one of those electronic maps mounted to the dashboard, which only ever succeeded in getting her lost—and had a pretty good sense of where Hodgson's construction site was located.

According to Hodgson's wife, he was building a studio above a garage in Tuxedo, one of Winnipeg's fancier neighborhoods. It was southwest of the downtown area, with the Assiniboine River to the north and Assiniboine Park to the west.

Nice.

She held her breath as she approached the overpass from which a sniper had shot McKell last year. He'd been aiming for her, but McKell had been driving her car.

The overpass was finished now but she saw no one on it.

Dear Lord. When she thought that he could have been killed... had come very *close* to being killed...

That had been the beginning of the end for her and Bert. He had gone into overprotective mode, which had driven her half-crazy, even though she understood his concern. It was as if that was the first time he had realized that her job was dangerous. Which spoke to a certain condescension on his part—what did he think they did as police officers in Mendenhall? Sit around and eat donuts? Did he think her constables weren't "real" police officers who faced dangers every day? Did he think only big city police officers were at risk?

She blew out her irritation on a gust of breath. Enough. There was no point in getting herself riled up again. Bert now knew that her job was riskier than his, and he couldn't handle that, even though he had changed his mind and said he could.

She didn't believe him. She had loved that man with a deep, abiding love, but she couldn't commit to a man who would try to make her change her mind about a job she loved. It would never have occurred to her to do that to him.

No, best to break it off before things got even harder. More heartbreaking.

Still. Amanda and Marco had found a way past that hurdle. Was it because they were still young enough to believe that love could conquer all?

She knew better.

Enough, enough, enough. It was time to focus on the job at hand.

She got off the highway and headed up Portage Avenue to the Moray St. bridge, then threaded her way through increasingly smaller roads in the general direction of Tuxedo. Finally, she turned up Beaverington Court and slowed down. All the houses were set back from the street, with lawns that were already green, thanks no doubt to lavish—and expensive—attention. Tall hedges screened many of the houses from indiscreet interest and almost all of the houses had elaborate posts on either side of the driveway entrance, proclaiming the street number.

It was only around eleven, but there were people on the street. When she looked closer, she saw that it was mostly young women pushing carriages or guiding little kids on bicycles. Nannies? Stay-at-home moms? She saw only one man, on a bicycle with a bundled-up toddler in a bike seat behind him.

She finally stopped in front of a house hidden behind six-foot cedar hedges. Only the black roof peeked over the top of the hedges so she couldn't tell what the house looked like.

She had almost expected gates on the driveway, but there weren't any—only brick columns with carriage lights on them, and the street number.

Very nice if you were into that sort of thing.

She got out of the Edge and placed her cap on her head before strolling up the driveway toward the house. Beyond the hedge, the lawn continued another fifty feet to the foot of a two-story red brick house with white columns and a set of hand-carved doors. A white panel van was parked nose out by a navy-blue king cab pickup next to the house. Both vehicles had "Hodgson Construction" painted on the side, with a Winnipeg phone number and email address underneath.

The sound of children laughing in the street competed with the sound of a pneumatic hammer coming from the back of the house.

There was no garage attached to the house. It had been built in the days before people expected to access their garage from inside the house.

She went around the vehicles and followed the paved driveway past a side door and staircase with a wrought iron railing. Narrow windows set in the foundation proclaimed the presence of a basement, or at least a half basement. She walked around the house to where the driveway ended at an old-fashioned garage with double doors that had to be opened by hand. A row of windows was set in each door.

The hammering was coming from the roof of the garage, where two men were putting up the skeleton of walls. The men had their backs to her. She briefly considered climbing the ladder leaning against the garage, then thought better of it.

The smell of sawdust was strong in the backyard, reminding her of her father and his workshop.

She glanced around and her eyebrows rose in appreciation. The backyard just kept going, filled with topiaries, flower beds, and narrow paths leading to a small gazebo. There was even a water feature in the center of the yard. She glanced behind her. A multi-level deck ran the length of the house, filled with patio furniture and lounge chairs. Finally, she looked back at the garage. Its siding looked like it could use a refresh. Probably part of the work the men were doing.

To the side of the garage on the lawn, a pile of two-by-fours rested on a plastic sheet next to a couple of sawhorses and a table saw. Sawdust covered the grass like some kind of mulch.

"Hello!" she called up. One man straightened but didn't look around. Clearly he had heard something but didn't know where it had come from.

"Down here!" she called, placing her hand on her cap to keep it from falling off as she craned her neck.

The two men stepped closer to the edge and looked down. They were both the same height and wore jeans and sweatshirts, with tool belts tied around their hips. That was where the resemblance ended.

The older one looked to be around forty, forty-five, and had an incipient paunch. The sleeves of his gray sweatshirt were pushed up to his elbows, revealing powerful forearms, still winter white. He was bareheaded, with short dark hair thinning on top. His face was red, especially his cheeks and nose.

The younger man was maybe twenty. Slender but with wide shoulders and a muscular build. His fair hair was held back from his face by a short ponytail, and the sides of his head were shaved. He looked like a Viking.

"Hello," said the older man. He looked her up and down, taking in her uniform. "Can I help you?"

"I'm looking for Leonard Hodgson," said Kate. "Would that be you?"

He looked taken aback for a moment, then shrugged. "Yes. Hang on. I'm coming down." He turned to the younger man and said something. The man nodded and returned to work.

Hodgson stepped over the framework of the wall they were building and swung himself onto the ladder with the ease of someone who used ladders every day of his life.

Kate swallowed hard and looked away. She was uncomfortable with heights. She could handle them if she had to, but climbing onto a roof from a ladder was a particular bane of hers. There was something about transitioning from the top of the ladder onto the roof—even if it was a flat roof—that gave her the heebie-jeebies.

Hodgson clambered down easily, jumping the last three feet, and walked over to her. He smelled of clean sweat and sunshine, and for a moment, the longing for Bert was almost overwhelming. She cleared her throat.

"I'm Kate Williams," she said. "Mendenhall Chief of Police."

He nodded and pulled a metal bottle out of one of the pouches on his tool belt. He unscrewed the lid.

"Elijah told me about the backhoe," he said. "I expected you to call, not drive all the way out here." He took a deep swallow and replaced the lid.

Of course the foreman would have called him.

"I like talking face-to-face," said Kate. She pulled her notebook and pen out of her jacket pocket. "Things are getting out of hand at the site."

A look of deep frustration settled on his face and he slipped the bottle back in its pouch.

"I can't begin to tell you how tired I am of that site," he said with quiet passion.

Kate grinned. "I can imagine," she said. "Just to confirm—you are a director of..." she flipped open her notebook to find the notation. "...128444, Incorporated?" She wondered briefly just how a receptionist for the company would answer the phone—the name was incredibly unwieldy.

"I am," he said with a nod.

"Who is insuring your construction site?" she asked, suddenly realizing she might save Charlotte some time if she got the information from him.

He looked up as if he could pluck the information from the air. After a moment, he looked down again.

"Why do you need to know?" he asked carefully.

"For our records," said Kate with surprise. "Is it a secret?"

He laughed, and looked suddenly younger.

"Of course not. We're dealing with Red River Insurance, here in town."

Kate nodded and wrote it down in her notebook.

"And are you responsible for the construction site?" she asked.

He looked at her as if trying to figure out what, exactly, she was asking him. He had pale brown eyes that stood out in his sunburned face.

"I'm the local contact point," he said. "Since I live the closest. Elijah Rudger is the foreman on the job and he keeps me informed. In turn, I keep my colleagues informed."

Kate nodded.

"The vandalism seems to be escalating," she said gently. "I recommend you beef up your security measures until the court case is settled."

Hodgson sighed and scratched the back of his neck. "You are

preaching to the choir, Chief Williams. I've been pushing for more security since the stop-work order was placed on the job." He put his hands on his hips and looked up at the roof of the garage, where his worker was bent over, hammering. "But I was outvoted. They don't want to spend more money on it than they absolutely have to."

He looked back at Kate and gave her a half smile. "To be honest, we don't think we'll win the case. The project manager we hired was a little... aggressive... and went ahead with beginning construction without obtaining the condo owners' agreement." He sighed again. "What a waste."

What a mess, more likely. Kate couldn't help but think this spoke more of greed than aggression. The company had clearly turned a blind eye to their project manager's shenanigans because the apartment building would bring in a lot of revenue. She was willing to bet they had planned to ask for forgiveness after it was a done deal, and hadn't counted on a judge who wasn't about to let them get away with it.

That was a matter for the courts to decide, but in the meantime, she was stuck dealing with the company's mess.

"Mr. Hodgson," she said sternly, "I can't stress enough the importance of having better security on the site. Porter Security is contracted to make one sweep of the site a night. That is clearly not enough. In fact, I recommend you hire someone to stay on-site at night to discourage the thieves."

Hodgson's eyebrows rose and he tilted his head slightly.

"With all due respect, Chief Williams," he said slowly, "I don't think it's your place to tell us how to run our business."

Kate stared at him. Gone was the *aw shucks* friendliness. The man who stared back at her now had resentment in his eyes.

So. That was the way of it, then. She shrugged.

"Maybe not, Mr. Hodgson," she said crisply, closing her notebook and replacing it in her pocket. "But it *will* be my business when someone gets hurt at your construction site, or someone burns it down. The recommendation I just made will be in my report, which I will share with your insurance company. Thank you for your time."

She turned on her heel and walked away.

* * *

Son of a *bitch.*

Kate drove out of Tuxedo and stopped at the nearest coffee shop she could find. She had learned a long time ago not to drive mad as she had a tendency to speed. She turned the engine off and sat behind the wheel, staring at the big picture windows of the coffee shop.

That company didn't give a damn what happened to their construction site. They knew they were going to lose the case and didn't want to throw more money into the project. They had to have very good insurance. Well, she was going to get in touch with Red River Insurance and explain the facts to them.

She finally slid out of the Edge and locked the door. The parking lot was half full, mostly with pickup trucks. The wind swirled grit around like a mini tornado and she kept her mouth firmly shut. The coffee shop—Joe's, according to the sign painted on the window—was right on Portage Avenue and the traffic noise was irritating. The smell of car exhaust reached her and she went up the three steps to the door quickly to get away from it.

A bell sounded as she pushed open the door and Kate stopped just inside. She removed her cap as she looked around. The place held maybe fifteen tables, some just big enough for two chairs but most accommodating four. There were maybe eight or nine customers seated at various tables, mostly men.

There was a counter to her right and a big display case with sandwiches, salads, and sweet treats. She made her way toward the counter and the young woman standing behind it.

"Hi," said the woman. She looked eighteen or nineteen and had long black hair in two neat braids. Her bright brown eyes shone with intelligence and interest. Her nose had a bit of a hook and was a little crooked, but her skin was clear and smooth and she had a pretty mouth.

"Hi," said Kate with a smile. "What have you got in sandwiches?"

"We've got an assortment of sandwiches," said the young woman. She waved Kate toward the display case and followed her. The sandwiches were all on mini baguettes and had all kinds of exotic ingredients. Kate finally settled on a Brie, chicken, and cranberry sandwich.

"And a cup of coffee," she added. She might regret it later, but right now, she needed the caffeine.

"Coffee's across the way," said the young woman, handing Kate the sandwich on a plate and taking her money. She nodded at a spot behind Kate's shoulder.

Kate turned around and saw a coffee station tucked in the corner. She fixed herself a mug of coffee and found a table as far away from the other customers as possible. She wanted to call the detachment.

Just as she was sitting down, her phone rang, startling her. A man a few tables over looked up from his own sandwich with a frown but Kate gave him her evil eye and he looked away.

She glanced down at the number and her lips tightened.

Bert.

For a moment, she considered not answering. Then she sighed and accepted the call.

"Kate Williams," she said.

"Hi, Kate, it's Bert."

His warm voice in her ear suddenly reminded her of where she had been the last time she spoke to him. She felt the heat crawl up her cheeks and closed her eyes in mortification.

"Hi Bert," she said calmly. "You have news?"

Because that was the only reason he would call. If he had news.

"Yes," he said. "Johann Mulvahill was definitely killed."

Kate's eyes opened slowly. She turned to stare blindly out the picture window and dropped her voice.

"You got the autopsy results already?" She *never* got autopsy results that quickly.

"Just the preliminary exam," said Bert. "The full autopsy has yet to be done. But when the medical examiner took a look at the body, she noticed bruising around the throat, bruises that took some time to show up, I guess. So she took a closer look. His hyoid bone was broken."

"Strangulation," said Kate. Huh. Someone had snuck into an old man's hospital room and strangled him.

"Yes. I figure it had to be a man, because Mulvahill was still pretty big for an old guy. He wouldn't have gone down without a fight."

Kate shook her head at her pale reflection in the window. It would take some kind of nerve to sneak into the man's hospital room, subdue him, and kill him while nurses and orderlies were just on the other side of the door.

Reckless or desperate?

A thought occurred to her.

"If he fought back…"

"I know," said Bert. "I'm getting the medical examiner to look under his nails. Maybe he scratched the bastard." He took a deep breath. "We need to notify his brother."

Kate thought about it for a moment. "Can we hold off on that?" she asked slowly, still thinking it through.

This time, it was Bert who hesitated. "For how long?"

"I'm not sure," Kate admitted. "But I don't want to lose the tactical advantage in case I need it."

"All right," he said finally. "It's only a preliminary result and we don't want to alarm anyone unnecessarily."

Kate smiled at the window. "Thanks, Bert."

CHAPTER 12

Kate decided against calling the detachment with Bert's news. She needed time to figure out what it meant. Besides, Samantha was probably not back from her interviews at the Mulvahill farm.

She got her sandwich wrapped up and poured her coffee into a to-go cup before climbing back into the Edge. She paused behind the wheel for a minute, running through what she knew so far, trying to decide if there was anything else she needed to do in Winnipeg. Finally she decided that there was nothing more she could do here at the moment.

Bert would call her if there was news. She tossed her cap onto the passenger seat next to her sandwich and buckled in. It was still beautiful out, but a few clouds were massing to the north, pushed by the wind. She glanced down at the dashboard. Only ten degrees Celsius. Charlotte's toes were going to stay cold.

She drove west on the highway, trying to keep her attention on the road, but the facts of both cases kept waylaying her.

Why had Johann Mulvahill been killed? Did he know something about the theft of the semen? How could he? He hadn't even been in town at the time. Or had that been the plan? Had someone waited until he was away to arrange for the theft?

Who would have known when Johann would be away? His

brother, certainly. And probably anybody else at the farm.

How likely was it that the semen would just happen to be delivered on the day Johann was away? Had Ernst Mulvahill arranged it that way?

A car passed her on the left and she glanced at her speedometer. Just as she sped up when she was angry, she slowed down when she was deep in thought. She nudged the gas pedal down an inch.

Who had decided when the tank would be delivered? Ernst Mulvahill or James Kendrick?

* * *

"We can't just assume that his murder is connected to the theft," said McKell around a mouthful of Kate's sandwich.

She, McKell, and Paterson had taken over the break room, pulling out the table so all three could sit around it with notebooks and food. Kate had cut her sandwich in half and shared it wordlessly with McKell, while Paterson had reheated leftover soup from home.

Kate and Paterson both turned to look at McKell. He shrugged.

"Someone has to play devil's advocate."

In the background, Kate could hear Martins talking with a man who had come in to report the theft of his motorcycle. Charlotte had gone for lunch, Trepalli was still at the construction site, and Friesen and Olinchuk were patrolling.

"All right," she said. "Let's admit the possibility. Did you find anything in your background checks that would indicate someone might have a reason to kill him?"

He shook his head and flipped through his notebook. Kate noted with interest that it was his regular, leather-bound notebook, the one he always carried on the job. "The man seems to have been well liked by everyone. He's never had an encounter with the law, never been sued. Paid his bills on time. He was seventy-one. Lost his wife to cancer about ten years ago. Three kids, ten grandkids. His kids are in Regina, Vancouver, and Kelowna. He owned the farm with his brother Ernst, who is fifty-eight. Ernst never married. He got into a little trouble when he was a teenager, but nothing since then."

"What about the staff?" asked Kate.

"Nothing popped out," he said promptly. "No arrests, no complaints."

"He's a bit of a strange duck," said Paterson. "Ernst. I can understand why he never married. I can't see him loving any woman as much as he loves that farm. But from there to killing his own brother..."

Kate sat back in her chair and looked out the window. The wind was rattling the bare branches of the oak tree. Clouds were massing and she wouldn't be surprised if it rained again.

"I think I'd like to meet Mr. Mulvahill," she said slowly. She turned to look at her colleagues. "Why don't we invite him to come in? Say, tomorrow?"

Paterson nodded. "It'll be interesting to get him out of his comfort zone."

Kate nodded. "And let's bring in the vet, too." She felt a little funny suggesting it, but Kendrick—charming as he was—was a part of this case. She couldn't neglect him as a witness, no matter how much she liked him. And she wanted to ask him—or have someone ask him—about leaving the tank behind.

McKell looked at her, and a slow grin spread over his face. "Shall we arrange to have them cross in the hallway?"

"Why, Rob McKell," said Kate in feigned shock. "You are a devious man."

A movement in the parking lot caught her eye. Charlotte was cutting across, head down, the hem of her blue car coat flapping in the wind, revealing glimpses of a bright yellow lining. She had changed into red running shoes. Just then, Marco pulled into the lot and parked in the assigned patrol car slot.

"What did we find out about the insurance on the semen?" she asked. Both cases—the theft of the semen and the vandalism at the construction site—seemed to orbit around insurance. Surely that couldn't be it. Could it?

The outside door opened and Charlotte entered as if shoved by the wind. Her hair looked as if it had been caught in a blender and she ran fingers through it, trying to put some order in it. She glanced inside the break room, saw them, and turned in, Marco Trepalli following right behind her, hanging on to his cap in one hand.

"Chief," he said with a nod. "DCs," he added with a grin.

"Is it done?" asked Kate.

"Yes, ma'am," he said. "It took some finessing, but they were able to haul the backhoe back up the slope. I called in Environmental Protection Services to check out the slope and see if there was spillage. The backhoe took some serious damage. I'm pretty sure it's a write-off."

"Did the company own it, or were they renting?" asked McKell.

Good question.

"Renting," said Trepalli. "According to Rudger, the foreman, insurance will cover the loss."

"Well, isn't that nice for them," said Kate.

Everyone turned to look at her and she shrugged.

"Everyone connected with Numbers Incorporated seems to like pointing out how well insured they are."

Charlotte stopped fussing with her hair and turned on her heel, walking out of the break room as if her phone were ringing. Before the others could do more than look at each other questioningly, she was back, lined notepad in hand.

"You asked me to research the directors of the company," she reminded Kate. "It's been around for about four years. Most of its projects are like the Riverview project—residential construction, mostly in Ontario. But fifteen years ago, Leonard Hodgson and the current CEO, Dwayne Landry, were directors in another construction company in Quebec, also a numbered company. And in between, Landry and Holman Rehayem were directors in yet another numbered company out of Alberta." She looked up from her notes. "About five companies in all, including Numbers Incorporated, over fifteen years, with various combinations of the same directors. None of the companies lasted more than five years. So far, four of them folded after their current projects were destroyed by fire. All four companies got major insurance payouts."

"Son of a bitch," said McKell.

"Yes," agreed Charlotte.

Trepalli looked around. "Maybe I should call the arson investigators in those cases and find out if they ever learned the cause of the fires." He glanced at the clock above the door. It was one forty-five. "It's still early enough to catch them at work, hopefully."

"Go ahead," said Kate just as Paterson said, "No."

McKell raised an eyebrow and Kate looked at Paterson.

"I can do that," said Paterson. Her color was high and there was an edge to her voice that hadn't been there in a while.

Kate waited to see if the acting DC was going to explain herself, but McKell stepped into the breach.

"Why?" he asked.

Paterson turned to look at him. "We're still short staffed. Trepalli needs to relieve Olinchuk and Friesen for lunch. We need at least one patrol car out there."

Kate found herself nodding. It made sense. Trepalli tried valiantly to control his expression, but she saw the frustration. She tucked the information away for further consideration. Was Trepalli's frustration with the acting DC, or with the fact that he wanted to do more than patrol?

"All right," she said, standing up to stretch her legs. It seemed that all she did lately was sit. It was time to start running outside again.

Charlotte raised her notepad in a mock salute. "I'll try to get the names of the arson investigators for you," she said and left the break room.

"Well," said McKell, stretching his arms out above his head. Kate wondered if the scar on his chest pulled when he did that. "I think I'll head back home. Let me know when you schedule the interviews," he said to Paterson. "I'd love to see what they have to say."

Paterson carefully didn't look at Kate. "Why don't you take one of the interviews on?" she asked.

McKell smiled crookedly. "Nope. I don't know the case as well as you do. This is your circus."

He was right, of course, though Kate admired Samantha for trying. They shouldn't push the man. He was clearly on his way back, and was wise enough to know he should walk, not run. Kate was thrilled that he had come this far.

She was getting him back.

Once McKell left, Trepalli dug through the refrigerator for anything of interest while Martins called Olinchuk and Friesen back in. Kate followed Paterson into her office and sat down in one of the visitors' chairs. Paterson hadn't removed any of McKell's pictures on the bulletin board by his desk. Clearly, she didn't think of the position as permanent.

"He's looking good," said Paterson, sitting down. She still looked tired, but her green eyes were bright with interest.

Kate nodded. "Yes, he does. You did a good job in getting him here, Samantha."

A faint pink overtook her freckles, and for a moment, Samantha Paterson looked beautiful.

"Thanks, Chief," she murmured. "But I think it took all of us working like dogs to get him here."

Kate burst out laughing and Paterson grinned sheepishly.

"All right," said Kate finally. "Did you learn anything new from the interviews?"

Paterson sighed and leaned back in her chair. She pulled her worn notebook toward her and flipped it open, searching for the right spot.

Paterson's window, like Kate's, looked out onto the parking lot. From Kate's angle in the visitor chair, she could see the back end of her red Edge in its parking spot, and Mendenhall Drive beyond it. Dust swirled in the air. Even though the sun still peeked through the clouds, the day had dulled. It looked cold out there.

"Mulvahill has three men working the farm with him, and a woman whose job is to keep the house clean and the men fed." She raised an eyebrow. "Mulvahill is a traditionalist."

Kate almost snorted but controlled herself in time. She nodded for Paterson to continue.

"Nothing stood out in the interviews with the men," she said. "They show up for work at seven every morning and leave at five. They're mostly working in the fields or in the barn and rarely go to the house. Ernst handles the grain operations while his brother handled the cattle. The workers knew that the vet was coming that day to drop off the tank." She looked up from her notes. "They're all new," she said. "They've only been on the job for a few months."

"All three?" said Kate in surprise. "Why? What happened to the old workers?"

Paterson shrugged. "When I asked Mulvahill, he said that one of them went back to school, one moved away, and he fired the third for incompetence."

Kate was nonplussed. Wasn't this a busy time of year for farmers? Bad time to change up the crew, she would have thought.

"And get this," added Paterson, her index finger resting on a spot on the page. "None of them have ever worked on a farm before."

Holy... "None of them?" she asked. "Isn't that a little strange?"

Paterson nodded. "That's what I thought, too. So I asked the housekeeper for the names of the three previous workers."

"Why didn't you ask Mulvahill?" asked Kate out of curiosity.

Paterson's mouth quirked up on one side. "He couldn't remember, offhand," she said. "He promised he'd get back to me once he checked his records."

"Well, that's not suspicious."

"Not at all," agreed Paterson.

"What about the housekeeper?" asked Kate. "Did she know their names?"

Paterson flipped a page. "Mrs. Einerson has a very good memory," she said. "She was able to give me their names without hesitation."

"Can you track them down?" asked Kate with a sigh. She was starting to get sick of interviewing people, for this case and for the vandalism case. But that was police work. You just never knew when the right question would jog the right answer and break the case wide open.

"Yes," said Paterson. "I'll ask Martins to find them and talk to them."

Out of the corner of her eye, Kate saw Friesen and Olinchuk arrive. She hoped McKell would decide to come back to work permanently, and soon. She couldn't keep running the detachment shorthanded.

"Anything else come out of the interviews?" she asked.

Paterson shook her head.

"Not really. Mulvahill gave one-word answers and was close to rude." She shrugged. "It could be grief."

Well, that was true. People didn't like dealing with the police at the best of times, let alone when a death was involved.

"You were there when he got the phone call that his brother had died, weren't you?" she asked slowly.

Paterson looked startled.

"Yes. He came out of the house holding the phone and announced it to the staff."

An idea was niggling at the edges of Kate's awareness, but she knew better than to try and force it.

A headache was beginning to form behind her eyes. She sighed and hauled herself to her feet.

"I have that meeting with the mayor's chief financial officer," she said glumly. "I'm taking Charlotte with me for protection. If she hasn't finished getting contact info for the arson investigators, get Martins to carry on. I'll ask him to arrange for Mulvahill and Kendrick to come in tomorrow afternoon."

"All right," said Paterson.

Kate headed out of the office but stopped in Paterson's doorway as a thought occurred to her.

"When we interview them," she said, working the thought out as she spoke, "let's find out when they decided on the date for the transfer of the semen to the farm. And who decided." She looked over her shoulder to find Samantha staring at her, clearly perplexed.

"It's been bothering me," said Kate.

Samantha nodded and jotted something down in her notebook. This was going to be her first formal interview. Every cop had experience with interviews, from talking to a driver pulled over for speeding to witnesses at the scene of an accident, but a formal interview was different. It took preparation and strategy. Samantha didn't show it, but she had to be nervous.

Kate hesitated, trying to find the right, nonthreatening, words.

"Tell you what," she said. "Let's both prepare a series of questions we want them to answer. Then we'll compare notes and make sure we've got everything covered."

Samantha nodded. "Good idea. Which one do you want me to take?"

Kate blinked, surprised by the question. She thought for a moment, staring blankly at her acting DC.

Samantha had spoken to both Ernst Mulvahill and Dr. Kendrick. Damn.

"Maybe you shouldn't interview either one of them," she said slowly. Samantha frowned and Kate hurried on. "You've already interviewed them both. It's probably more valuable to see what they would say to a new person."

Samantha sat still for a moment, mulling it over. Then she nodded. "I agree. You should probably take Ernst Mulvahill. What about the vet? Should we ask the DC if he would do it?"

Kate shook her head. "He's already said no," she said. "And for good reason. Martins knows as much about the case as we do. He can interview the vet." Martins had only taken the preliminary information in the case when the vet first came in. Samantha had done the brunt of the talking to the vet.

"All right." Samantha stood up. "I'll talk to Martins and review questions with him. Then we can compare with yours."

"Sounds like a plan," said Kate.

As Samantha went to speak with Martins, Kate walked over to Charlotte's desk.

"Time to go?" asked Charlotte, glancing at the clock.

"Just about," said Kate. "Did you have a chance to speak to the insurance companies for Mulvahill and Kendrick?"

Charlotte shook her head. "Sorry, Chief. I left messages at both companies but I haven't had a chance to follow up."

Kate shrugged. "You can try when we get back from the meeting."

Charlotte nodded but the frown didn't leave her face.

"What is it?" asked Kate.

The girl sighed. "It's probably nothing," she said.

"What's probably nothing?" asked Kate. The door to the detachment opened and the clump of booted feet came down the hall, preceding Olinchuk and Friesen. Their cheeks were ruddy with the cold.

"It's just..." started Charlotte, reclaiming Kate's attention. "It's just... well, you know how Josh has to travel all around southern Manitoba for his work?"

Kate nodded. As an itinerant veterinarian, Josh worked out of various clinics in Winnipeg, Brandon, and Mendenhall. He could travel hundreds of kilometers in a day.

"Well, he depends on his truck," continued Charlotte, turning in her chair to face Kate. "And if the truck breaks down, he has to be able to get it to the service station as soon as possible. That's why he's a member of CAA."

The Canadian Automobile Association. Yes, that made sense. But what did that have to do with the price of tea in China?

Kate nodded again, silently encouraging Charlotte to continue.

"Well, Dr. Kendrick must have something similar," said Charlotte. "Why didn't he call CAA and wait for the tow truck?"

Kate stared at Charlotte. There might be a perfectly logical explanation. Martins would have to ask the good vet.

CHAPTER 13

The meeting with the city's chief financial officer went about as well as Kate had expected. He bemoaned the fact that the city had very little money and Kate pointed out that a police department couldn't function with squad cars that kept breaking down and out-of-date computers. Charlotte presented their budget figures and pointed out that there was no fat left to trim in it. After an hour and a half, the CFO promised to take the request to the next council meeting and that was that.

This was the part of her job that she hated, this constant paperwork and fighting for every penny. Well, that and scheduling.

Kate and Charlotte drove back to the detachment in silence. Kate was pretty sure Charlotte was already working out a strategy for obtaining what they needed from the city. She sure hoped Josh wouldn't take the girl away from Mendenhall.

By the time they arrived, the rain had started up, washing away the eternal prairie dust that seemed to live on Kate's car, no matter how often she washed it.

Both squad cars were out and the parking lot looked deserted.

Charlotte glanced at her watch as she got out of the Edge.

"It's past four o'clock," she said. "If Nick hasn't been able to contact the arson investigators yet, we may have to wait until tomorrow morning."

Kate nodded. Couldn't be helped. There was too much work to do and too few people to do it. She should have requested additional constables from the CFO—then he probably wouldn't have quibbled about the relatively minor cost of new equipment. She sighed.

"Can't be helped," she said glumly, leading the way to the detachment's door. "Until we get McKell back, everyone's stretched."

Charlotte nodded and went through the door Kate held open.

Martins looked up as they walked by.

"That bad, eh?" he said sympathetically at the look on Kate's face.

"It's not looking good," said Kate grimly.

Charlotte turned to look at her, her eyebrows raised.

"I thought it went very well," she said with surprise, "for an initial meeting."

Kate's own eyebrows rose. "Maybe we weren't at the same meeting?"

Charlotte grinned. "It's the CFO's job to keep the city's books in balance," she said. "It's up to the mayor and council to rearrange priorities. We just laid the groundwork that will allow the mayor to do that." She looked at Martins. "We'll get our new squad car yet. And new computers, too, I'll bet." She walked over to her desk, removing her coat.

Martins laughed. "If anyone can do it, Charlotte, it's you."

Kate glanced at the DC's empty office. "Where's Samantha?"

"She's in Brandon," he said. "We located the employee the Mulvahills fired. She's gone to see if she can interview him."

"Good," said Kate. Maybe they were finally going to get somewhere on this case. "Any luck with locating the arson investigators?"

He shook his head. "Found all their names and phone numbers, but haven't been able to reach them. I left messages."

Kate sighed. Patience, she told herself, is a virtue.

"All right. What about the interviews with Mulvahill and Kendrick?"

"Mulvahill refused to come in tomorrow. He said he's arranging for his brother's funeral as soon as the hospital releases his body. The best he would do was agree to come in on Friday morning. Short of arresting him, I figured we'd settle for that. He's coming in at ten thirty on Friday. I left a message at Kendrick's clinic asking him to come in at eleven. I figure Kendrick will have to wait a bit, which will help us arrange for Mulvahill to see him on his way out." His mouth quirked up on one side. "Mr. Mulvahill was *very* reluctant to come in but he finally agreed when I pointed out that his insurance company would be receiving our report."

Huh. Martins had had to threaten Mulvahill in the same way she had threatened Hodgson at the construction site. Again, things seemed to revolve around insurance.

"I would like to talk to the insurers," she said slowly. "Hodgson told me that Red River Insurance covers Numbers, Inc. Can you get me the name and number for Kendrick's insurer? And the Mulvahills'?"

"Yes," said Martins, turning to the computer. "It'll just take a minute."

"How are the questions for the interviews coming along?" asked Kate.

Martins looked up from the keyboard.

"The DC left me her list and I've combined it with mine. It's on the common drive under 'interview questions.' You should probably take a look and make sure we haven't forgotten anything."

Kate nodded and headed for her office. Her brain felt fried and mushy at the same time. It occurred to her that she hadn't had a vacation in a while. As she dropped her cap on top of her filing cabinet, she sighed.

It would be a while before any of them could take a vacation.

* * *

By the time she'd gone over the interview questions, added her own, and rearranged them in the order she felt would make sense, Kate knew she was done for the day. She printed out the questions for Martins, herself, and Samantha, then grabbed her cap and left her office.

"I'm going to see if I can interview Jason Cromarty on my way home," she told Martins. Charlotte had already left, popping into Kate's office to say goodbye. Samantha was still gone, but Kate couldn't wait any longer. She was going cross-eyed, and she still needed to pop by Amanda's place to make sure she didn't need help.

All she really wanted was a hot bath and eight hours' sleep. Surely that wasn't asking too much of the universe?

"Who's Jason Cromarty?" asked Martins. He was looking a little peaky, too, and Kate hoped he wasn't coming down with the flu. This was only day three of his four days on. Three busy days. He needed his time off. They all did.

"The other security guard," she said. "His shift started on Monday night. Nobody's talked to him yet about the vandalism and thefts."

Martins blinked at her, then frowned. "Sorry, Chief. I should have remembered."

She cocked her head slightly and gave him a half smile. "We both should have."

He sighed and ran a hand through his copper-wire hair, succeeding in making it look like a Brillo pad.

"You know," he said, "if something else comes up, we're screwed."

Kate nodded. That had occurred to her.

* * *

To her astonishment, Jason Cromarty lived in the Riverview condo development.

She had driven directly to the Riverview from the detachment and slowly cruised by the construction site, trying to be as visible as possible. Martins was going to talk to Albertson when he came on shift about making sure there were numerous patrols of the area again tonight. She didn't want a repeat of the Cat-tipping incident.

Once she'd finished her patrol, she drove out of the condo development and pulled over to the side of the street under a street lamp. She saw a woman walking a dog—a big thing, all white with splotches of black—that must eat her out of house and home, and a couple of teenagers getting off the city bus, but otherwise Mendenhall seemed to be settling in for the night.

Now she sat in her Edge as evening gathered around her and stared at the address on the yellow sticky note. It was a measure of how tired she was—how tired they *all* were—that she hadn't noticed before where he lived.

She had taken the sticky note from the receptionist at Porter Security on Monday and stuck it on the inside back cover of her notebook without noting the address, then promptly placed the sticky note with Pinkley's address on top of it. Until this moment, she hadn't had occasion to pull the Pinkley address off and look at Cromarty's address.

She remembered planning to interview him—when was that? Monday? But so much had happened since then that she hadn't had a chance to search for his address.

And now here it was, smack dab in the middle of her investigation.

But really, how significant was it? Mendenhall, for all the thousands of acres of farmland surrounding it, was a small town. Everybody lived near everybody else, in one way or another. It was probably just a coincidence that Cromarty lived in the condo development.

A really weird coincidence.

Finally, she set the notebook down on the seat next to her and put the Edge in gear. She pulled into the road and found a place to turn around. The street was still damp from the earlier shower and now the light from the street lamps reflected off the wet surface.

Driving at night, especially in the rain, always left her a little melancholy, as if she was all alone in the world and no one was expecting her home.

Oh, wait, she thought. No one was.

It was just past six o'clock. Most people would be at dinner or just finishing up. Cromarty's shift started at seven. She would probably catch him at home, getting ready.

His unit was on the other side of the development from the construction site and abutted the green space. All the units on this side were separated from the green space by a fence, which gave individual owners access to a personal backyard. An older model, gray Cherokee was parked in one of the two parking spots in front of Cromarty's house, and a light shone above his door. She pulled into the empty parking spot next to the Cherokee and walked up the sidewalk. The damp immediately penetrated her uniform jacket and she shivered.

Just before knocking, she turned and looked around. Other units blocked Cromarty's view of the construction site, even from his balcony.

Turning back to his door, she knocked firmly three times and waited.

She was just raising her hand to knock again when the door pulled open suddenly, startling her. A tall, broad-shouldered man filled the doorway and she controlled a sudden urge to step back. He was younger than Pinkley, with blond hair trimmed neatly and blue, blue eyes that put her in mind of Marco's eyes. His angular jaw was freshly shaved and he smelled faintly citrusy. He wore jeans and a fitted white shirt with a black jacket over top that read PORTER SECURITY in white embroidery over the left breast.

He stared at her for a few seconds, then his gaze dropped to her shoulder flash.

"Chief Williams?" he asked, grinning at her. "I wondered when you guys would come around to me."

It could have been a criticism but it was said with such humor that Kate found herself grinning back at him.

"Jason Cromarty, I take it?" At his nod, she continued. "Do you have a few minutes?"

He stepped back, allowing Kate to enter, then closed the door behind her. Next to the door, a pair of men's running shoes—size ten or eleven, she figured—sat on a small mat, next to pair of black dress boots, same size. She took off her cap and tucked it under her arm.

His kitchen layout duplicated Mr. McClusky's. Same terra-cotta tile floor, same white granite countertops. Instead of a square table, however, Cromarty's kitchen sported a small round one with two wrought iron chairs that looked like they belonged on a patio. The sink had dirty dishes in it and the only appliance she could see on his counter was a fancy coffee machine with lots of levers and buttons.

Bachelor pad.

"I only have a few minutes, Chief Williams," said Cromarty apologetically. "I'm on shift at seven and I still need to pick up something to eat for lunch. Or breakfast. Whatever."

He smiled self-deprecatingly and shrugged. Kate remembered night shifts only too well—the indecision around what kind of food would be suitable for a meal break that was in the middle of the night, the dreaded three o'clock droopy eyelids...

"I don't miss night shifts at all," she told him honestly.

He laughed. It was a very nice laugh and it made her look at him more closely. He couldn't be older than thirty and was obviously fit. Any woman would pause to give him the once over. Why wasn't this fellow married?

He might be divorced, she told herself. Or even have a girlfriend somewhere. Just because he lived on his own didn't mean he *was* on his own.

"If you can spare me a few minutes," she continued, "I'd just like to ask you a few questions about the incidents at the construction site." She nodded over her shoulder at the door.

To her surprise, Cromarty crossed his arms over his chest and looked down at his booted feet. Then he sighed and looked up at her.

He was blushing.

"It's very embarrassing to have this happening where I *live*," he said glumly. "My neighbors are giving me a hard time."

She barely controlled a smile. Instead she nodded. "I can imagine. Have you seen or heard anything that might help us?"

He shook his head. He smelled good, like sweet lemonade.

"Nothing that I can think of. After nothing happened on Monday, I thought maybe whoever it was had smartened up, but then last night..." He shook his head again. "How the *hell* did they push the Cat over the edge without anyone noticing?"

Kate shrugged. "Luck and sound sleepers is my guess. What time did you patrol on both nights?"

He pulled a smart phone out of his pocket and quickly flicked through a couple of screens, then started reading.

He'd patrolled three times the first night, once before midnight, then once at two thirty and once at four. Then last night he'd patrolled four times, again once before midnight and the other times between one and five.

"Was the backhoe still there at your last patrol?" she asked, jotting down his information.

She looked up when he didn't answer right away. Now his face was beet red.

"I can't honestly say," he finally told her. "I wasn't looking for it. I certainly didn't notice that it was gone. I stopped the car and got out, shining the Maglite through the window openings and on the storage container, but I didn't notice the backhoe. Or the lack of the backhoe."

"Not even the fence pulled out of its moorings?" asked Kate.

He shook his head, his face a study in misery. She wondered fleetingly if he was about to lose his job over this. Surely not. Four patrols when they were only contracted for one patrol nightly showed conscientiousness. Not a good sense of observation, maybe, but definitely conscientiousness.

She flipped her notebook closed and slid it back in her jacket pocket.

"All right, Mr. Cromarty, I won't keep you any longer. We'll be increasing patrols tonight. If you notice anything—anything at all—that might be of concern, please call the detachment and report it. We'll be there right away."

He nodded and sighed. "Thank you, Chief Williams. I'll do that."

* * *

The last thing Kate wanted to do once she got home was go back out again, but Amanda's friends and family do was tomorrow night, and there would be a lot of last-minute work to do at their house.

Kate dropped her keys on the little table by the door and bent over to unlace her boots. When she straightened, her back protested a little. Definitely time to start running outside again.

She kicked the boots into the closet and padded down the dark hall to her bedroom. She was a little hungry, but if she stopped in the kitchen first, she knew she would never get out the door.

The house felt cold and a wave of melancholy swept over her. This was the way it was going to be now. No more coming home to a warm house redolent with savory smells. Amanda and Marco were going to move in together as soon as the rest of their house was finished, and Kate would be on her own again.

Wah-wah-wah, she mocked herself. She'd been on her own most of her life and she was doing fine.

It was true. She was accustomed to being on her own, to dealing with her problems by herself, to making her own decisions without consulting anyone else.

But having Amanda around had spoiled her. Not to mention having Bert around.

The traitorous thought surprised her and she stopped in her bedroom doorway, staring blindly into the dark room.

It *had* been nice having Bert around. He was smart and funny and kind. And a really good kisser.

Shaking her head at herself, she flicked on the light and quickly changed into jeans and an old sweatshirt. Not glamorous, but practical.

Minutes later, she slipped on her running shoes and was back in the Edge, having avoided the kitchen successfully. Hopefully, Amanda would have some food at the house for the workers.

She saw a few of her neighbors walking their dogs as she drove down the road, but mostly the street was quiet as families finished their dinners and kids their homework.

The driveway at Amanda's house was packed with cars again, none of which were Bert's green Honda CRV. She parked across the street and got out, glancing up and down the street as she did so. She didn't see Bert's car anywhere.

She didn't know if she was disappointed or relieved.

All the lights were on in the house and she could see figures moving in front of the big picture window in the living room—dining room now. Winding her way between the cars in the driveway—Marco's, Amanda's, Friesen's, and Julianne's, Amanda's best friend—she made her way to the backyard. There were no lights on and it took a few moments for her eyes to adjust enough to make her way to the deck stairs.

The backyard smelled of damp earth and wet grass, and the breeze had a bit of bite to it. The clouds had finally moved off, leaving a sky filled with stars dimmed by the light pollution leaking from the street.

She climbed the steps to the deck, noting that the trellis was up around the entire railing, completing the cozy look. Someone had even threaded the mini lights Amanda had wanted through the overhead trellis.

Light spilled from the empty kitchen onto the deck. There were no tables or chairs on the deck yet—it was too cold still, and besides, Kate wasn't sure Amanda and Marco had even bought any yet.

Damn it. She had forgotten to buy a gift certificate when she was in Winnipeg.

With a sigh, she opened the back door and let herself into the kitchen.

At that moment, the kitchen light went on as Julianne entered the kitchen, carrying a pail full of dirty water. She stopped in surprise and grinned at Kate.

She was a tiny thing, barely five feet tall, with long, dark hair that fell in a sweep halfway down her back. Her dark eyes and high cheekbones spoke of aboriginal ancestry, and her full lips always looked ready to smile. Tonight, her hair was in a single braid down her back and since Kate had last seen her, she'd added bangs to her haircut. It made her look all of seventeen, though Kate knew she was closer to Amanda's twenty-five.

"Hello, Chief Williams," said Julianne cheerfully. "Come to help?"

Kate grinned at her and raised her hands, palm up. "These are all yours," she said. "What do you want me to do?"

Hearing Kate's voice, Amanda popped her head into the kitchen.

"Aunt Kate!" She came into the room, carrying a damp rag in one hand. "I wasn't expecting you."

Julianne hefted the pail to the sink and poured its contents out. Kate shrugged. "I figured there would be a bunch of last minute stuff."

Although now that she looked around, everything seemed to be in place and clean. She toed her running shoes off and walked over to the dining room. Amanda stepped aside to let her by and followed her in.

The room had been transformed. Amanda and Marco had refinished the oak floors and now they gleamed in the light of the two chandeliers dripping with crystal drops. Six round tables were interspersed around the room, four of them able to accommodate two people and two that could seat four or five people. Most of the tables had chairs around them but two tables were still missing theirs.

Amanda and Marco had traveled to every estate sale, pawn shop, and secondhand furniture store in southern Manitoba to find chairs for their home restaurant. As a result, no two chairs were the same, but the overall effect was charming.

One long rectangular table had been pushed against the inside wall. All the tables were covered with white tablecloths and the rectangular table had an additional multicolored, embroidered runner that ran the length of the table. Small candlesticks sat on each table and a candelabra sat on the big table. A built-in hutch with glass doors on top and drawers and cupboards on the bottom filled the far wall. It was filled with dishes, cutlery, napkins, and tablecloths.

"It looks great," said Kate, impressed. They had even extended the coat closet at the front door so their guests could hang their coats.

"It does, doesn't it?" said Amanda happily as she surveilled her handiwork. "We're all done, Aunt Kate. The bathroom is ready with guest towels and soaps, and even candles. We're just doing the final cleanup. Tomorrow is cooking day and tomorrow night is party night!"

Marco chose that moment to come up the stairs by the front door, carrying a pair of chairs.

"Oh, hey, Chief," he said when he spotted her. He edged past the two of them and set the chairs down at a one of the tables. Friesen came up the stairs a moment later with two more chairs.

The front door opened suddenly and they all turned to see Bert standing in the doorway. He blinked at the attention concentrated on him, and a grin started to form. Then his gaze found Kate.

Her heart started beating faster and her breath caught in her throat. He looked thinner than the last time she'd seen him in her sister's backyard in Quebec, seven months ago. His red hair was maybe a little grayer than she remembered, but those copper penny eyes were still as brilliant and penetrating as ever.

She wished he would stop staring at her so she could catch her breath.

"Hi Bert," said Marco cheerfully. He seemed to sense no awkwardness—apparently, it was perfectly normal for her and Bert to be in the same room at the same time.

And why wouldn't it? They were both adults.

"Reporting for duty, ma'am," Bert told Amanda with a mock salute.

Kate found herself smiling. She shouldn't be surprised to see him. A small part of her had expected him to be here. After all, the job wasn't done.

Amanda went to Bert and planted a kiss on his cheek.

"I'm so sorry, Bert," she said contritely. "If I'd known you were planning to come, I would have called you. We're done." She swept a hand around the room to show him.

Bert gave her a crooked smile.

"No worries, Amanda. But now that I'm here, maybe I can talk to your aunt."

Everyone turned to look at Kate. She blushed.

"About what?" she asked abruptly.

"Our case," he replied grimly. "Let's talk outside and let the kids finish up here."

He went to walk into the dining room but Amanda placed a hand firmly on his chest. "Oh, no, you don't. We just washed this floor."

Bert grinned at her, then looked at Kate. "Meet me on the deck," he said.

Kate nodded and retreated to the back door to put on her running shoes.

Bert was coming up the steps as she closed the door behind her. He stopped a few feet from her.

"You can't possibly have the DNA analysis so soon," said Kate. It took weeks, sometimes months, to get the results of a DNA analysis, if one got done at all. They weren't cheap.

Bert shook his head.

"Too soon," he agreed. "All we got was the fact that the DNA belongs to a man."

Kate walked over to the railing and leaned back against it, careful of the trellis. She crossed her arms and stared down at her running shoes. That it was a man's DNA wasn't surprising. After all, a man had been seen leaving Johann Mulvahill's room.

"What males are connected to this case?" asked Bert, approaching. "The nurse who saw a man leaving the hospital room never saw his face. She said he was tall and wore Carhartts, a black windbreaker, and a black ball cap low over his eyes." He sighed.

She understood his frustration. It could well be that the man seen leaving the room was a friend who came to visit. Or he could have been the murderer.

She looked up at him. "As far as I know," she began carefully, "just the three farm workers, his brother, and the vet."

Bert looked at her blankly. "The vet?"

"The tank was stolen from his truck."

Bert nodded and stood staring off to the side, clearly thinking it through. Finally, he looked back at her.

"Isn't it time we told Mulvahill that his brother was murdered?"

Kate nodded. They couldn't put it off any longer. Bert had agreed to hold off on notifying Ernst Mulvahill until they knew more, a courtesy that could be seen in some quarters as cruel to the brother. But this was a murder investigation, and sometimes, police had to make tough calls.

"He's coming in on Friday morning for an interview. If it's okay with you, I can tell him then and watch his reaction. The vet's coming in, too." He didn't have to agree, of course. Johann's murder had taken place in his bailiwick, after all. But it made sense to collaborate, since the murder might be linked to the theft of the semen tank, which was in her jurisdiction.

She wasn't surprised when he reluctantly nodded his agreement. He clearly didn't like it, but he'd go along with it. Then she remembered something.

"Bert, do you think you could find out from Grace Hospital when they informed Ernst Mulvahill that his brother had died?" She could try to get the information herself, but Winnipeg wasn't her jurisdiction and hospital administrators could get sticky with releasing information.

He stared at her for a moment, then slowly asked, "What are you thinking?"

She shrugged. "Probably nothing. I don't know. But it's been niggling at me."

"I'll make the call first thing tomorrow," he promised. "Now, do you mind if I observe the interview?"

Kate's eyebrows rose. "If you like," she said slowly. "But I would tell you everything he said."

"I know." He grinned at her. "But you said it yourself, I want to observe his reaction."

"All right," she said with a shrug. "He's coming in at ten thirty Friday morning. Kendrick, the vet, is coming in at eleven."

"I'll be there," he said, and suddenly leaned in to kiss her on the cheek. She got a whiff of his spicy aftershave on a gust of warmth. "It's good to see you, Katie," he murmured.

Then he turned and ran down the stairs to disappear into the shadows of the backyard.

* * *

To Kate's delight, Amanda came home that night. They had a late dinner of omelets and sat around the kitchen table for hours talking about the upcoming opening of Amanda's Folly and her plans for the future. Kate mostly just listened, enjoying her niece's company and basking in the girl's joy.

When she couldn't keep her eyes open anymore, she retreated to her bed, where she fell asleep listening to Amanda getting ready for bed and reliving the feel of Bert's lips on her cheek.

CHAPTER 14

Kate's eyes sprang open at the sound of trumpets in her bedroom. She stared at the darkness, blinking in incomprehension until she noticed the curtains forming a faint square on her wall. It was still night.

The trumpet sounded again and she sat up suddenly, realizing it was her phone. She turned the bedside light on just as her bedroom door opened.

"Aunt Kate?"

"Mph."

"Are you awake?"

The trumpet sounded again. If she'd had a hammer, she would have smashed the phone to bits. If she could have found it.

"It's on your dresser," said Amanda, coming into the room. She wore a ratty tee-shirt and a pair of fuzzy pajama bottoms with little penguins on them. She plucked the phone from the dresser and handed it to Kate.

Kate's eyelids finally parted enough for her to focus on the phone's screen. She didn't know the number. She slid her finger over the screen to accept the call.

"What?" she said indistinctly. Amanda let herself out of the room and closed the door behind her.

"Chief Williams?" said a scratchy male voice.

"Yes. Who is this?" She knew her tone was abrupt, but it was—she glanced at her bedside clock and stifled a groan—almost two-bloody-thirty in the morning.

"Fergus McClusky. You told me to call you if anything happened."

And just like that, Kate was wide awake.

"What's happening, Mr. McClusky?"

"I just saw the cyclist pass by my house, heading for the building site."

Excitement speared through her and she found herself on her feet. "Thank you, Mr. McClusky. I'll have someone check it out right away."

"Good," he said, and hung up.

Kate immediately called the detachment and hit the speaker phone icon. As the phone rang, she pulled down her pajama bottoms and left them in a pool on the floor. She snagged the jeans she'd tossed on the wooden chair that she kept in the corner by the dresser.

"Mendenhall Po—Chief," said Albertson's voice. "What's wrong?"

She never called in the middle of the night so the concern shouldn't have been surprising, but there was something else in his voice.

"What's happening, Stan?" She zipped up her jeans and pulled her pajama top off while she padded to the dresser for a bra.

"We've had a couple of incidents," said Albertson. "Small ones," he hurried to add. "Some idiot set fire to the gazebo in Joe Carter Park. "Tourmeline and Boychuk are on-site, along with the fire department. Then, twenty minutes ago, there was a break-in at the jewelry store on Main."

Kate finished pulling her sweatshirt on and sat on the bed with a pair of clean socks.

"Fallon and Oppenheimer are on that one?" she asked. When Albertson said yes, she continued. "Did Porter Security respond?"

"No. It's not one of their clients."

Kate stood up again and took Albertson off speaker phone. She quickly told him about the phone call she'd just received.

"Call Porter Security and tell them to meet me at the construction site," said Kate.

"All right," said Albertson. "I'll send one of the constables as soon as I can. You wait for them," he warned.

"Of course," said Kate.

"I mean it, Chief. Wait for backup."

They rang off and she hurried to the front door, pulled open the closet door and quickly donned her running shoes. It was odd that two incidents had happened at roughly the same time. Pretty serious incidents, for Mendenhall. Especially on a Wednesday night. The regular yahoos usually waited for Friday or Saturday nights to pull their moves.

The incidents were a diversion, meant to pull the police away from Riverview.

She was just putting her jacket on when Amanda emerged from the kitchen with a thermos mug in hand.

"Here," she said, handing it to Kate. "You could use the caffeine."

Bless the girl. No questions asked, just doing what needed to be done. She would make a fine police officer's wife.

"Go back to bed," said Kate. "You've got a big day ahead of you." She opened the door and said over her shoulder, "Thanks for the coffee."

At two forty in the morning, the streets of Mendenhall were deserted. Kate raced to Riverview, only slowing down once she entered the condo development. There were no lights on in any of the little houses. The streets were still damp on the edges where they met the lawns, but otherwise it looked like they were drying up. There were no cars out and about, and no bicycle that she could see.

Her Glock pressed into the small of her back where the holster was covered by her jacket. It was good to have it even though she probably wouldn't need it. The vandal hadn't shown any tendencies toward violence.

Her mouth tasted stale and she realized she hadn't combed her hair. Oh, well. This wasn't a fashion show. Still, she quickly ran her fingers through her hair, trying to work the worst of the knots out.

She parked where she and Trepalli had parked the last time, on the main road, and dug out her foot-long flashlight from under the driver's seat.

She silently closed the driver's door, put her phone on mute, and ran on the balls of her feet past Mr. McClusky's house. She hoped the old man was inside where it was safe, but didn't take the time to look up at his balcony.

Her ears and hands immediately felt the cold, and she could see her breath in the faint light. Her heart beat fast with either fear or excitement—she couldn't tell. It had been a while since she'd done anything like this. She reached the last house in the row and stopped. Crouching to make herself the least visible possible, she peered past the edge of the wall at the construction site.

The place looked completely deserted. She could see no car parked nearby, and no bicycle, although a bicycle could be hidden around the far wall of the half-constructed building. She studied the wire mesh fence but couldn't see anywhere it might have been cut or even disconnected from a neighboring panel.

The only things she could hear were the sound of the river rushing by far below and her breathing, which was fast and shallow. She made an effort to take deep breaths and let them out slowly to calm herself.

Was she too late? Had the vandal come and gone already? Or was the cyclist just some random guy coming home from a late shift?

Disappointment tightened her lips and she stood up. Well, she was here now. Might as well check it out.

The metal shaft of the flashlight was freezing cold, but she kept her hand wrapped around it as she silently ran across the road to the fence. The flashlight was heavy with the batteries filling it, and would serve as a good close-up weapon if she needed it. The only outside lighting in the development was on the balconies, from the lights that came on at nightfall. It was enough to see where she was going, but not enough to see in great detail, especially at the construction site.

But if anyone was inside the building, they would be able to see her clearly through the empty holes of the window cutouts on the front. If they were looking.

The rain over the past few days had softened the ground around the fence and turned some spots into muck. She scanned the ground as she made her way around the fence, trying to see in the incidental light from the nearby homes. She didn't want to turn the flashlight on yet. Her feet sank slightly at every step and she had to work at keeping her running shoes on.

The first time she had been here, she had found an entry point on the left, where someone had snipped the metal ties that kept two panels together. It had since been repaired, but now one panel gaped open again. Her heartbeat accelerated and her hand tightened on the flashlight. Someone had been here. She studied the ground around the fence and saw footprints where someone's feet had sunk deeply in the wet ground. There was a flurry of prints, probably as the perpetrator fiddled with the fence bindings, and the footprints then carried on inside the fence.

There were none coming back out.

Kate looked up at the side of the building, which presented a blank face to her. There were no windows cut out on this side, either because none had been planned, or because the builder hadn't gotten around to it yet. She would have to follow the footprints around the building to the back.

Glancing around, Kate listened hard for any sound that would tell her where the vandal was. Nothing. Just the wind and the river rushing by.

She was so *tired* of the whole Riverview case. She wanted to catch the bugger and put him behind bars.

Taking out her phone, she quickly punched in the duty desk number.

"Chief," said Albertson. His voice was tight.

"I'm at the site," she whispered. "Someone's inside. This is now an active crime scene. Who's coming?"

"Tourmeline and Boychuk are ten minutes away," said Albertson promptly.

"No sirens," warned Kate in a whisper. "But the sooner they can get here, the better."

"Yes, ma'am," he said. "Wait for them and stay out of sight."

Yes, Dad, she wanted to say. Instead, she hung up and slipped the phone back in her pocket.

What was he *doing* in there?

If she retreated to the nearest little house and hid behind the corner, she would be able to see both ends of the construction site. He couldn't make his escape on the cliff side, so he would have to come out the way he'd gone in or shove the fence out on the other side.

If she caught him by surprise, she might be able to stop him before he got away on his bike.

Hurry up, she silently urged her constables.

She was about to retrace her steps and wait for backup when she caught a faint whiff of gasoline. Her head swiveled automatically toward the shell of the building.

Son of a bitch. Was he lighting a *fire*?

Without another thought, she followed the footsteps past the fencing.

This close to the building, the smell of damp wood was almost overwhelming, along with the stink of muck. There was standing water in the ditch all around the building. As she rounded the corner of the building, the wind suddenly whipped her face, snatching at her breath.

They should tear the bloody thing down and plant trees as a windbreak. It would stabilize the ground at the same time.

Despite being closer to the building, she could no longer smell gasoline. Had she imagined it?

Then her searching gaze caught on something that hadn't been there the last time she had been at the back of the building. Halfway down, where the back door opening yawned open, someone had placed a two-by-eight plank of wood to bridge the four-feet-wide, five-feet-deep ditch.

He was definitely inside.

The hand holding the dark flashlight rose reflexively and she set out again. To her dismay, her shoes made a soft sucking noise as they pulled out of the mud. Had he heard?

She crept closer to the back door, achingly aware of the window openings on either side of it. She wanted to catch whoever it was in the act, which meant she had to make her way up that plank before turning on the flashlight to peer inside. With any luck, whoever it was would be too busy to notice her.

Should she pull her weapon out? Not yet, she decided. No need to pull the weapon out unless and until she needed it. And then only if she was prepared to use it.

It might be a kid in there.

She placed a foot on the plank and began to shuffle up the forty-five-degree angle to the doorway. The plank sagged a little as she approached the middle and her muddy running shoes had trouble getting a grip on the wood. At every step she paused to listen, but could only hear the wind and the sound of the river. Back here, it was almost total darkness, in spite of the starry sky. She peered into the black hole of the door opening, trying to make out any movement.

She caught a ghost of a smell, something vaguely familiar, before the pungent stink of gasoline reached her from inside.

Holy... Her heartbeat accelerated suddenly and she took a couple of deep breaths.

Stay calm.

She reached the two-by-four frame of the opening and placed one foot on the base for greater stability just as she turned on the flashlight and swept the beam through the interior darkness.

"Mendenhall police!" she called out in a loud voice. "Show yourself!"

She caught a glimpse of sawhorses and sheets of plywood stacked on two-by-fours. Then two big hands reached out of the darkness by her feet, grabbed her ankles, and yanked.

She had time to yell, "Son of a bitch!"

Then she lost her balance and toppled over backward. The flashlight tumbled end over end as she lost her grip on it and it disappeared inside the building. Then her shoulder caught the plank on her way down and her head slammed into the corner of the board.

She had a vague sense of someone yelling, of mud and water filling her nose and mouth, and then nothing.

* * *

The cold water in the ditch shocked her back to consciousness. She got to her hands and knees, coughing and spluttering, shaking her head. The whole front of her was soaking wet and she immediately started shivering.

She thought at first her shoulder was broken, it hurt so much, but that couldn't be, since she was using both arms to keep herself above the water.

Her coughing worsened, and she managed to get to her feet, covered in mud and soaked to the skin. She wiped the worst of the mud off her face and spat it out of her mouth, only then realizing that she was cursing.

The Glock. In a panic, she twisted as if to see behind her, then reached back to feel for the holster. Her relief at finding the familiar hard metal of the Glock still safely tucked in the holster almost drove her to her knees again.

Cough, curse. Cough, curse. Her head pounded with every cough. If she caught that bastard...

At last, she realized that what was causing her cough was smoke. She whirled to face the building and almost passed out again. She had to lean back against the ditch wall and wait for the stars to stop spinning. When she was finally able to open her eyes, she saw thick plumes of pale smoke emerging from the door and window openings.

The bastard had done it. He'd set a fire.

She had to call this in. Her hands automatically reached for her phone but it wasn't in the pocket she always used. She patted her pants pockets and the rest of her jacket, but the phone was gone.

Crap, crap, crap.

If it had fallen into the ditch, she would never find it. It was black as Hades in back of the building, and the bottom of the ditch might as well have been hell's floor.

The smoke was getting worse and she was breathing it in.

She cast about for the plank but couldn't see it anywhere. He'd probably slid it back inside after he got out. Which meant she had no way of getting out of the ditch. The ditch wall was too high, as was the opening of the door. Not that she wanted to go inside the building. As she watched, a tongue of flame appeared from inside the smoky doorway. The stink of gasoline competed with the choking smell of smoke.

She had to get out of here.

With one hand trailing the cold dirt of the ditch wall, she began to make her way down the ditch toward the side of the building. Once she was at the front, she might find some way of climbing out. And if she didn't, at least she'd could let her constables know where she was, once they arrived, or once Porter Security arrived.

What was taking Porter Security so long? Albertson would have called them soon after she hung up with him the first time. What was taking her constables so long, for that matter?

The mud at the bottom of the ditch kept trying to pry her running shoes off her feet, slowing her progress. Her feet were so cold from the six inches of water at the bottom that she couldn't feel them. As she trudged, she felt the back of her head gingerly. There was no broken skin that she could feel—her fingers were ice cold and probably not as reliable as usual—but a huge lump was forming behind her left ear.

Great.

Just as she turned the corner, she heard the sound of sucking mud and stopped. Someone was above her. Above the ditch. Had the perpetrator come back? Had he even left? Behind her, the sound of flames crackling grew louder as the fire caught in gasoline-splashed wood. She looked up but could only see a few feet past the top of the ditch wall.

She glanced around looking for anything she could use as a weapon. Nothing. She was a sitting duck.

A pair of pajama-clad legs suddenly appeared at the top of the ditch and Kate followed them up to find Mr. McClusky staring down at her. He had thrown on a jacket over his pajamas and was carrying a hammer.

"Chief Williams," he said politely.

"Mr. McClusky," she replied, trying not to cough.

They stared at each other for a moment, then McClusky blinked.

"Would you like some help getting out of there?"

A bubble of hysterical laughter threatened to escape Kate and she swallowed it back.

"That would be lovely, thank you."

And then he left.

Kate stared at where he had been, wondering where the hell the old man had gone. When he didn't reappear, she continued on her way around the side to the front. While there was more light at the front of the building, none of it reached the bottom of the ditch.

The fire had caught well and was now crackling and roaring

behind her. Heat pulsed from the building, warming her. Pretty soon, it would roast her. Or maybe steam her.

As she passed one of the lower window openings, she could see the fire feeding on the back wall. Soon it would make its way around to the front of the building. She had to be out of the ditch before that.

"Where did you go?" called Mr. McClusky, a note of panic in his voice.

"Around the front," she yelled back and was immensely relieved to see him hurrying toward her, awkwardly carrying a metal ladder. He immediately dropped it into the ditch and held it steady against the slippery wall while she clambered up. He grabbed her arm to steady her and she almost yelped at the pain in her shoulder. Then she was off the ladder and on the ground.

"Did you call nine one one?" she asked the old man just as, behind them, the fire caught in the plywood floor and raced toward the front of the building. They both grabbed the ladder and hauled it up as voices called out from the nearest house and lights turned on in houses all around the construction site. People came out on their balconies.

"Call nine one one!" Mr. McClusky yelled to the nearest neighbor, who nodded and ran back inside.

Just then Kate noticed a small, black SUV parked next to the fence. It had PORTER SECURITY written on the passenger door in big white vinyl letters, with the phone number underneath. She looked around just as she heard a voice call out.

"Chief Williams!"

It was Jason Cromarty. He had come through the fence at the same spot she and Mr. McClusky had used and was now sucking his way toward them.

"Let's get out of here," said Mr. McClusky, hauling up one end of the ladder.

Kate couldn't agree more. She leaned down to pick up the other end and almost keeled over, barely bracing herself in time. More carefully, she reached down and picked up the end of the ladder and headed toward the break in the fence.

Cromarty saw them coming and turned around to lead the way

back out. There wasn't enough room between the fence and the ditch for them to pass him.

She heard the first sirens when they finally were back on pavement. Kate looked down at her shoes. They were caked with mud, ruined, and must have weighed ten pounds each. Cromarty's spit-polished work boots were probably ruined, too.

Mr. McClusky, God bless him, stood staring at the burning building, holding his ladder upright, barefoot.

She looked up from his muddy feet to find him staring solemnly at her.

"See?" she said softly as people from the neighboring houses ran up to them. "I knew you still had some vinegar left in you."

CHAPTER 15

The firefighters weren't able to save the structure, but they had kept the fire confined. None of the nearby homes were in danger.

The emergency medical technicians who arrived at the same time as the firefighters tried to convince Kate to go to the hospital with them, but she refused. All she had was a bit of smoke inhalation—nothing, really—a sore shoulder, and a bump on the head. Her breathing was a little raw but it would clear up.

She'd had worse.

The headache, however, was making her grumpy. Or maybe it was the fact that the firefighters were making a bloody mess of her crime scene.

John Tourmeline and Dan Boychuk arrived together, pulled off their respective cases by Albertson. Boychuk made a beeline for her while Tourmeline headed for the crowd of neighbors who kept creeping closer to the fire.

She was glad Tourmeline was here. For all he always looked like a deer caught in the headlights, the man never missed a detail. If there was anything to find at the site—once the firefighters were finished corrupting it—Tourmeline would find it. She heard him order people to move back, back, and even further back.

"Chief," said Boychuk, approaching her. Then he got a good

look at her. "Holy crap."

"Let's get out of the way," said Kate, refusing to be embarrassed. She led the way to the nearest little house and stood under the balcony where they could talk more privately. She was pretty sure the owner was among the crowd of twenty or so people being kept at bay by Tourmeline.

"Are you hurt?" asked Boychuk. Not waiting for her answer, he stepped closer and examined her from head to foot. She allowed it because she recognized the impulse, and frankly, she felt a little guilty.

Albertson would think she had ignored his request to wait for backup. Technically, she had, but only because she felt a crime was about to be committed. Which it was. She just wasn't sure she had handled the situation in the best way possible.

She probably looked like the creature from the black lagoon. The only good thing was that the drying mud on her clothes now formed a windbreak.

"I'm fine," she said gently as he kept trying to see through the mud.

"I doubt that," said Mr. McClusky, who had snuck past Tourmeline's one-man cordon and now approached them.

She had sent the old man back home before he came down with hypothermia. Instead of staying home, of course, he had cleaned himself off, changed into warm clothes, and come back out with a thermos of coffee. He handed Kate the thermos lid full of coffee pale with cream, and when she took a sip, sweet with sugar. She almost closed her eyes in bliss.

"Thank you," she murmured in gratitude.

Mr. McClusky turned to Boychuk.

"She's been dizzy. I think she hit her head, but she won't tell you. And I don't know how long she was lying in the water at the bottom of the ditch. And her shoulder is funny."

Kate gave the old man a reproachful look.

"Never mind that," she said sternly. "Did you see the cyclist leave?"

They hadn't had a chance to debrief after he pulled her out of the ditch, what with the arrival of the firefighters and the crowd of neighbors.

He shook his head and tucked the thermos in the crook of his arm. "I saw you go around the building. Then I saw smoke coming out and I heard someone yell. That's when I came to see."

With a hammer, Kate suddenly remembered. He'd thrown a coat over his pajamas and come out to help with nothing but a hammer for protection. Her respect for him grew.

"What cyclist?" asked Boychuk, confused.

Kate quickly filled him in, though he would have been aware of the cyclist if he'd read the duty log for the past four days. Albertson had known right away what the significance was.

But Boychuk wasn't slow. He listened to her report, then scowled.

"So, the bastard set fire to the gazebo and threw a brick at the jewelry store window as a distraction?"

This time, it was Mr. McClusky who looked confused, but Kate nodded, then reminded herself not to do that again.

"That's what I'm thinking."

At that moment, Samantha Paterson and Marco Trepalli came running around the corner from where Kate had parked her Edge. They were both dressed in uniform, even though neither one was on duty. They jerked to a stop when they saw the crowd and Tourmeline doing crowd control. The fire was pretty much over by then, but smoke still belched from the building as the firefighters poured water on it.

Then Trepalli saw Kate and his mouth dropped open. He grabbed Paterson's arm and tugged her toward Kate.

Paterson saw Kate and her eyes widened in alarm.

When they arrived under the balcony, Kate stepped forward, looking at Samantha expectantly. But Samantha was having none of it.

"You look like hell," she said harshly. "Did you get yourself checked out?"

"Yes." Kate nodded and winced. Next to her, Mr. McClusky snorted.

"She wouldn't let them take her to the hospital," he tattled.

Samantha's lips thinned, and for the first time, Kate realized the woman was angry.

Kate opened her mouth to speak but Samantha put a hand up.

"What would you say to one of your constables who refused to go to the hospital after getting hurt?"

Kate closed her mouth and looked to Trepalli for help, but he was busy studying her, clearly aghast at what he was seeing.

"Exactly," said Samantha grimly, as if Kate had answered her. "Marco's going to take you to the hospital. No argument!" she added as Kate began to object. "And no coming back until you get the okay from the docs."

Boychuk tried to hide a smile, not very successfully. Mr. McClusky just nodded sharply in agreement, and Trepalli grabbed her firmly by the arm.

"You need to debrief Mr. McClusky," she told Samantha as Marco pulled her away. "About the cyclist."

And then Marco dragged her out from under the balcony toward her car.

* * *

At five o'clock on a Thursday morning, the emergency department of Mendenhall Hospital was deserted. The doctor on duty was one Kate had worked with on one of her first cases in Mendenhall, Dr. Kijawa, a tall, heavy-boned black woman, fiercely intelligent, in her mid-sixties.

"Chief Williams," said Dr. Kijawa, walking into the examination room. Her eyebrows rose as she took in the sight—and smell—of a mud-caked Kate. "What *have* you been up to?" she murmured.

Trepalli cleared his throat and the doctor looked at him.

"Ma'am," he said, "the chief was exposed to smoke from a burning building. She has a shoulder injury and we suspect she hit her head." He glanced worriedly at Kate.

She blushed, though no one could see it beneath the mud. *Had* she made the right call? She'd failed to stop the arson and didn't even get a glimpse of the arsonist's face. But she couldn't have just stood there and watched it go down. Could she?

"Bumps and bruises," she said, and barely controlled a shrug. She had to admit that the shoulder was starting to ache. Her left arm felt like it weighed a hundred pounds.

Dr. Kijawa studied Kate as if she were a specimen under a microscope. A not very promising specimen, at that.

"Well," she said doubtfully, "first I have to see what I'm dealing with." She pointed to the small sink in the room. "Clean yourself up." She glanced at the trail of dried mud that had followed Kate in. "And take off your clothing, please. I will bring you a hospital gown."

* * *

Kate sent Trepalli to her house to pick up a change of clothes. She had a spare uniform in her office, but she didn't relish putting the mud-caked jeans back on for the trip to the detachment. She told him to reassure Amanda that she was fine.

It wasn't the first time she'd sent the boy to fetch a change of clothes for her. Nor was it the first time he'd taken her to the hospital.

Amanda had called Marco as soon as Kate left the house, and Marco had called Albertson, who filled him in. Then Albertson called Samantha in when he realized that Kate might need the help.

So now Samantha Paterson was mad at Kate, and Albertson wouldn't be too pleased, either.

As she tried to wash the worst of the mud off her face and shake it out of her hair, Kate grimaced at herself. She'd gone into a dangerous situation without backup and had had to be rescued. True, she would likely have found a way to pull herself out of that ditch, but with a fire roaring at her back, there was no guarantee she could have done it in time.

Was it a mistake? She stared at herself, the cloth pressed to her cheek. *Should* she have waited?

Every instinct told her no. She was a police officer. Her job was to protect and prevent. If she had to do it over again, she suspected she would. Hopefully better.

Still, a nagging little voice asked, what had she accomplished, really? She hadn't kept the building from burning down, and she'd managed to get hurt in the process. She hadn't even seen the perpetrator's face.

Staring at herself in the small mirror, Kate couldn't help but sigh.

She had certainly mucked this one up.

* * *

Dr. Kijawa poked and prodded her and finally declared that there were no broken bones or concussion, much to Kate's relief. The shoulder was badly bruised and the doctor fashioned a sling for her left arm, which immediately relieved the pain in the shoulder.

"Put cold compresses on the bump on your head," said Dr. Kijawa when she finished probing her skull. "Alternating heat and cold on your shoulder. Ibuprofen for the pain."

Her South African accent still charmed Kate, despite the doctor's abruptness.

"I would tell you to go home and rest, but I know you won't listen," continued Dr. Kijawa.

The thin hospital gown left Kate at a disadvantage but she didn't have time for weakness right now.

"I'll rest later today," she assured the doctor.

Dr. Kijawa looked down her curved nose at Kate, her full lips compressed. When Kate first met her, she was conducting an autopsy on a body discovered during an emergency measures exercise in the middle of winter. It was only much later that Kate learned the doctor also had a regular practise in Mendenhall.

"Of course, you will," said Dr. Kijawa. She pulled a tank of oxygen on a cart toward the bed and unhooked the mask. "Use this for a few minutes. It will help your lungs."

Kate meekly accepted the mask and was still using it when Marco finally returned with her clothes and utility belt.

"Thank you," she said, pulling the mask off.

He stood exactly where Dr. Kijawa had stood, eyeing her critically.

"Chief, you look like hell. Let me take you home."

"I'll take a shower at the detachment," said Kate, clutching her clothes to her chest. "I promise I'll look better then."

He shook his head.

"Ma'am, Amanda is really worried about you and DC Paterson instructed me to take you home—"

All right. That was enough.

"Constable Trepalli, I need to get dressed. Please leave the room." She slid off the bed to make her point. The thin cotton shift crept perilously high on her legs.

Trepalli turned a bright red and left the room without another word.

For Pete's sake.

* * *

It was past seven thirty by the time Kate and Trepalli arrived at the detachment in her Edge, well past shift change. Trepalli drove, since Kate's left shoulder had begun to stiffen up. She took off the sling and left it on the seat before sliding out of the car. Trepalli pretended he didn't notice.

Albertson was still at the duty desk even though Martins had arrived to take over for day shift. Martins stood on the platform behind Albertson's chair, looking over the man's shoulder at the computer screen. They both looked up as Kate and Trepalli walked in.

"Chief," said Martins, nodding at her. He took in her clean clothes, her utility belt, her hair, but didn't say another word.

"Good morning, gentlemen," she said crisply. She turned to Albertson. "Report."

Sergeant Stan Albertson was older than her. He had agreed to postpone his retirement until Rob McKell was back on strength. She would miss him. Albertson was a steady man, smart, calm, good in a crisis. But this morning, his usually neat gray hair was ruffled as if he had run his fingers through it, and he had bags under his eyes.

Now the look he gave her was troubled, and for a moment, she thought he would start berating her. Instead he took a deep breath and began his report.

"The fire at the construction site is out, but the site is still too hot to examine. The owner of the jewelry shop reports nothing taken. Fallon took the report. No witnesses. Traffic cameras in that area are at the wrong angle to see what happened. The gazebo fire was put out quickly. No cameras in the park. The fire marshal will come down from Winnipeg later today, for the gazebo fire and the one at the construction site, but the incident commander reported that he thought an accelerant was used on the gazebo—gasoline. Oppenheimer is still on-site, along with Friesen. They're combing the grounds, just to be sure."

He sounded discouraged and angry, and Kate knew exactly how he felt. She wished now that she and Trepalli had brought in coffee for everyone.

"Gasoline was used as an accelerant at the construction site, too," said Kate. "I could smell it. That's why I went in."

Albertson nodded and jotted the information down on the pad of paper on the duty desk.

"Where are the others?" asked Kate.

Albertson turned back to face her, brushing past Martins as he swiveled, and ticked the information off on the fingers of one hand.

"Paterson is still at the Riverview site, along with Olinchuk, Fallon, Boychuk, and Tourmeline. They've cordoned off the perimeter while waiting for the site to cool down. In the meantime, they're interviewing everybody they can find."

Kate nodded. Standard procedure. Her traitorous mind reminded her that a coffee would be so good right now.

"What about Mr. McClusky?" she asked. "Did he provide any more details?"

Albertson leaned past Martins again and grabbed his notepad. He read for a few seconds then shook his head.

"No. He saw the bike go past his house and turn the corner. Called you. Saw you arrive and go into the construction site." His voice was carefully neutral, but Martins glanced at him. "Then he heard a yell." He looked up at Kate. "He couldn't tell if it was male or female."

Kate nodded. She didn't remember yelling, but she might well have.

"That's when he left the balcony and went downstairs to get his coat," continued Albertson. "He says it may have taken him thirty seconds to get out the door. He figures that's when the perpetrator got away."

Kate waited but he was done. Once again, they were stuck.

She sighed. "All right," she finally said. "As soon as we can free up the night shift crew, send them home. But I want their preliminary reports before they leave." She didn't bother telling Albertson to go home. He wouldn't leave until his squad was relieved.

"Yes, ma'am," said Albertson.

"I'm going to take a shower," she said, and headed for her office.

Half an hour later, she finally felt clean. It had taken a surprisingly long time for the water sluicing off her to run clear, but at last she put on her clean uniform and stood in front of the steamed-up mirror. She wiped it down with her damp towel.

Only then did she see the long red welt that traveled the left side of her face from the corner of her eye to her jawline.

Holy cow. How did she manage to hit the back of her head *and* the side of her face? And why hadn't she seen that at the hospital? She leaned in to examine herself more carefully. That was going to bruise, she thought glumly. Between that, her bloodshot eyes, and the dark circles under them, she looked like death warmed over.

At least her shoulder felt better for having all that heat poured on it.

She folded her civilian clothes and picked them up, along with the spare set of running shoes Trepalli had brought her. It might be an idea to keep a change of civilian clothes in her office, too.

She opened the door of the locker room, letting the steam escape, only to find Albertson, Martins, Trepalli, and Charlotte standing in the duty room, looking at her. Charlotte's arms were crossed. The expression on her face flitted from anxiety to anger to finally settle on relief.

Kate sighed and shook her head, and was about to say something when the door to the detachment squeaked open. They all turned to face the opening in front of the duty desk.

Rob McKell didn't glance up from the two trays of take-away coffee he was carrying as he walked past the opening. He entered the duty room and set the trays down by the log book on the counter, along with a paper bag for the sugar and cream. Only then did he look around.

"I figured it was going to be a long day," he said with a small smile.

No one said a word. His smile faltered and he looked from person to person. Finally, his gaze settled on the welt on Kate's face.

"What the hell," he sighed.

CHAPTER 16

R ob, I think I'm a little bit in love with you right now," said Kate.

"That's just the coffee talking," said McKell, grinning.

He sat in her guest chair, hair trimmed, freshly shaved, so much like his old self that Kate's heart squeezed in gratitude.

She took a sip of her coffee. It smelled like heaven in a cup. She'd added sugar and lots of cream, and she'd never tasted anything better, except maybe Mr. McClusky's thermos coffee earlier that morning.

"Now," said McKell, suddenly serious, "what the hell *happened*?"

Kate took a deep breath and blew it out. "Who called you?"

"Samantha. She said there'd been a rash of incidents overnight and could I come in earlier. She didn't go into details except to say you'd been hurt." His gaze strayed to the side of her face and she almost touched it.

Beyond the closed door, Kate could hear boots thumping on the linoleum floor and voices in conversation. Some of the constables had returned.

She filled Rob in on what had happened, leaving nothing out. When she had finished, she leaned back in her chair and drank more coffee while he digested the information. Finally, he set his cup on the desk and linked his fingers in his lap.

"Why do you say *he*?" he asked.

Kate blinked. "Pardon?"

"You keep calling the perpetrator a *he*, even though you never saw his face."

She thought about it for a moment. "Mr. McClusky had the impression it was a man on the bike," she said slowly. "And the hands that grabbed my ankles were big like a man's hands."

McKell nodded. "Do you think he meant to kill you?"

His question hit her like a punch in the gut and for a moment she couldn't breathe. Her hands began to shake and she held onto the chair's armrests.

Had he meant to kill her? Finally, she shook her head.

"No. If he had meant to kill, he could have done it once I fell in the ditch. I think I passed out for a minute. No, I think that I surprised him. Suddenly he was trapped inside the building and he panicked." So, the guy wasn't a professional, then. At least, not a professional criminal.

McKell nodded slowly.

"Still," he said softly. "He left you there to drown."

"Well, I didn't," she said promptly. She pushed back from her chair to stand up, then sat back abruptly. "Did I screw up, Rob?" She would never have asked any of her constables, but Rob would be honest with her.

And she really wanted to know what he thought.

He looked surprised.

"For going in?" At her nod, he sat back and stared at her. After a moment, he shrugged. "I would have done the same," he said. "Maybe what you did wasn't technically by the book, but what were you supposed to do? Let him torch the place without even trying to stop him?"

Kate nodded sharply and stood up. "Let's go see what the constables found out."

McKell stood up and they went out into the duty room. Terry Fallon, Dan Boychuk, and Russ Oppenheimer looked up from the computers at which they were typing. She felt their gazes on her face and knew they had noticed the welt. Then they saw McKell and grinned.

Charlotte wasn't at her desk but Martins was at the duty desk. He looked up from his hunting and pecking on the keyboard and nodded at her and McKell.

"We're just typing up our reports, Chief," said Boychuk. "We'll have them for you soon."

"Thank you, Constable," said Kate. "Where's Tourmeline?"

"Still on-site," said Oppenheimer. He was Trepalli's age, but where Trepalli was arrestingly handsome, Oppenheimer was a plain-looking sort, with thick dark hair and brown eyes. He was neither tall nor short. Average, until he smiled. When he smiled, his face lit up and his eyes crinkled up at the corners. Kate doubted that any woman could resist that dimple.

"He's with Paterson," he continued. "They're waiting for the fire marshal."

"And day shift?"

Martins swiveled on his stool to face them.

"Friesen just finished up the last of the interviews at Riverview. He's coming in to type up his report. Trepalli and Olinchuk are on patrol."

Stan Albertson wandered past the duty desk opening, holding a cup of coffee. Only then did Kate smell fresh coffee. It was going to be that kind of day.

It was time for night shift to go home, she decided. She had McKell and Paterson to help with the fine details. But she knew Albertson wouldn't leave until all his men were back, which meant she had to pull Tourmeline off the Riverview site.

Before she could say anything to Martins, McKell turned to her.

"I think we need to pull Tourmeline," he said. "He'll be back on again soon enough and will need rest. And you and I both know it'll be hours before the site is safe to enter. And there's no telling when the fire marshal will arrive."

Kate closed her mouth and hid a grin. She nodded solemnly. It was true that they were at the mercy of the fire marshal's schedule.

"All right," she said. She looked at Martins. "Are the firefighters still on-site?"

"One truck and two firefighters," confirmed Martins.

"Ask the firefighters to let us know before they leave, and we can pull one of the constables off patrol to stay on-site," she said. "And ask Samantha to return to the detachment, too." It was pointless waiting at Riverview.

"And Charlotte?" she asked the room in general.

"She had an appointment," said Martins.

All right then, that was everyone accounted for.

Half an hour later, Albertson and his night shift were gone, leaving the duty room feeling curiously empty. Kate kept coming out of her office to see if Paterson was back yet. McKell had gone over the interview questions for Kendrick and Ernst Mulvahill but hadn't thought of anything else to add.

She read through the reports from night shift, including the various interviews conducted with the Riverview residents. They were all depressingly similar. No one had seen anyone suspicious, or known what was happening until they smelled smoke. Then neighbor woke neighbor until everyone was outside, gawking.

And then there was the death of Johann Mulvahill and the theft of the semen destined for his farm.

Her mind swirled with facts and questions, both cases merging and dividing in an insane dance in her head. She began to worry that maybe it was unethical to keep Johann's murder from his brother, but she wanted to see his face and judge his reactions for herself. It was only for one more day.

Finally, the door to the detachment opened and she abandoned her computer and the fruitless reports.

She walked into the duty room to see Martins talking with Samantha. McKell had retreated to one of the common desks and Samantha lifted a hand in greeting.

Kate caught her eye and nodded her toward the office. Samantha patted Martins on the shoulder and followed Kate into her office. She closed the door behind her and sat down facing Kate.

"The DC is looking better and better," said Samantha.

Kate couldn't read any expression on the woman's face. She nodded.

"Do you think he's ready to step back in?" continued Samantha.

Kate shrugged. "I wouldn't be surprised," she admitted. Then she studied Samantha's face. "Would that disappoint you?"

"Of course not," said Samantha. Then her gaze dropped to the desk. After a moment, she shrugged and looked up at Kate. "Well, maybe a little." She grinned.

Kate laughed. "So, it isn't all bad?"

Samantha looked her in the eye.

"No. It isn't." A small smile tugged at her lips. "In fact, I mostly enjoy it."

Kate nodded. "And I enjoy working with you. Mostly."

This time, Samantha laughed, her pretty green eyes crinkling up. Then she sobered.

"I spoke to two of the three former employees of Mulvahill Farm," she said. "Yesterday." She leaned back in her chair, crossed her long legs, and folded her hands in her lap. "Sebastien Artemis is twenty-three. He moved here from Ontario right after high school and decided to go back to school this winter. He's at university in Nova Scotia right now, and has been since January. I checked with the dean."

Kate nodded. "What did he have to say about life on the Mulvahill farm?"

Samantha pulled her notebook out of her jacket pocket, and as an afterthought, unzipped the jacket. She flipped to the right page.

"He said he usually had nothing to do with the house. Sometimes, if they were working in the farmyard, Mrs. Einerson would bring them baked treats and coffee, but otherwise, he mostly worked with Johann Mulvahill with the cattle." She glanced up. "He said Ernst and Johann argued a lot."

The mention of coffee reminded Kate and she took another sip of hers.

"What kind of arguments?" she asked.

"Farm stuff," said Samantha promptly. "Johann was thirteen years older and had the final say, since their dad left the majority of the farm to him. The two brothers didn't always see eye to eye, apparently."

"Anything serious?" As in, serious enough to warrant Ernst killing his brother?

"No," said Samantha. "Not that Artemis said. He said it reminded him of his own family."

Kate nodded. She would ask Martins if he could track down a will for Johann Mulvahill. In all the busy-ness of the past few days, it had completely slipped her mind.

"Then I tracked down Henry Nunez," continued Samantha, "thanks to Mrs. Einerson, again. Nunez is married and his wife was expecting their first child. They wanted to be close to family and moved back to southern British Columbia, near Vancouver."

"What did he have to say?"

Samantha shrugged. "He was a little cagier. Said things like, the Mulvahills were wonderful to work for and very generous, and gave him an excellent reference."

Kate looked at Samantha expectantly.

"I just got the feeling that he felt obligated to say nice things about his bosses because of the 'generous' payout."

"Or payoff," murmured Kate.

"Exactly."

"Did he quit or was he fired?"

Samantha shrugged. "Hard to tell. Mrs. Einerson says he was fired, but Nunez says he quit." She flipped the page. "Now, Barry Mongrain, the guy who was fired for incompetence, that was a whole different matter." She looked up at Kate and grinned. "Mrs. Einerson almost had steam coming out of her ears when she talked about Barry, who apparently had been on the farm for fifteen years. He's thirty-eight, single, and a little... well, maybe 'simple' is the best way to describe him."

Kate raised her eyebrows in question.

"Mrs. Einerson told me that Johann Mulvahill had hired Barry through a work program at a nonprofit agency in town. He lives in a group home for adults who are developmentally challenged. When the program ended, Johann kept Barry on. According to Mrs. Einerson, Barry Mongrain was," she looked down at her notes, " 'as hard-working, competent, and kind a man' as she had ever met." She smiled a little. "I think Mrs. Einerson thought of Barry as a son."

"But, he was fired?" asked Kate.

Samantha shrugged. "Mrs. Einerson didn't know for sure. She did say that she overheard Johann and Ernst fighting about it. I went to the group home but Barry was at work." She looked up at Kate. "Apparently another farmer snapped him up as soon as word got out that he was available."

Huh. Why had Ernst Mulvahill fired a "hard-working, competent, and kind man" only to replace him with someone who had no farming experience?

An abrupt knock at the door startled them both and they looked around as Martins stuck his head in. Although he kept his voice neutral, his eyes almost danced.

"We got a hit on our website. Someone responded to our post about the theft."

CHAPTER 17

Ellie Blackjack had provided her work number in Brandon as well as her home number in Mendenhall. Samantha called her at work, since no one wanted to wait until she was back home before talking to her.

Kate, Martins, and McKell stood next to the duty counter, arms crossed, waiting impatiently for Samantha, who was using one of the duty desks, to finish talking to Blackjack.

Charlotte was still away and they had the duty room to themselves. Even the general detachment line was quiet.

The sun had yet to make its way around the building and the duty room was in shade. Kate glanced at the clock. Almost ten o'clock.

It was going to be a long day.

At last, Samantha finished her interview and hung up. She looked up at the three of them and shook her head.

"She didn't see much," she said glumly.

Only as her hopes came crashing down did Kate realize how high they had been.

"Ellie Blackstone was driving in from Gladstone," continued Samantha, "where she'd spent the weekend at her sister's. Ellie lives in Mendenhall but works in Brandon, so she had to leave Gladstone early. She said she passed a truck that matched the description of the vet's truck on a farm's side road. It was about five forty-five." She took a sip of coffee. "She caught a glimpse of a man leaving the woods that border the road and heading for the parked truck, but she couldn't give me a description except to say he wore brown pants."

Martins' shoulders slumped a little and Kate felt for him.

"That could be anybody," she said out loud.

Samantha nodded. "But the fact that he was walking out of the woods toward the truck, that might mean something."

"Does the timeline work?" asked McKell.

Martins held up a hand and started ticking off points on his fingers. "So, she saw the truck at five forty-five. That works with what Kendrick told us. Flat tire around five thirty, he had to wait for someone to pick him up and drive him to the service station, then back to the truck. Then he drives to Mendenhall to report the theft." He dropped his hand to his lap. "He's the one she would have seen. His assistant wouldn't have had time to pick him up yet."

Yes, but that still wasn't enough, was it?

"Did you search the woods when you went to the site?" Kate asked Samantha.

Samantha frowned, but answered readily enough. "No, ma'am. I didn't see any reason to."

"I wouldn't have either," said Kate, and clamped a hand over her mouth as a huge yawn threatened to engulf the room. "But it's probably worth checking out now."

"Yes," said McKell. "He might have hidden the tank in the woods until he could get back to it. Even though he's had ample time to go back for it, he might have left behind some evidence."

Kate was surprised at how she resisted the idea of the vet being a thief. She liked the man. Still, her job was to keep her mind open to all possibilities. No matter how disappointing.

"Let's all remember that this is just hypothetical," she warned. "If he did steal it, he must have had plans to sell it. It's worth fifty thousand dollars. Even if he sells it for half, someone would be getting a heck of a bargain."

"He might still have it," said Martins suddenly. They all turned to look at him and he shrugged. "He wouldn't want to do anything to draw suspicion to himself. He'd hang on to it until the investigation dies down."

It made sense. Kendrick would want to keep it somewhere secure. His clinic, under lock and key? His home?

McKell straightened away from the counter. "You know, he'd have to be in pretty desperate circumstances to risk doing something like this." He looked at Kate. "Maybe we should get a warrant to look at his finances."

That would be ideal, but... "There's no way we'll get a justice of the peace to sign off on a warrant," said Kate, shaking her head. "We have no real evidence. And for all we know, it wasn't Kendrick the woman saw."

The room grew quiet as they considered her words. Kate was too tired to feel frustrated. This case, and the Riverview one—they were making her old before her time.

"Keep digging," she said finally. "I'd like to have more information before we interview Mulvahill and Kendrick tomorrow."

* * *

A few hours later, the fire marshal arrived in Mendenhall and Samantha sent Olinchuk to meet with her at Joe Carter Park. Charlotte remained on the duty desk while Martins took over one of the general desks, trying to speak to the various insurance companies connected with both cases. While Martins worked at that, Samantha sent Trepalli and Friesen back to the site of the theft to search the neighboring woods.

It was past lunchtime, but Kate was too exhausted to have much of an appetite. She'd had so much coffee already today that she could feel it burning a hole in her stomach. She was grateful that Martins had taken on talking to the insurance companies—she wasn't sure she would have made sense over the telephone.

Samantha had excused herself shortly after Trepalli and Friesen left and closed the door to her office. She still needed to talk to the arson investigators from the old fires related to the Riverview arson case.

Kate stood in the middle of the duty room, feeling suddenly at a loss. Martins and Charlotte were both on the phone. She looked up suddenly, aware that she was being watched. McKell leaned against the doorjamb between the hallway and the duty room, watching her with a frown. He nodded toward the hallway and she followed him into the break room.

Five feet inside the room he turned to look at her.

"You look like hell," he said bluntly. "Go home, get some rest."

Kate was too tired to bristle, or even to joke.

"Can't," she said, swallowing a yawn. "Things are coming to a head. I need to be here."

"We can call you if anything develops," he argued. "You can't expect to make smart decisions in your state."

He said *we*, she thought. This time she did grin at him. As if she could leave when Samantha and Trepalli were clearly as exhausted as she was.

"That's why you're here," she said. "To keep me on my toes."

He stared at her for a moment more, irritated, then shook his head. "Fine. What can I do to help?"

Kate thought about it and finally said, "Check with Charlotte to see if she's had a chance to call the housekeeper about Johann's will. Find out if she's talked to the lawyer. If not, you could call and find out who the beneficiary is."

"All right," he said. "In the meantime, you go to your office and close the door. If you put your head down for a few minutes, no one will know and it will help."

"Yes, Mother," she said meekly and smiled at the look he gave her.

* * *

The endless afternoon eventually ended and Kate dragged herself back home to catch a nap and shower before heading out to Amanda's Folly for the friends and family party. Trepalli had already booked off time so he could leave a little early and help Amanda with the final setup.

Despite feeling like something that had been left to dry out in the desert, Kate was looking forward to the evening. It wasn't often the whole crew had a chance to socialize and it was nice to catch up with the wives—and Samantha's husband. As she unlaced her work boots and padded down the hallway toward her bedroom, it occurred to her that flu was already working its way through her detachment and that this little party, with its close quarters, might just hasten it along.

She sighed.

The long, hot shower rejuvenated her and as the water sluiced down her body, almost too hot to bear, she reviewed what her constables—and Charlotte—had learned from a long afternoon of phone calls, searches, and interviews.

Mrs. Einerson, Mulvahill's housekeeper, had readily given McKell the name of Johann's lawyer in Winnipeg. The lawyer, in turn, had been persuaded that it was in everybody's best interest to share the contents of Johann's will with McKell.

Johann had left his majority share of the farm to his brother. No surprise there, really. Johann's kids had made it clear by moving out of the province that they weren't interested in the farm. There was a provision in the will that once Ernst died, the farm was to go to Johann's three kids, since Ernst had none. Johann had had investments that totaled up to almost a hundred thousand dollars, which he had left to his children, along with individual behests to friends and other family members. There was an insurance policy that would help his brother over the transition period.

It might be motive enough for Ernst to kill his brother, but he had been on the farm when his brother was killed.

So. What did that leave?

Trepalli and Friesen had found nothing in their search of the woods near where Kendrick's truck had been left with the flat tire. Maybe the vet had gone into the woods just to relieve himself. Or maybe the man Ellie Blackjack had seen wasn't the vet at all.

Kate sighed. They needed more than suspicions. Getting a look at his finances would help, but they wouldn't be able to get a warrant. And they couldn't go around talking to the vet's suppliers to see if he'd been having money problems without affecting his reputation—not to mention tipping him off. They could try talking to the bank—assuming they could figure out who he banked with without alerting him—but Kate doubted any bank would share information without a warrant.

And it would be a gross invasion of his privacy if, as she suspected, he was innocent.

She turned the water off and stood in the steamy bathtub for a moment, staring at nothing.

As for Johann's murder... while that was Winnipeg's case, she couldn't help but believe it was connected to the theft, if she could only figure out *how*.

This damned case...

She sighed and pulled the shower curtain open. As she toweled herself off, she admitted that she hoped the vet wasn't connected to the theft, and by extension, to the murder.

She pulled the towel around her wet hair and twisted it into a modified turban, then straightened to find herself staring back in the steamy mirror. She wiped at the mirror and peered.

Yep, the welt was still there. And her shoulder was turning black and blue. Her gaze was drawn to her right shoulder, where a small, puckered scar would forever remind her of her first year here.

Sliding into her fleece robe, she opened the bathroom door and let all the steam escape. Cool air swirled around her bare feet and ankles and her feet left damp imprints on the hardwood floor as she padded to her bedroom.

As for the Riverview case, well, Paterson had spoken to two of the three arson investigators from previous projects Leonard Hodgson and his cronies had been involved in. Both investigators had declared the fires arson, but they'd had no proof about who the perpetrators were. Kate doubted that Hodgson or his company cronies would have done the deed themselves, but they were the ones who had profited when the insurance companies paid out.

Three arson cases attached to the same man—same men—were just too much of a coincidence.

* * *

Despite her best efforts, it was almost seven thirty by the time Kate parked down the road from Amanda's house, almost two blocks away. The house's windows streamed light, and as she walked back, she could see people spilling out the front door and into the front yard. She hoped the neighbors had been invited.

It was a cool evening, maybe ten Celsius, and she was glad she'd worn her wool jacket and the blue silk scarf Amanda had given her for Christmas. Underneath she wore a pretty silk blouse with a wild pattern in blues and greens and yellows, an impulse buy that she rarely wore since it made her feel like a walking painting. But tonight was a party, surely a good time to wear it. She had hesitated over dress slacks or jeans, and finally decided on black dress slacks.

With her hair down and fluffed up, she figured she'd pass muster.

Just in case Bert's there? a little voice asked.

Oh, shut up, she told it.

She reached the house and turned up the walkway. A dozen people lounged on the porch or sat on the steps, chatting, some of them smoking. Kate decided that she didn't need to know if the drinks in their hands were alcoholic. The front door was wide open, leaking light and music and laughter. Through the plate glass window, she could see people milling about in the dining room.

Warmth hit her as soon as she entered. That explained the open door. Through the opening into the kitchen, she could see that the door to the back deck was open, too. A few people turned as she walked in and she smiled in greeting. There had to be thirty people in the room and between the shifting bodies, the heat, and the throb of something vaguely rap-like from the speakers tucked in the corners, Kate had to take a deep breath to quell the incipient claustrophobia.

"Aunt Kate!" said Amanda, walking out of the kitchen with a tray of pastries in hand. She handed the tray to Marco, who was following behind her. Marco grinned at Kate and headed for the big buffet table against the wall while Amanda threaded her way toward Kate.

The girl wore a bright red vee-necked tunic top that hugged her trim figure and a pair of black leggings and flat shoes. She'd pulled her lovely blonde hair into a twist at the back of her head, opening up her face and showing off her long, slim neck. The only makeup she wore was red lipstick that drew attention to her lips. That, and the colorful, beaded earrings she wore completed her outfit.

"Don't you look nice," said Kate as her niece hugged her. She had to raise her voice to be heard over the din of people talking and laughing and whatever the heck that was playing over the speakers.

"Let me take your coat," said Amanda, helping Kate out of her jacket. Kate tried not to wince as her shoulder protested the movement. Amanda hung the coat up in the closet and tucked Kate's scarf inside the sleeve before turning back to her aunt. Then she did a double take.

"What happened?" she asked, touching the fading welt on Kate's face.

Somebody came in behind Kate with a murmured "sorry" and she moved out of the way.

"Nothing serious," Kate assured Amanda. She looked around the room again. "Did you invite everyone in town?"

Amanda laughed.

"Just about," she said. "But I didn't expect them all to show up."

"Hi, Chief," said a familiar voice next to her, and Kate turned to see Stan Albertson with his wife, Beth.

"Hi, Stan," said Kate. She'd forgotten that Stan's crew were now off for the next four days. "Hello, Beth," she said warmly.

"Hi, Kate," said Beth, leaning over to hug Kate.

She and Beth Albertson had hit it off from the first time they met. Beth was a freelance writer. Mostly, that consisted of helping nonprofit organizations write grant applications, and writing annual reports for businesses all around the province. She and Stan had three kids, grown up and long gone from the nest. Every once in a while, Beth kidnapped Kate from work for a long lunch. No wonder Kate liked her.

"Dear, why don't you get us each a glass of wine?" suggested Beth to her husband. "We'll be by the buffet table."

"Work, work, work," grumbled Albertson good-naturedly. He wore jeans and a striped blue shirt. He glanced at Kate's welt, then quickly looked away. "I'll be right back."

Kate grinned over her shoulder at Amanda as Beth pulled her away toward the buffet table. Beth was a few years younger than Kate, but her hair was completely gray and she wore it in soft spikes that framed her face and showed off her high cheekbones.

"You have to try these date things," said Beth, practically shouldering people out of her way. She might be only five feet two inches tall, but Beth had grown up with four brothers.

They stopped at the table and Kate blinked at the array of food on it, everything from crackers and various cheeses to maple-drenched Brie with walnuts to moose meat skewers with roasted vegetables to mini pita pockets filled with feta, olives and basil...

Kate's mouth watered and her stomach rumbled so loudly she

looked around to see if anyone had noticed. But Beth was busy filling up a small plate with a variety of hors d'oeuvres and the noise level seemed even louder than it had been.

Someone jostled her to get closer to the table and she looked around. A strange man smiled apologetically and reached for a plate. Now that her claustrophobia was under control, she saw many strange faces among the familiar.

Exactly how many invitations had Amanda and Marco handed out?

Someone at the far end of the room gave her a little wave and she recognized Martins standing by the hutch. He had a beer in one hand and a napkin with bits of food on it in the other. The man he was talking to kept waving his hands as he talked and Martins kept moving his napkin out of range.

She caught sight of a uniform and recognized one of her constables, Brendan Jones, chatting with Amanda. As always, he looked as if he hadn't slept well in days. Someone clapped him on the shoulder and Kate realized it was Josh, Charlotte's young vet. She looked around and sure enough, Charlotte was close by. Even as he chatted with Jones, Josh's gaze searched until he found Charlotte.

Kate sighed.

"Here you go," said Beth, handing Kate a plate heaped with food that smelled so good Kate was afraid she would start drooling. She really should have eaten something before coming over.

"Thanks," said Kate. "How—"

"Here you go," said Albertson, coming up to them. He held a glass of wine in each hand. "I didn't know what you preferred, Chief, so I took a chance on white."

"Good choice, Stan," said Kate with a smile. "Thanks."

Albertson handed his wife the other glass, then leaned in to Kate's ear. "You'll never guess who's here."

Kate barely controlled an urge to look around.

"Who?" she asked.

"Dr. Kendrick."

Kate tilted her head as if it would help her absorb the surprise. What the heck was the veterinarian doing *here*? Did Amanda and

Marco know him? No, of course not. Marco would have told her.

Of course, Amanda might know him. The girl seemed to know everyone in Mendenhall.

She and Stan exchanged a look. Neither one of them knew what it meant that the veterinarian was here but suddenly the evening felt weird.

"Beth!" someone cried and a woman grabbed Beth by the hand and pulled her away.

"Catch up later!" said Beth over her shoulder before she disappeared among the taller bodies.

"Great," muttered Albertson, peering into the crowd. "Now I'll never find her."

Kate laughed and he grinned before following his wife.

The noise level suddenly seemed to increase and Kate felt like tucking her head into her shoulders. Instead, she threaded her way toward the kitchen. Surely there would be fewer people there. But that room was full of people, too, some helping Trepalli place food on serving plates, but most just hanging around and chatting.

Desperate, Kate glanced at the doorway to the back deck. None of the trellis lights were on and only the light from the kitchen provided any kind of illumination. The cool emptiness of the deck beckoned like an oasis of quiet.

She smiled and nodded her way past half a dozen people before finally stepping through the doorway and onto the deck. She paused in the sudden gloom, waiting for her eyes to adjust and letting the coolness of the night wash over her overheated body.

She was not going to last long in that crowd.

A soft laugh alerted her to the presence of others and she looked around. At the far end of the deck, where only a faint glimmer of light reached, Friesen stood close to Julianne, Amanda's friend. They were oblivious to Kate's presence.

Julianne had left her long black hair loose and it fell in a smooth, shadowy curtain down her back. She stood looking up at Friesen, smiling, as he delicately smoothed a strand of hair away from her face and tucked it behind her ear. His fingers lingered over the curve of her ear in a gesture so intimate that Kate looked away.

She briefly considered leaving the deck to them and returning inside but she just couldn't face the crowd. Instead, she coughed and headed for the other side of the deck as if she hadn't seen them. Clearly Amanda hadn't expected people to want to spend time on the deck on such a cool night, but nevertheless, a few round tables had been set up on the deck and Kate set her plate and wine glass down on the tablecloth.

"Evening, Chief," said Friesen behind her and Kate turned to find the constable walking toward her with Julianne. Kate's glance fell on their clasped hands and she raised an eyebrow at her young constable.

"Evening, Constable Friesen," she said formally, then ruined the effect by grinning. "I see you're having a good one."

He grinned at her and Julianne laughed. They both looked so happy that Kate almost sighed again. She'd never been that young.

Then Julianne shivered.

"It's cold out here," she announced. "Let's go back inside."

Friesen released her hand and put his arm around her. "You got it. Chief? You coming in?"

Kate shook her head. It *was* getting a little cool, especially in her silk top, but it was still better than the oven that was the inside of the house.

"You two go in," she said. "I'm going to cool down for a bit."

They left and she sat down at the table to apply herself to her food. The moose meat skewers in particular were delicious and Kate devoured the savory morsels between sips of wine. She found herself wondering where the heck Amanda had gotten moose meat. A breeze brought the scent of sweet hay, damp soil, and faintly, the smell of meat grilling on a barbecue. Someone in the neighborhood was anxious for summer.

She faced out into the dark backyard. Tall hedges grew at the back, beyond which was another house. A light flickered on in one of the small windows, maybe in a bathroom or a bedroom.

She was just licking her fingers—having forgotten to grab a napkin—when someone came up behind her.

"I thought I'd seen you," said Dr. Kendrick. "What are you doing sitting here alone in the dark?"

Kate turned to face the vet, a smile already on her face. Backlit by the kitchen light, he looked big and imposing. She couldn't see his face, but there was a smile in his voice. She got up.

"You make it sound like a bad thing," she said. "I didn't expect to see you here."

The veterinarian approached and smiled down at her. He had combed that mane of his and looked a little rakish in the night.

"I only just learned that our hostess is your niece. Small world, eh?"

Yes, indeed.

"How do you know Amanda?" she asked.

He lifted a tall glass and took a drink before answering.

"I don't," he replied. "Or didn't. I ran into Josh Gallant this morning, and he invited me. I wasn't going to come, but in the end, it seemed like a good way to clear my head after the last few days."

A small part of Kate wondered if the reason really was that innocent, but finally she decided that his presence here had to be nothing more than a coincidence. She couldn't imagine why else he would have shown up, knowing that Kate and most of the police department would be here.

"Good food always clears my mind," she agreed solemnly.

He laughed.

"Except that now it feels a little weird," he admitted. He wore jeans tonight with, for once, a solid color shirt, though she couldn't tell what color.

"How do you mean?" she asked cautiously.

He shrugged.

"Well, I'm seeing you tomorrow to give a formal statement. It almost seems... I mean... I wouldn't want you to think..." He sighed. "Look, Kate. When this is all over, I would love to take you out for dinner. That's what I mean."

Heat rushed up to Kate's face in a way that made her grateful for the dim light on the deck.

"Dr. Kendrick..." she began.

"James. I know." He waved away her words. "I told you. Weird." He leaned in suddenly, startling her, then straightened. "You've got something by your mouth," he said.

Kate swiped at her mouth, but he shook his head.

"Still there."

She swiped again, and he shook his head again. "May I?" he murmured, raising his hand and waiting for permission.

Kate hesitated, suddenly uncomfortable, but it would be worse if she said no. Instead, she smiled her permission and his thumb reached out to stroke the side of her mouth.

"There," he said, his voice low.

Disturbed, Kate took a step back, but before she could say anything, a voice spoke up from the steps leading to the backyard.

"Kate?"

She looked around, wondering why she had ever thought she'd find peace and quiet out here. Bert stood on the top step, looking at her. The light from the kitchen didn't reach his face, but something in his voice warned her.

"Hello, Bert," she said calmly. "Have you met Dr. Kendrick?"

CHAPTER 18

If she hadn't been so tired, Kate might have handled the situation differently.

"He's a suspect," said Bert, his voice carefully controlled.

"All he did was brush something off my cheek," explained Kate, for what seemed like the fourth time, barely hanging on to her patience. What business was it of Bert's who touched her, anyway?

Dr. Kendrick, no slouch, had read the situation correctly and beat a hasty retreat. Kate hoped he'd actually left the house but she couldn't check as she was still trapped on the deck with Bert.

"It looked like more than that," he said. He stood two feet away from Kate, wearing jeans and a black leather bomber-style jacket. Clearly, he'd only just arrived from Winnipeg.

"Bert, why does this matter?" she asked.

"Because, Kate," he replied grimly. "He's at the very least a witness in a theft and he may possibly be a suspect in a murder investigation. Developing a relationship with a murder suspect would give the Crown counsel cause to doubt your testimony."

Whoa.

"That's quite the leap," she pointed out slowly. "You went from having him as a witness in a theft—which is my case, by the way— to having him on trial for murder. Why don't we finish investigating before you slam the jail door on him?"

His chin lifted, and in the dim light, she saw his mouth twist.

"I see," he said quietly. "You shouldn't be involved in investigating him at all since you are clearly compromised."

Compromised?

For a moment, every bad word Kate had ever heard filled her mind. Then she got a grip on herself.

She picked up her still-full plate and the half empty glass of wine. "You'll be present for the interview, Bert. Since you now doubt my professionalism, the Crown counsel can always call on you to testify instead of me. Now, if you'll excuse me, I'm getting cold."

She turned away, suddenly feeling the cold like a knife through her thin shirt. Bert grabbed her forearm, causing her to slosh the wine onto her hand.

"Kate, wait."

"Aunt Kate?" Amanda's voice called from the doorway.

"Over here," said Kate, shaking Bert off and succeeding in sloshing more wine over herself. Damn it all.

Amanda stepped onto the deck, followed by Trepalli, Charlotte, and Josh. Kate heard Bert sigh.

"Sorry for interrupting, Chief," said Trepalli as he neared. He kept his voice low so that everybody had to crowd in to hear him.

"No problem," said Kate. She replaced the plate on the table along with the glass of wine. Somewhere along the way, she'd lost her appetite. The wind quickly dried the wine on her hand and she crossed her arms over her chest in an effort to stay warm. "What's the matter?"

Trepalli turned and grabbed Josh by the arm to pull him closer.

"Did you know that Kendrick was here?" asked Trepalli.

"Yes," said Kate shortly.

"Turns out Josh invited him," said Charlotte, nudging in next to Josh. "He didn't know."

Josh looked at Kate and even in the dim light she could see the earnest expression on his face.

"I'm sorry, ma'am," he said. "I didn't know it would be a problem. It just seemed like a nice thing to do, considering the trouble he's been having these past few months."

Kate perked up, as did Bert next to her.

"What kind of trouble?" asked Bert.

Josh hesitated a moment. He was a tall man, taller even than Trepalli, and he was thin but well muscled. Only a few years older than Charlotte, he had black, curly hair and green eyes. Yes, indeed, he and Charlotte would make pretty babies.

"Josh, you have to tell them," urged Charlotte, placing a hand on his arm. He sighed.

"All right." He looked from Bert to Kate. "You have to understand— this is just... I mean, I don't have *facts*..."

"Just say it!" said Amanda, startling them all.

"I think Doc Kendrick is in financial trouble," said Josh, his voice low so that it would carry no further than their little group.

"Why do you say that?" asked Kate.

Josh shrugged. "Little things. I've worked for him on and off for the past few years. I've taken the odd phone call from pharmaceutical companies asking why their bills hadn't been paid. I know he's laid off staff in the last few months. And the last two times he's called me in, he hasn't paid me."

Well.

Kate thought for a moment, then turned to Trepalli.

"Is Jones still here?"

"No, ma'am," said Trepalli. "He's back on patrol. Fallon's here, though."

Kate nodded. "All right. Can you find him and bring him here? I'd like him to interview Josh for details."

Trepalli hesitated. "Ma'am, I can do it. I'm familiar with the case. I'd have to bring Fallon up to speed."

That made sense. Kate shivered as the last of her body heat dissipated. She hated to pull Trepalli from his party.

"Wait," said Bert suddenly. "Have you been drinking?"

Trepalli shook his head.

"No, sir. I've been too busy schlepping for Amanda."

Everybody laughed and Kate jumped as something warm suddenly settled around her shoulders and back. Bert had placed his jacket over her. She nodded a curt thanks and turned back to Trepalli.

"All right. Do it in your car. That may be the only quiet place you'll find here tonight."

* * *

She was back home by nine o'clock, exhausted, irritated, and still angry at Bert. She'd left soon after Trepalli promised to email her the gist of his interview with Josh. Amanda had promised to be home as soon as the place was cleaned up. Kate had felt a little guilty at abandoning her niece to the cleanup but there would be plenty of bodies around to help. Kate needed to get some rest. She needed to be at her sharpest for tomorrow's interviews.

Josh's revelation was interesting, but a justice of the peace would call it hearsay. Still, it gave a direction to the next day's interview.

She changed into her pajamas as soon as she got home and ended up in the kitchen with her pad of paper. Pulling out the stool, she sat down at the counter and jotted down more questions she wanted Martins to ask the veterinarian. Martins would be officially on days off, but he had insisted on coming in for the interview and Kate hadn't had the heart to refuse him.

She kept glancing longingly at the coffee pot, but that way lay disaster. Instead, she got up and poured herself a glass of water. Not nearly as satisfying but it wouldn't keep her up.

Her thoughts kept circling back to James Kendrick and his behavior. She liked him. He seemed like an easy, open, what-you-see-is-what-you-get kind of guy, but his assertion that he wanted to take her out for dinner and then his touching her... that had felt forced. It wasn't the normal escalation of a man who liked a woman.

It had been a while, but Kate was pretty sure she could still recognize when a man was interested in her. And she didn't think Kendrick was interested in her. Not in that way.

And the moment he touched her, any interest she'd had in him disappeared as her instincts sat up and took notice.

So, why the charade? Why pretend he was interested in her if he wasn't?

To sway her to his side? In hopes that she wouldn't investigate the theft?

Or something worse?

With a sigh, she pushed the pad and pencil away and stood up. Amanda would be coming home tonight, but Kate just didn't have the energy to wait up.

As she made her way to her bedroom, she was honest enough with herself to admit that part of her had expected Bert to follow her home.

She couldn't tell if she was disappointed or relieved that he hadn't.

CHAPTER 19

At ten fifteen the next morning, Kate was standing in the middle of the duty room, talking with Martins and Samantha, when Bert walked in. He nodded in greeting and Kate nodded back coolly.

"Good morning," he said to the room in general. "How late did things go last night?"

O'Hara, on the duty desk this morning, looked around from the keyboard.

"I showed up at eight thirty and things were still in full swing," he said.

Charlotte piped up from her desk, where she was reconciling invoices.

"I stayed to the bitter end," she said primly, "all of nine thirty. A dozen of us stayed behind to help clean up and set up for tonight's grand opening. By ten thirty, everyone was gone."

Kate had been so tired last night that she had fallen asleep before her head hit the pillow. She hadn't even heard Amanda come in.

Bert came to stand next to her as if that was his place. He wore a different aftershave than she was used to, still spicy but with undertones of cedar.

He had some nerve. He had been a complete jerk last night and now he acted as if nothing had happened. She wanted to step away from him but didn't. It wouldn't be professional. Instead she kept her expression bland and looked directly at him.

He focused suddenly on the welt on her face and she realized that this was the first time he'd had a chance to see it. Last night it had been too dark on the deck.

"What happened?" he demanded.

Kate found herself bristling at his tone. The memory of all their old arguments came rushing back to her. She turned away from him.

"Nothing worth mentioning," she said crisply.

The outside door opened again and they all turned to face the hallway.

McKell walked by, glanced in, and did a double take at seeing everyone staring at him. He gave them a small smile and walked into the duty room carrying a tray full of coffee cups.

"Good morning," he said cheerfully, depositing the tray on the counter. "How did it go last night?" He wore jeans and a white shirt open at the collar, with a light green-and-black jacket that looked like it might be left over from his high school days.

"We missed you," said Charlotte. "Half the town was there. And you missed some great food."

"Half the town, eh?" said McKell. "Glad I missed it, then."

Kate gave him a half smile. Yes, indeed.

"You're looking good, Rob," said Bert, giving McKell the once over. Kate wondered if this was the first time Bert had seen McKell since the shooting.

"Thanks," said McKell with a shrug.

"What time are they getting here?" Bert asked Kate.

"Mr. Mulvahill will be here any time now. Dr. Kendrick will be in at eleven." Her heart was beating fast, whether from irritation or from the fact that Bert was in uniform, she couldn't tell. It had been months since she'd seen him in uniform. The Winnipeg Police Services uniform was black with a yellow stripe down the leg and a white shirt open at the collar. Like Mendenhall, Winnipeg had adopted the lighter bomber jacket as a good solution for warmer weather. On the men, especially, the uniform made them look like flyboys out of a World War II movie.

It bothered her that he could still have such an effect on her, even after seven months. Even after last night.

"If you'll excuse me, I have a call to make before Mr. Mulvahill gets here."

She grabbed one of McKell's coffees and headed for her office as an uncomfortable silence settled on the group.

She didn't care. Bert was here to witness the interviews in case they learned something pertinent to his murder case. Nothing else.

And she needed time to regain her balance.

She had planned to call Rose and find out how she was dealing with Mom moving in with Alfred but she just stared at the phone, instead. The thought of dealing with Rose's drama was more than she could handle right now. Instead, she stood by the window, looking out at the parking lot and the street beyond, and sipping her coffee. It was a clear morning and the sun actually had some warmth to it.

She had ordered an arrangement of yellow and white flowers—none of which she could name—to be delivered at Amanda's Folly this afternoon. Her real gift, the gift certificate, would have to wait until she could call around and find the best supplier. It suddenly occurred to her that Julianne might be able to help.

She was about to turn back to her desk and scribble a reminder to herself when a tan and white pickup truck turned into the parking lot. She perked up. That looked like the kind of truck a farmer might drive, pocked with rust and dented. A working truck. It pulled into the visitor parking spot and sat there for a moment. The sunlight hit the passenger window at the wrong angle for her to see inside but she would have bet a week's wages that Ernst Mulvahill sat in the driver's seat.

She turned away as the driver's door opened, and headed into the duty room, first grabbing a pen and pad.

O'Hara was the only one in the duty room. He was on the phone. Kate popped her head into Samantha's office. The acting DC was typing away and looked up, startled.

"Mulvahill is here," said Kate.

Samantha stood up and followed Kate out of her office just as the outside door opened. A moment later, a man appeared at the duty desk window. O'Hara, still on the phone, nodded to him and lifted a finger to indicate he would be a minute. The man wore a jean jacket over a blue-and-gray plaid shirt that looked like it had come straight from the package. He was maybe five feet ten and stocky, with heavy shoulders and a shock of thick, unruly gray hair that was swept back from his face. He wasn't wearing a hat but the imprint of a brim in his hair told her he'd been wearing one a few minutes ago, as if he had taken off his ball cap and tossed it on the truck seat before coming into the detachment.

He nodded at O'Hara, then glanced inside the duty room. He took in Kate, then his gaze settled on Samantha.

"Mr. Mulvahill," said Samantha. "Thank you for coming in." She rounded the duty desk and headed for the hallway.

"I don't have much time," said Mulvahill stiffly. "I'm still trying to get my brother's body released from the hospital, and I have to get back to the farm."

"No worries," said Samantha calmly. "We won't be keeping you long. Would you like a coffee?"

Kate studied Ernst Mulvahill carefully as Samantha led him away through the ident room to the back, where the small interview room was. McKell had said the man was fifty-eight, but Kate would have pegged him at closer to sixty-five. Most farmers looked older. It was the hard work, and spending most of their days outside in all weather.

O'Hara finally hung up and turned to look at her.

"Are they all hiding in the break room?" asked Kate.

He grinned.

"For Pete's sake," grumbled Kate, heading into the hallway. Someone had closed the door to the break room so Mulvahill couldn't see in when he walked by. Kate pushed it open and stood staring at Charlotte, McKell, Martins, and Bert.

"We didn't want him to see us staring at him like some kind of exhibit," explained Charlotte sheepishly.

Kate nodded and headed for the coffee pot. She poured some into a cup and picked up her pad and pen. She doubted all five of them—including Samantha—would fit in the tiny space in front of the interview room's one-way glass. Samantha appeared in the doorway and Kate raised the cup.

"Ready?"

"Yes, he's ready," said Samantha. "Grumpy, but ready."

Well, she'd be grumpy, too, thought Kate, if she'd just lost her brother and now had to go to the police station. She handed Samantha Mulvahill's coffee cup.

"Wait until I'm behind closed doors with him," she told them, "and for Pete's sake, keep the lights off."

If they turned the lights on in the ident room, Mulvahill would see them through the glass. While nobody could expect privacy in a police detachment, he might be less willing to talk if he knew half the detachment was watching his interview.

"It's not our first rodeo, Kate," Bert reminded her patiently. His gaze flickered to her welt and she knew—*knew*—he would ask McKell about it the moment she was behind the door. She almost sighed. Instead she nodded and followed Samantha to the back of the ident room and into the interview room.

Samantha stood by the open door of the interview room, letting Kate walk in. Mulvahill had taken a seat at the small table, facing the window. He wrapped his big, scarred hands around the cup Samantha handed him as if they were cold. He looked up at Kate, his dark gray eyes bloodshot under bristly black eyebrows. He had puffy dark circles under his eyes.

"Chief," said Samantha, "this is Ernst Mulvahill. Mr. Mulvahill, this is Chief Williams. She will be taking your statement today." With a cordial nod, she stepped aside to let Kate past, then left the room, closing the door behind her.

Kate smiled politely at Mulvahill as she pulled her chair out.

"Chief Williams," he said. "Can we not do this another time? My brother has just died and there is much to do."

Kate placed her pad on the table, laid the sheet of paper with her questions face down on top, then sat down.

"I realize that, Mr. Mulvahill," she said gently. "And I am very sorry for your loss. I assure you I won't keep you any longer than necessary."

She reached for the recorder sitting at the end of the table, turned it on, and moved the mike closer to Mulvahill.

"Mr. Mulvahill, we will be recording this conversation. Do you have any objections?"

Mulvahill's eyebrows had risen in surprise as she adjusted the mike. Now he shrugged.

"No," he said after a moment. "Why do you need to record it?"

Kate smiled. "Our conversation will form part of the official investigation into the theft of the... straws." She couldn't bring herself to say "semen" in front of this dour-looking man. "It's standard." She hesitated briefly. She didn't truly think the man was a suspect in his brother's murder, but still... she had to make sure his rights were respected, especially as she had deliberately delayed telling him his brother had been murdered.

"Since this will form part of the official record," she told him, "do you wish to have an attorney present?"

He studied her face as if evaluating her words. Then he shook his head. "No. I want to get this over with."

She stated the date clearly for the recording, then glanced at her watch. "It is ten thirty-five. Present are Ernst Mulvahill and Mendenhall Chief of Police Kate Williams."

She set the page with the questions aside and wrote the date at the top of the notepad.

"In the interest of getting you out of here as soon as possible," she began pleasantly, "let's get right to it. Can you tell me when you first learned that the tank containing the straws had been stolen?"

Mulvahill sat back in the oak chair, his hands still wrapped around the mug.

"It was Monday morning," he said. He had a faint accent but she couldn't place it. "Not sure what time, the first time. Kendrick called twice. The first time to tell me he'd be delayed. Then he called again, soon after the seven o'clock news, to tell me about the theft." His mouth tightened.

Huh. So the vet had let Mulvahill know before reporting the theft to the detachment. Not that it meant anything.

"What did he say?"

"The first time," said Mulvahill, "he told me he had to get his flat tire fixed and would be late. The second time he told me the tank had been stolen." This time he crossed his arms over his chest in a gesture even a blind man could have read.

"You seem angry, Mr. Mulvahill," said Kate matter-of-factly.

He stared at her out of those bloodshot eyes and for the first time, she noticed that most of the lines on his face were frown lines. Even the corners of his mouth had a downturn at rest. Finally, he shrugged.

"I do not understand why the man left the tank unattended," he said.

Neither do I, thought Kate.

"What is the value of the tank?"

"Fifty-one thousand, three hundred and forty-five dollars," he replied promptly.

"And are you insured for the loss?"

He raised one eyebrow in an eloquent gesture.

"You know this already, I think," he said stiffly. "Yes, of course, I have insurance. They will reimburse me the cost of the semen and claim the value from Kendrick's insurance company."

She nodded. She did indeed know this already. She looked up from her pad.

"Tell me, Mr. Mulvahill," she asked out of curiosity, "why do you use a veterinarian out of Mendenhall? Wouldn't a vet out of Brandon be closer to your farm?"

He shook his head slightly and sighed. His arms uncrossed and he rested his hands on the table.

"My brother..." He swallowed suddenly and looked away, but not before she saw the sheen in his eyes.

Kate gave him a moment, surprised and oddly moved by his display of emotion, slight as it was. She got the sense that Ernst Mulvahill didn't leave himself open to emotions easily. The small room was growing warm and she took a moment to roll up her sleeves, giving him more time to recover. A faint, sweet smell reached her. Baby shampoo. Ernst Mulvahill used baby shampoo.

He cleared his throat. "My brother is—was a very loyal man," he said. His voice sounded normal and she wondered what kind of effort it took to control himself like that. "Kendrick used to work out of Brandon. He moved to Mendenhall about fifteen years ago, but my brother saw no reason to change veterinarians."

There was a note of frustration in his voice.

"I take you didn't agree?" asked Kate.

He studied her for a moment. "What does this have to do with the theft?" he asked bluntly.

Kate shrugged easily.

"Maybe nothing," she admitted. "But we won't know until we have all the information. That's why we have to ask all these intrusive questions. You never know which one will give us the clue we're missing."

His mouth tightened again and suddenly she realized that this man was exhausted. He probably hadn't slept much—if at all—since his brother's death.

"It was just another sign of Johann's stubbornness," he said finally. "He had trouble seeing that we had to move with the times."

Kate's eyebrows rose.

"You didn't agree on the running of the farm?"

The arms crossed again and he stared at her reproachfully. "Not that this is any concern of yours, Chief Williams," he said stiffly, "but no, we did not agree."

Kate's head cocked to one side as a thought occurred to her.

"And yet, you did as he wished."

To her surprise, he smiled, and he no longer looked so forbidding.

"As I have said, my brother was stubborn. He liked things the way he liked them. And he was the eldest. So yes, I did as he wished."

Kate smiled at him. "And yet," she said softly, "you fired your three long-term employees and hired three inexperienced workers."

He looked at her in surprise. Then he frowned.

"Again, Chief Williams, I fail to see how this is any of your business."

She tapped the pen on the pad as she looked at him.

"Humor me. Please."

For a moment, he got a stubborn look on his face, then he shrugged.

"The boy had only been with us for two years," he said. "And he wanted to go back to school. Nunez wanted to be closer to his wife's family. I was sorry to see him go. He was a good worker."

"And Barry Mongrain?"

Again, the tightening of the mouth.

"Barry was a good worker, too," he said grudgingly. "But he was devoted to my brother and would only take direction from him. That was fine until—"

He broke off suddenly and looked away. Kate waited a moment, then prompted him.

"Until?"

Mulvahill looked at his watch.

"I need to go," he said.

"Just a few more questions," said Kate, and circled back. "That was fine until what?"

Ernst Mulvahill closed his eyes and took a deep breath. Kate waited and finally he looked at her.

"Until my brother began showing signs of dementia. I believe that is why Nunez and young Artemis left. They worked every day with my brother, and his directions were becoming more and more erratic. But Barry followed every one of Johann's orders, no matter how idiotic. The day Barry lit a bale of straw on fire because Johann told him to..." Mulvahill shook his head. "I couldn't keep him on."

The frustration and despair emanating from him felt sincere. Kate couldn't imagine what it would be like to have Mom start to lose her mind. To lose herself.

"I'm sorry," she said softly. "That must have been very hard."

Mulvahill sighed and rubbed his face with both hands as if erasing the memory.

"Well, all that was lost was a bale of hay. It could have been worse." He leaned forward a little. "It wasn't Barry's fault, you understand. That's why I got him a job with another farmer."

Kate glanced down at her list of questions. She was being derailed by sympathy.

"When did Dr. Kendrick receive the tank from the supplier?"

Mulvahill's eyebrows rose at the change of direction but he answered readily enough.

"I'm not sure," he said. "Late last week, I think."

"Why didn't he bring it over right away?"

"There was no rush," said Mulvahill. "We had to wait for the cows to be ready anyway."

Well, that made sense.

But something else had been niggling at her for a few days, and it finally rose to the surface.

"Mr. Mulvahill," she said, leaning forward slightly, "forgive me if this is a naïve question. I don't know much about cows, but why inseminate the cows now? Doesn't that mean the calves will be born in January?" She might not know anything about farming, but she knew about January. Newborn calves would have a hard time surviving outside at that time of the year.

Mulvahill's shoulders suddenly slumped and he looked defeated. Then he straightened.

"Yes, it does. It is... not wise. Dairy cows would just stay in the barn all winter but we have beef cows. They—and their calves—would be outside. Under normal circumstances, we could store the tank safely and use the semen later in the year. But that... that was a lot of money."

"Why didn't Dr. Kendrick try to talk your brother out of it?" she asked. "Or talk to you?"

"That, Chief Williams, is a very good question."

Holy cow. Fifty-some-odd thousand dollars on the whim of a man with dementia. And the vet just went along with it.

Then she blinked.

"So, the theft was actually a godsend."

He looked at her, bloodshot eyes serious, and nodded slowly.

"Yes, Chief Williams. I am not sorry that someone stole the tank."

Well, wasn't he the honest one.

Mulvahill sighed. "I did not steal it, Chief Williams. Nor did I arrange for the theft. But I can't pretend that I'm sorry."

Fine. Time to change tacks.

"Tell me about your brother's tests. I take it they had to do with his dementia?"

Mulvahill shook his head.

"No, actually. The doctor was concerned about his prostate. We have a history of cancer in our family. Johann was supposed to be in the hospital overnight only." His voice thickened at the end and he cleared his throat.

Not yet, she told herself firmly. One more question before she told him.

"Did Johann drive himself in to Winnipeg?"

"Of course not," he said with a smile. "Although he put up a fight. Mrs. Einerson drove him in first thing on Monday and I was going to pick him up on Tuesday, once the hospital called. That's what I thought they were calling about..." He looked at her, a lost expression on his face. "How could he have died from running *tests*?"

All right. She'd delayed long enough.

"Mr. Mulvahill," she said softly, "I'm so sorry, but I have some terrible news for you."

He blinked at her, clearly wondering what fresh hell this was, and Kate took a deep breath.

"Your brother was murdered."

He stared at her, the words clearly not registering. Then his face blanched. For a moment, she thought he would pitch over and she almost stood up to go around the table. Then his hands clamped on the edge of the table and he seemed to steady himself. His mouth opened but no words came out. His gray eyes looked darker, maybe an effect of his lowering brow.

He clearly couldn't speak, so she filled him in on the Grace Hospital doctor's suspicions and the results of the preliminary examination of his brother's body. She took her time, but watched him carefully. She'd seen people succumb to shock at receiving bad news.

But Ernst Mulvahill was tough. Color returned to his cheeks and the shock receded, to be replaced by anger.

"Why?" he said, as if that was the only word he could get out. Then, "Who?"

"We don't know yet," she said. "Winnipeg police are in charge of the investigation. They will be in touch with you soon."

His eyes narrowed then and the look he gave her was unfriendly. "My brother was murdered on Tuesday and you waited two and a half days to tell me?"

Kate shook her head.

"No, sir. We only received confirmation yesterday that he had been murdered. Can you think of anyone who might want him dead?"

"No," he said coldly. "He was a good man. I can think of no one who would want him dead. But you, you suspect me, don't you?"

She returned his hard gaze unflinchingly.

"Not really, but until we know who did it, Mr. Mulvahill, everyone connected to this case is a suspect. And to be honest, you would have one of the best motives. He was becoming a liability on the farm. With him gone, you become the sole owner of the farm and can run it the way you want."

Mulvahill suddenly slapped the table. His cheeks bloomed with color and anger filled his eyes. He stood up.

"That's enough," he said, his voice sharp. "I have come here in good faith to answer your questions when I should be arranging to have my brother's body brought home. Now I find myself a suspect? In the murder of my *brother*? A murder you waited a day to tell me about?" He took a deep breath and she saw that his hands were shaking. "I am leaving now, Chief Williams, and will not come back here without a lawyer."

He stalked around the table and flung the door open. To Kate's deep relief, no one was outside the interview room. She followed him out of the ident room and into the hallway, where Dr. Kendrick was seated at one of the chairs. Mulvahill stopped abruptly and Kendrick looked at him in surprise. Out of the corner of her eye, Kate saw O'Hara sitting at the duty desk, staring at the two men in the hallway. She didn't want to look in the duty room for the others. In particular, she didn't want to draw Mulvahill's attention to Bert's Winnipeg Police Services uniform. Bert was already going to have to do some fancy footwork to explain why Winnipeg didn't advise Mulvahill right away that his brother had been murdered.

"Ernst," said Kendrick, standing up. He wore Carhartts and the regulation plaid shirt, this one red and black. Clearly, he had interrupted his workday to be here. He'd taken his coat off while he was waiting, as sunlight flooded the hallway. "I'm so sorry to hear about Johann's death."

Mulvahill nodded stiffly and managed a strangled "Thank you," and then he was out the door.

Kendrick looked at the closed storm door for a moment, then turned to look at Kate. His eyebrows rose and he leaned in a little.

"Is he mad at *me*?"

Kate shrugged, refusing to respond to his unspoken invitation to intimacy. "I expect he's mad at the world right now. Thank you for coming in, Dr. Kendrick. If you'll just follow me, please."

She led him into the interview room recently vacated by Mulvahill.

"Officer Martins will be right with you," she said, and closed the door on him.

She hurried back to the duty room to find Martins sitting at one of the common desks and Bert standing in Samantha's doorway.

"I didn't think it was a good idea to let him see me," he explained, his eyebrows raised.

Kate nodded. "Where are the others?"

He hooked a thumb toward Samantha's office. "Paterson's on the phone. McKell's in the break room with Charlotte."

All right. She turned to Nick Martins.

"Are you ready?"

He nodded and stood up. McKell and Charlotte emerged from the break room at that moment.

"Ready?" asked McKell.

"Looks like it," said Kate, nodding at Martins. Charlotte smiled at her and sat down at her own desk. Clearly, she didn't want to be squished with four other people in the back room.

"Did you watch the interview?" Kate asked McKell. "Anything pop out at you?"

He shook his head. "You pretty much covered everything," he said. "Unless he's a damned good actor, I don't think he killed his brother."

Kate looked at Bert, who shrugged. "The hospital confirmed that they notified Ernst of his brother's death at almost three o'clock on Tuesday afternoon."

"That's consistent with when he came out to tell us," said Samantha, coming up behind Bert. He moved out of the doorway to let her pass. "That alone would rule him out."

Well, that was the last piece, then. Ernst Mulvahill could not have killed his brother and been back on the farm in time to receive the hospital's call.

But he could have hired someone to do it.

Kate turned back to Martins. "Don't forget to tell him you're recording," she said, and they waited until he had closed the door to the interview room before following him.

Martins was already seated and talking when they silently arrayed themselves in front of the one-way glass. Kendrick, who was facing them, seemed perfectly relaxed, nodding at something Martins was saying. Samantha reached across Bert and flicked the speaker on.

"...standard procedure," Martins was saying. "I know you're busy, so let's get started."

"Sure," said Kendrick. His shirtsleeves were rolled up, revealing muscled, white forearms. He'd gotten a haircut before coming in. His graying, sandy hair had a tendency to curl. He had an easy smile that reached his eyes. The effect was boyish.

To her irritation, Bert stood just behind her right shoulder in the cramped quarters and she could feel the heat emanating from him.

"Let's start with the basics," said Martins. "You ordered the semen on behalf of the Mulvahills?"

"I thought I did," said Kendrick. "But it turns out Ernst knew nothing about it."

"How do you mean?" Martins' pen was poised above the notepad.

Kendrick shrugged. "I normally deal with Johann." He paused for a moment, then started again. "I used to deal with Johann. He was the one who worked most with the herd. So when he told me he wanted to inseminate the Angus cows, I worked with him to determine the best bulls to use and then I placed the order."

Martins nodded and scribbled something before looking up again. All they could see of him was the back of his head and a bit of the side of his face.

"When did you find out that Ernst knew nothing about it?"

Kendrick sighed. On Monday, his eyes had looked gray, but today they definitely looked hazel. An attractive man.

"When I called the farm last week to tell them the tank had arrived.

I left the message with the housekeeper. Within minutes Ernst called me back. He was some upset," he said with feeling.

"Really?" said Martins with interest. "How do you mean?"

"Called me an idiot for not checking with him. But I've been dealing with Johann Mulvahill for over twenty years and I'd never had reason to doubt his decisions."

"Even when he wanted to inseminate at this time of year?"

Kendrick gave Martins a sharp look.

"I admit it was unusual. I did ask Johann about it, but he insisted." He shrugged. "All I can do is give my best advice. If the client doesn't want to take it..."

"They decided to go ahead with the insemination?" asked Martins.

Kendrick nodded. "Yes. They could hold the tank safely as long as they topped it up with liquid nitrogen once a month. Besides, it was too late to cancel. Johann had signed the contract to purchase and the semen was already on its way. Once the tank leaves the supplier's control, they won't take it back. Because they can't guarantee continuous quality control."

"I see," said Martins, though Kate doubted he did. Bert's warm breath feathered the small hairs at the back of her neck and she barely controlled a shiver. The room was growing very warm.

"When did the tank arrive at your clinic?"

Kendrick looked up at the ceiling. After a moment, he said, "Wednesday. No, Thursday."

"Why didn't you bring it to the farm right away?" asked Martins in an almost word-for-word echo of her own question.

Kendrick shrugged. "There was no rush. I called to tell them it was in and that I'd bring it in on Monday. And then... well, you know what happened then."

"Yes," Martins nodded. He looked up at the veterinarian and Kate saw the corner of his mouth rise in a smile. "I noticed an automobile association sticker on your windshield, Dr. Kendrick. Why didn't you call them when you saw you didn't have a spare?"

Was that a flinch? Kate felt the other three lean in with her, as if they could hit replay to see the vet's reaction again.

"My membership lapsed," admitted Kendrick. "My assistant lives in Mendenhall, so it made sense to call her."

Huh. Kate glanced sideways and found Bert watching her, his eyes alight with curiosity.

"I see," said Martins, and wrote something down. Kendrick tried to see what he was writing. Martins looked up suddenly and Kendrick's gaze shifted away.

"What I don't understand," said Martins as if nothing had happened, "is why you didn't take the tank with you, or stay with it while your assistant got your tire repaired."

Kate glanced at McKell but he was staring at the veterinarian. There it was, the question that had been bothering her since McKell brought it up. Why hadn't the vet stayed with the damned tank?

The four of them watched with bated breath as a tide of red crept up Kendrick's neck.

"Excuse me?" he said stiffly. "What exactly are you accusing me of?"

Martins' head rose as if in surprise and he waved a hand as if to ward off the question.

"No accusation, doctor. But these are questions we need to ask. Your insurance company will ask them, too, no doubt."

The crimson tide now crept over the vet's face. He stood up and looked down at Martins.

"Is this why Ernst left so mad? Did you accuse him of insurance scam, too?"

Bert suddenly grabbed her arm and pulled, McKell and Samantha right behind them. They barely managed to scramble out of the ident room and into the duty room before Dr. Kendrick stormed out, not sparing a glance to the right or the left, his black jacket clasped in one fist and flapping behind him. The storm door slammed shut behind him and they all turned to watch Martins saunter out of the ident room.

"Well," he said cheerfully. "That was interesting."

CHAPTER 20

Interesting how he assumed you were accusing him of insurance fraud," said Samantha. She swallowed a yawn and sat up straighter on the love seat. Obviously her kids were still keeping her up at night.

They were back in the break room to debrief. Kate had just finished pouring coffee into five cups. Martins picked up one cup and went to sit at the table across from Bert. His eyes were bloodshot, too, but Kate suspected that had more to do with incipient flu than with tiredness.

She automatically added cream and sugar to Bert's cup and handed it to him. He smiled his thanks, and it was only when she saw his smile that she realized what she had done.

Seven months and she still knew how the damned man liked his coffee. She ignored him and returned to the counter.

"That's because it's on his mind," said Bert.

McKell joined her at the counter and poured a little cream into one of the cups, which he then handed to Samantha. He picked up the remaining cup and leaned a hip on the counter while Kate went to sit next to Samantha with her own cup.

Kate nodded reluctantly. "And it's on his mind because he's guilty."

McKell nodded, too. "Oh, yes. Now we have to figure out how he did it."

"Hang on," said Samantha. "There's no evidence that he stole the tank."

Martins shrugged. "Not yet."

Then something occurred to Kate and she looked at Bert.

"What did you say the hospital footage showed?"

He stared at her. "What footage?"

"Of the man leaving Johann's room."

Bert shook his head. "No footage. There's no video surveillance on the ward. It was a nurse who saw a man leaving Johann's room. She said the man wore... hang on..." He pulled his notebook out of his back pants pocket and flipped through it until he got to the right page. "Carhartts, a black jacket and a black ball cap," he finished slowly. He looked up at Kate.

"Huh," she said.

"Huh," said McKell at the same time. "Kendrick was wearing Carhartts today."

"Wait a minute," said Samantha. "It's a pretty big leap to go from insurance scam to murder." She glanced at Kate. "A *lot* of people wear Carhartts."

Kate nodded slowly. That was true. And while she was suspicious of the vet's motives for coming on to her, that didn't make him a murderer.

"Your justice of the peace might be more inclined to grant your warrant for his finances if they knew that Winnipeg was seeking a warrant to search the vet's house and clinic."

Maybe, thought Kate, but their evidence was flimsy, at best. And it would be hard for Winnipeg to convince a justice of the peace to grant a search warrant for another jurisdiction. Just as it would be hard for Mendenhall to convince a JP to grant them a search warrant for Kendrick's financials.

Then again, Kendrick had admitted to letting his automobile association membership lapse, which could speak to financial stress. And thanks to Josh, they now had a list of suppliers who dealt with Kendrick's veterinary clinic.

Those suppliers might be willing to discuss just how deep Kendrick's financial woes were.

* * *

"He's divorced," said Samantha, walking into Kate's office and sitting down.

Kate looked up from her screen and blinked at the acting deputy chief.

"Who's divorced?"

"Kendrick," said Samantha, a small smile on her face.

"You look like the cat that ate the canary," said Kate. "How did we miss this?"

Samantha shrugged.

"He was married out of province. We put the call out to all provinces and territories, and it took time for the information to trickle back to us." She glanced down at her notebook. "Twenty years ago he lived in Regina."

Huh. Kate didn't know why she was surprised, but she was.

"Kids?"

"Still trying to find out," admitted Samantha. "Also, we're trying to find out what the terms of the divorce were. Maybe he's paying alimony."

Alimony would add stress to an already stressed financial situation. Still, fifteen years ago he was living in Brandon, and no longer married. Fifteen years was a long time to be paying support, even if there were kids. The information brought them no further ahead.

Bert had left an hour earlier, promising to let her know if he managed to get a warrant. Kate wasn't holding her breath. In the meantime, McKell and Charlotte were on the phone with Kendrick's suppliers.

They were close. She could feel it in her inability to settle into her work. She sighed. This was the part she hated. The waiting.

"What about the fire marshal?" she asked Samantha. "Did she reach any conclusions?"

Samantha blinked as if she had to search her memory. Then she nodded.

"Clear-cut case of arson. Both the construction site and the gazebo."

Well, they already knew that.

"Did she give us anything to work with?"

Samantha shrugged.

"Not much. Accelerant in both cases was gasoline. The plastic jerry cans were left on-site in both places. They were too melted to pick out any prints."

"All right," said Kate on a sigh. "Keep me posted."

Samantha left and Kate found the phone number for Red River Insurance, the company insuring 128444, Inc. She spent the next fifteen minutes talking to the senior claims adjuster, sharing what she had learned about the officers of the company and their link to the various projects that had succumbed to arson. He was very grateful and she promised to send him a copy of her report when she was done. Maybe they would have more success at stopping these buggers than she was having.

As she hung up, she heard a murmur of voices in the duty room and got up to stretch her legs. To her surprise, Trepalli was leaning against the counter by the log book, talking in a low voice with O'Hara. Charlotte was still on the phone, murmuring and typing at the same time. McKell was busy scribbling on a pad, the phone tucked between his ear and shoulder.

Trepalli looked up when she walked in. He wore jeans and a faded gray sweatshirt with the sleeves pushed up his forearms, and still managed to look like he belonged in GQ.

"Afternoon, Chief."

"Marco," she said. "I thought you'd be busy helping Amanda." She tried not to put any censure in her tone, but really, why wasn't he helping Amanda?

"She kicked me out," he said with a shrug. "Everything's ready except for the cooking and she never lets me help with that." He glanced at McKell, then back at Kate. "So, how's the case going?"

"Which one?" asked Kate with some frustration. "Never mind. Neither one is going well."

Samantha came out of her office and leaned against the door jamb, her arms crossed.

"We're waiting to see what comes out of the interviews Charlotte and the DC are doing," she told Trepalli. "That may give us enough for a search warrant of Kendrick's financials."

The phone rang and O'Hara turned to answer it. Trepalli stepped closer to Samantha and Kate so as not to disturb O'Hara.

"You know," said Trepalli in a low voice, "we interviewed Kendrick's assistant the day after the theft and she confirmed that she picked him up and got him to the service station. I've been thinking that maybe we should ask her where Kendrick was the day Johann Mulvahill died."

Huh.

Kate glanced at Samantha, who returned the look with raised eyebrows.

"That's a very good idea, Marco," said Samantha slowly.

"Yes," agreed Kate. Detecting 101. Check out the alibi. "In fact," she said, suddenly deciding, "I'm going to go over there right now. If he's out of the clinic, I'll interview the assistant."

"Why not call ahead and find out if he's there?" asked Samantha, uncrossing her arms and straightening.

Kate shook her head.

"This is a covert operation," she said with a grin. "I don't want to tip him off that we're coming, and I don't want her to have a chance to tip him off, either." She thought for a moment. "Besides, it'll give me a chance to look around. You never know what I might see."

Before Samantha could say anything, Trepalli spoke up.

"I'll come with you."

Kate looked at him.

"You're off duty, Marco."

"I have five hours to kill," he replied. "And this case is making us all crazy. Let me come with you."

Kate considered it for a moment. Then she smiled.

"I guess it depends on whether or not you've retained any of your old charms."

He blinked at her and Samantha hid a smile behind her hand. Then he blushed.

"I may still have a few ounces left," he said modestly.

Samantha rolled her eyes.

"Shall I come, too?" asked Samantha.

Kate glanced at the clock. It was just past two o'clock.

"No," she said finally, looking at Samantha. "I think I'd like you to do some checking for me."

"On what?" Samantha's eyes were bloodshot and she looked a little pale. Kate controlled an urge to step away from the woman.

"Mark Pinkley and Jason Cromarty, the two security guards at Porter Security. Let's find out more about their backgrounds."

"Okay," said Samantha. "What are you expecting to find?"

"Nothing," admitted Kate glumly. "Just more Ts to cross." Might as well be thorough.

* * *

The clinic was barely within town limits. It took Kate twenty minutes to drive through town and emerge at the northern end, well past the subdivision where the mayor lived. They took her car, as a patrol car would be too noticeable. The day had turned warm, with the sun beaming out of a clear blue sky like a promise.

She knew where the vet's clinic was, of course—she knew where everything was in her town—but she'd never had occasion to actually go there. It was at the end of a long dirt driveway. There was a pretty white farmhouse with green trim at the end of the driveway and an old barn that looked like it had been converted into his clinic. A sign above the incongruous white metal door of the barn read KENDRICK VETERINARY SERVICES in faded black letters on a white background. Next to the man-sized door were the traditional extra wide doors through which the farmer who had originally owned this farm would have driven his tractor.

Beyond the house and barn were fields that ran right up to a screen of trees—too far to identify. She had no idea what was growing in the fields. She defied anyone to identify what the crop would be from the twelve-inch-high green stalks.

"He lives in the farmhouse," said Trepalli as they turned down the long driveway. Tall elm trees marched down either side of the driveway, their tiny leaves glistening with that particularly fresh shade of green that only came from new leaves in springtime.

There were no cars by the house, and only one car parked in front of the barn, a gray Smart car covered in dust.

"His truck could be parked behind the house," warned Trepalli.

"Yep," said Kate. "We won't know until we get closer." By which point, any chance of discretion would be blown.

She pulled up to the barn and parked by the Smart car. She could see the back of the house in her side view mirror. Just grass, shrubs, and a deck. No white Silverado.

"Lucky," murmured Trepalli, getting out of the car.

Yes, indeed. And they had better take advantage of that luck while they could.

She got out and closed the door behind her, crunching over the gravel driveway to join Trepalli. She paused by the Smart car and looked in. Only two seats, with a bit of space in the back. A plastic bin with containers of windshield wiper fluid and motor oil, and rags filled almost half the space. There might be enough room to carry a tire and a tank if they removed the bin.

"She knows you," she said as they walked toward the door. A window was set in the door, but it reflected the day back at them, making it impossible to see inside. "So you take the lead."

He nodded and opened the door for her.

Inside she found herself in a small waiting room with a speckled industrial linoleum on the floor and beige plastic chairs set around the perimeter of two walls. A counter set in the wall directly ahead of them looked into a small office, empty right now. There was a door in the far wall of the office, and another door set to the right of the counter, presumably to let the pets into the examination rooms.

The place had a faint, wet-dog smell that Kate found off-putting.

Trepalli didn't seem bothered by it. He walked over to the counter, leaned in, and called out.

"Hello? Miss Wesolowski?"

Kate moved off to the side so she wouldn't be immediately visible to anyone coming in from the back.

From the back came a shuffling sound and the door in the office suddenly opened to reveal a middle-aged woman with frazzled blonde curls pulled back in a loose bun at the back of her head. The hair had dark, inch-long roots. She was maybe ten pounds overweight and wore a short-sleeved green smock over a black, long-sleeved tee-shirt and black pants. She came through the doorway pulling off rubber gloves and stopped when she caught sight of Trepalli.

"Officer Trepalli," she said with surprise. "This is an unexpected pleasure." She gave him a wide smile that transformed her into a beauty, in spite of her slightly crooked teeth.

Trepalli grinned at her.

"Too kind, ma'am," he said modestly.

"And you brought a friend," said Wesolowski, catching sight of Kate.

"Ma'am," said Trepalli, "this is Chief Williams. I hope you don't mind, but I've got a few more questions for you."

Wesolowski smiled again.

"How can I refuse that handsome face?" she asked rhetorically. "Come on back. I'll put the kettle on." She walked back out the door, and a moment later, the door to the side of the counter opened.

They followed her down a short hallway with two doors on either side and one at the far end. Presumably they were examination rooms. The wet-dog smell was stronger back here.

Wesolowski stopped at the first door on the right and opened it. To Kate's surprise, it opened onto a small, neat kitchen with a short counter, microwave, kettle, and fridge. A small round table sat in front of a large window that looked out at a field. A chain-link fence enclosed a small area, presumably some kind of exercise pen.

"Have a seat," said Wesolowski, waving them to the table. She dropped the rubber gloves she'd been carrying into the sink and washed her hands.

"I was just cleaning the examination rooms," she explained over her shoulder. "It's been fairly quiet, for once, and I thought I'd take advantage and do a thorough cleaning." She wiped her hands on a paper towel and then pulled the kettle over to fill from the tap.

"Why is it so quiet?" asked Trepalli as she placed tea bags in a Brown Betty.

Wesolowski shrugged.

"We've cut down the small animal clinic to drop-ins, once a week. Most people take their pets to vets who specialize in dogs and cats. The doc mostly handles farm calls."

The room felt stuffy to Kate and the dog smell that seemed to permeate the building was making her a little queasy. She really, really wanted to open the window, but didn't want to interrupt Trepalli's flow.

"Is that where the doc is now?" asked Trepalli, getting up to help her carry the teapot and cups to the table.

"Yes," she nodded. "Horse with a limp." She set the cups out in front of everyone and sat down across from Trepalli. "Now, what did you forget to ask?"

Kate tried not to tense. This was the tricky part. Asking the woman about the vet's schedule on Tuesday, when the theft of the tank had taken place on Monday.

"I just need to fill in some blanks for my report," he said easily. "It would be useful if I could attach the doc's schedule for this week to the file. Do you think you could print it out for me?"

He made it sound so casual, so incidental, that Kate almost believed him. But Wesolowski sat there blinking at Trepalli, her brown eyes slightly narrowed. She took in his civilian clothes, then looked sideways at Kate.

Kate's heart sank a little.

"Now, why would you need a copy of his schedule?" asked Wesolowski slowly. She nodded at Trepalli without taking her eyes off Kate. "And why would the chief of police come along for something so… mundane?"

To his credit, Trepalli didn't even look at Kate. He nodded at Wesolowski, acknowledging the validity of her question.

"Ma'am, we have some concerns surrounding the theft."

"What kind of concerns?" asked the woman, sitting back in her chair and crossing her arms.

Trepalli shrugged.

"Well, for one thing, we are wondering why he didn't take the tank with him when you picked him up."

Wesolowski stared at him for a moment, then dropped her gaze, and suddenly Kate had a very good idea why.

"Were you wondering the same thing?" she asked Wesolowski softly.

Wesolowski glanced up quickly at Kate.

"No, I wasn't," she said firmly. "Did you see the Smart car parked outside? I barely had room for the truck's tire."

"I noticed you had a bin back there for a jack, windshield wiper fluid, that sort of thing—was that in the car when you picked up Dr. Kendrick?" asked Kate.

Wesolowski paused for a moment, then nodded jerkily.

"Could you not have removed the bin to make room for the tank?" asked Kate reasonably.

Wesolowski shifted uncomfortably in her chair and didn't answer.

"Ma'am?" pressed Trepalli.

Finally, Wesolowski sighed.

"I didn't know he had the tank with him," she admitted. She glanced out the window, then back at the top of the table. "He had the tire off and was waiting for me by the side of the road. He shoved the bin over to make room for the tire."

Well, well, well.

"You didn't know he was going to the Mulvahill farm that morning?" asked Trepalli.

Wesolowski nodded.

"Yes, but I didn't know why. He doesn't tell me everything, you know."

Kate nodded as if she understood.

"How long have you been with Dr. Kendrick?" she asked.

Wesolowski shot her a glance.

"Four months. Why?"

Kate shrugged.

"You're his only employee. Are you a vet tech?"

The woman shook her head no.

"I do cleanup and I take care of his appointments. He does pretty much everything else."

"Is that usual?" asked Trepalli. "Doesn't a vet usually have more staff?"

Wesolowski took a deep breath and let it out slowly. She looked as if she were debating with herself. Finally she looked at Kate.

"I think he's been having money problems," she admitted. "I don't think he can afford to hire anyone else."

Kate nodded. The aroma of orange-flavoured tea wafted over to her, merging with the dog smell.

"Could we see his schedule for this week, please?" she asked softly. This woman was smart. She would know that the police couldn't demand to see the schedule without the legal authority of a warrant. But at the same time, something about the whole incident clearly bothered her.

Wesolowski studied Kate's face for a long moment, then glanced at Trepalli. He said nothing, but stared back at her seriously. Finally she got up and left the room without a word.

The door closed softly behind her and Trepalli looked at Kate.

"Do you think she's gone to call him?"

Kate shrugged. If she called her boss, she called her boss. Kate couldn't prevent her. But maybe now was a good time to snoop around, while Wesolowski was away. She pushed away from the table and was about to stand up when the door opened again and Wesolowski strode in, carrying an old-fashioned agenda book. Kate blinked in surprise. Even she used an electronic agenda these days.

Wesolowski placed the agenda open on the table in front of Kate.

Trepalli pulled out his phone and stood up, leaning over to take a few pictures.

"Thank you," said Kate gratefully. She glanced down at the vet's weekly schedule, spread out over the two pages.

On Monday morning, someone had scribbled in "Mulvahill" next to the seven thirty time slot. Nothing else that day. Tuesday morning at eight was "Stuttgart—vaccinations, cows." After lunch, at two o'clock, "Marty—pig."

She looked up at Wesolowski.

"Who is Marty?" she asked, pointing at the entry.

Wesolowski glanced down at the agenda.

"That's Martin Janssen. He's a pig farmer near the military base. His pig was poorly."

So. If Kendrick went to the pig farm at two o'clock, there was no way he could have dealt with the pig and made it to Winnipeg by three o'clock, in time to murder Johann Mulvahill.

Wesolowski frowned slightly as her finger tapped the entry.

"Mr. Janssen called," she said slowly, as if just remembering. "At about two thirty. He wanted to know if the doc was on his way."

Kate looked at her, trying not to show her excitement.

"Why was he delayed?"

"I don't know," said Wesolowski with a shrug. "I tried calling him but his phone was probably out of juice. When the doc didn't show up back at the office by quitting time, I called Mr. Janssen back and he said that the doc had just left."

Trepalli leaned forward slightly, transfixing the woman with his gaze.

"What time did you call Mr. Janssen?"

"About five o'clock," she said, clearly nonplussed. "Why?"

Trepalli turned to look at Kate and she felt the familiar tingle up her spine.

* * *

Kate called Samantha from the parking lot of the mall. It was going on four o'clock and the sun was on its way down, but for the moment, it sent long shadows across the half-empty parking lot and filled the sky with a golden haze.

"Samantha," said Kate when her acting DC answered, "I need you to send someone to check an alibi." And she proceeded to explain what they had learned at the veterinary clinic. Next to her, Trepalli was busy scribbling in Kate's notebook, since he didn't have his with him.

Samantha listened quietly while Kate finished talking, and only then spoke up.

"I'll ask the DC if he'll do it," she said. "He and Charlotte found out that the vet owes at least twenty thousand dollars to a variety of suppliers. Most of them are refusing to send him more until he clears his accounts."

Maybe that explained why his clinic was so quiet.

"If McKell can't," said Kate, "maybe send Tattersall." At once, she realized that she should leave it up to Samantha to decide. "Sorry, Samantha," she said. "Send whoever you want."

There was a brief silence at the other end.

"I agree," said Samantha. "Tattersall is a good choice."

Kate nodded, even though the other woman couldn't see.

"Any joy on Pinkley and Cromarty?" she asked.

"Pinkley's been with Porter Security for over five years. Before that, he worked for Smith and Smith, a high-end security company in Winnipeg, for about ten years."

"Why did he move?" asked Kate. Going from a high-end security company in the capital to rinky-dink Porter Security in Mendenhall was quite the change.

"Family," said Samantha. "His wife's folks are in Mendenhall."

"Okay. What about Cromarty?"

"Still working on it," said Samantha. "I'll let you know what I find out."

"All right," said Kate. "But first, find me a justice of the peace who'll sign off on a search warrant for Kendrick's financials, and his property." They had enough right now to deal with the theft and the suspicion of fraud. As for the murder, well, she'd have to talk to Bert once McKell or Tattersall confirmed what time Kendrick had shown up at the pig farm.

They hung up and Kate turned to Trepalli. He handed her the notebook and her pen, which she tucked away.

"I'm sorry," he said suddenly.

Kate looked at him.

"For what?"

"I guess I don't have as much of my old charm left as I thought." He looked a little woebegone.

Just before they'd left the vet's clinic, he had turned the full force of those blue eyes on Miss Wesolowski and asked if they could look around the clinic. Kate had seen that look turn grandmothers into schoolgirls. But Wesolowski was made of sterner stuff, and she had apparently reached the limit of her willingness to cooperate. She refused.

Now Kate grinned at her constable and considered that being taken down a peg or two was probably good for him.

"Don't worry, Constable," she assured him. "I won't tell Amanda."

"And I appreciate that." He grinned back at her. "Now what?"

"Now," said Kate firmly, "you go back to being on days off."

His face fell.

"Chief," he protested. "We're so close—I can almost taste it. Once the DC confirms that Kendrick could have been in Winnipeg, we'll have no problem getting a warrant. Even without the confirmation, we have enough for a warrant. We can't waste any time, or Kendrick could get away."

Well, even if he ran, he wouldn't get away for long. But Trepalli was right. They were very close.

"The murder is Winnipeg's case," she reminded him. "We need to concern ourselves with the theft."

For a moment, he looked like a little boy who'd been told he couldn't go to the amusement park. Kate had to work at not smiling.

"That said," she continued calmly, "Winnipeg will likely get their warrant before we do. And they will need us to accompany them when they serve the warrant. But it'll be hours before it comes through. And you have an opening night."

His eyes narrowed slightly and his lips thinned into a smile that gave his face an unaccustomed ferocity.

"Amanda understands," he said. "Julianne will be helping her."

Kate studied his face for long moments as something cool and unnerving washed over her. His focus wasn't on Amanda's dreams. His focus was on catching a murderer. Kate wondered if Amanda truly understood the man she was about to marry.

CHAPTER 21

It was almost nine o'clock that night before Bert finally arrived from Winnipeg with the warrant. He walked into the detachment, his boots thumping on the linoleum of the hallway, and found Kate, Trepalli, and McKell waiting for him.

He nodded a greeting at Emile St. Ives, who was on the duty desk, and waved a folded piece of paper at Kate.

"Ready?" he asked. He was still in uniform and his eyes were alight with excitement. Kate had to work hard at not catching it from him. She had to stay calm. Steady.

"Yes," she said. "You, Trepalli, and I will take one of the patrol cars. Fredrickson and Jones are already parked near the clinic, waiting for us." Samantha had left hours ago, reluctantly, at Kate's insistence. She had enough bodies to help, and Samantha was clearly getting sicker. She needed her rest.

Bert's eyebrows rose and he turned to look at McKell.

"You're not coming?"

McKell remained silent but he turned a gimlet eye on Kate, who shrugged.

"He's not officially on strength yet," she said. She felt like a hypocrite, seeing as he'd been at the detachment most of the week, helping out. But it was one thing to sit at a desk and make phone calls, and quite another to implement a search warrant on a murder suspect.

"You don't expect your veterinarian to be armed, do you?" asked Bert skeptically.

Kate felt the heat rising in her cheeks and she stared hard at him. *Her* veterinarian? Was he honestly questioning her judgment? Again?

Trepalli chose that moment to walk over to the duty desk where he and St. Ives busied themselves finding the right key for the patrol car. Trepalli had changed into his uniform. Like most of the constables, he kept a spare uniform in his locker.

As the silence stretched, McKell cleared his throat.

"If you're going to go," he said gruffly, "go. I want to get to bed before midnight and I'm not leaving until this is done."

Kate turned and walked out of the duty room, her stomach churning with anger. Since when did Bert Langdon question her judgment? Her professionalism? She walked out of the detachment into the night, the cold air like a balm on her cheeks.

The clear day had turned into a clear night, and the temperature had plummeted to barely a few degrees above freezing. A half-moon hung low in the sky and she could see a few stars past the wash of light from the street and nearby buildings.

Trepalli stepped out behind her, forcing her off the stoop and toward the patrol car parked in one of the assigned spots. Bert had driven to Mendenhall in a Winnipeg Police Services patrol car, which he'd parked in a visitor parking spot. They would take Mendenhall cars to serve the warrant, but if they ended up arresting Kendrick, he wanted to be ready with a patrol car.

She looked over her shoulder at Trepalli and he wordlessly handed her the keys. She expected him to take the back seat in deference to Bert's rank, but he took the passenger seat, leaving Bert to get into the back. A little passive aggressive, maybe, but the petty part of her wanted to smile.

At that time of night, there was hardly any traffic on the streets of Mendenhall and it took barely fifteen minutes to make it to the top of the veterinary clinic's driveway. She had passed Jones and Fredrickson on the way, and they had pulled in behind her. She pulled to a stop past the driveway and turned the engine off. They had decided to walk down to the house—less chance of alerting the vet to their presence.

She reached under her front seat and pulled out the spare flashlight she had taken from the detachment. Her own was buried under the wreck of the construction site at the condo development but this one was similar in size and heft. She attached it to her web belt.

Fredrickson and Jones approached as Bert extricated himself from the back seat.

"We did a drive by a few minutes ago," said Fredrickson. There was no risk of being overhead from the house, but he still kept his voice low. Jonah Fredrickson was a tall, thin man whose nickname—which Kate never used—was Ichabod. He had sandy blond hair, straight and fine, and pale blue eyes. He had the palest skin she had ever seen on a person. Like Tourmeline, he had a good eye for details.

"Anything stand out?" asked Bert before Kate could. She could feel Trepalli bristling next to her.

"No, sir," said Fredrickson.

"It looks like he's in for the night," Jones picked up. In contrast to Fredrickson, Brendan Jones was a little heavy, a little jowly. She knew from his file that he was only thirty-five, but he looked closer to early forties. "The clinic looks closed, with no lights, and there's only one light on in the farmhouse. His truck is parked out front."

"Any dogs?" asked Trepalli.

Kate almost shuddered. On her first case in Mendenhall, she'd been attacked by a dog while trying to apprehend a suspect. It wasn't an experience she cared to repeat.

"None that we saw or heard," said Fredrickson. "Could be inside, though. He *is* a vet, after all."

"All right," said Kate. "I'll take the front with DC Langdon. The three of you take the back. Make sure those are the only two doors," she added. Some of these old farmhouses had a storm cellar door that gave onto the outside. "Ready?"

They all nodded and headed down the driveway, the younger men at a faster clip than Bert and Kate so as to arrive at their respective doors at about the same time. The new leaves on the elm trees lining both sides of the driveway whispered in the wind. At the far end, Kendrick's farmhouse gleamed a pale gray in the moonlight.

This is probably overkill, thought Kate as she walked silently next to Bert. Five people to deal with one mild-mannered veterinarian. While she was angry with Bert, she had to admit that James Kendrick did not strike her as a violent man. But... that big, charming, seemingly gentle man might have placed his hands around an old man's neck and squeezed the life out of him.

"Katie—" began Bert softly next to her. His sleeve brushed hers and she moved away.

The three constables had split up, two of them taking the right side of the house and the other one crouching low as he made his way past the front of the house toward the other side. Trepalli.

"Better hurry," she said, and increased her pace. A little part of her wondered what the hell kind of game Bert was playing. He seemed to be all over the place when it came to her, and she was getting sick of it.

But this wasn't the time to deal with Bert and his seesawing attitudes. They reached the front steps and Kate glanced at Bert and nodded him forward. His warrant. His lead.

Without a word, Bert climbed the six steps to the front porch and knocked firmly on the door. Kate stayed on the top step.

"Mendenhall police!" called Trepalli suddenly from the side of the house. "Stop!"

Kate and Bert turned as one and ran down the steps toward the side of the house, in the direction Trepalli had taken. Kate crushed a few plants in front of the house in her hurry.

"He's running!" cried Trepalli. Then came a shout of pain and Kate's heart lurched in fear.

"Trepalli!" she shouted.

She and Bert rounded the house at the same time and saw a figure crumpled to the ground ten feet away from the open doors of an underground storm cellar.

"He's running!" called one of the constables from the back of the house just as the figure on the ground groaned and sat up.

"Are you hurt?" asked Bert, dropping to one knee and pulling Trepalli's chin up.

In the moonlight, the boy's blue eyes looked black. And mad.

"Bastard has a cattle prod," said Trepalli, adding a foul word that would have made Amanda blush. "Go! I'm fine! Go!"

Taking him at his word, Bert took off running. Kate took a moment to help Trepalli up, then, when she saw that he was steady on his feet, she went after Bert. She reached the backyard in time to see Bert vault the picket fence and would have been impressed if she could have spared the time. The backyard consisted of lawn right up to the low picket fence, beyond which was a field.

A quick glance showed no crouching figure in the backyard, and no gate in the fence. She wasted precious time looking around for something to stand on so she could climb over it.

A garden had been dug by the side fence, its turned soil looking like a fresh grave. Next to it, a bunch of stacked five-gallon buckets stood waiting. She grabbed the stack and turned it upside down, emptying soil and dead plants next to the back fence, and climbed on top. Then she climbed over the fence, careful of the pickets.

The moon washed the field in pale glory, with the foot-high stalks all bending in the direction of the wind. The soil sank a little underfoot, thanks to the abundance of rain they'd had this spring.

A hundred feet away, Fredrickson, Jones, and Bert were clustered together, looking toward the trees that formed a windbreak at the back of the field. There was no sign of Kendrick.

She heard Trepalli coming up behind her but didn't wait for him, instead running awkwardly through the field to join the men.

"He's gone into the trees," said Bert when she reached them.

"We can spread out," said Kate. "The windbreak is long, but it isn't very deep. If we don't catch him soon, he'll make it out the other side and into the neighboring field." And they would lose him.

Trepalli joined them, and they quickly spread out at twenty-foot intervals, the five of them advancing toward the screen of trees.

"Dr. Kendrick!" Kate called as she jogged toward the trees. The mini forest was dark and filled with shadows that the moon did nothing to dispel. "Come out," she continued, raising her voice to be heard over the rustling of the new leaves. They were only fifty feet away from the trees now. "Please don't make this worse than it already is."

She felt Bert's gaze on her but ignored him. The point was to get the man to give himself up without anyone else getting hurt. She glanced sideways at Trepalli, but he was at the far end of the line and she couldn't make him out clearly. He had run up to join them, so clearly he wasn't badly hurt.

Kendrick didn't answer and she grimaced. Fine. They'd do it the hard way.

"Be careful as you enter," she warned Fredrickson and Jones. "He's got a cattle prod and he's already used it. No firearms," she warned. It was too dangerous in the dark. "And remember that turning on your flashlight will tell him exactly where you are."

In other words, they were going into the woods blind.

"Yes, ma'am," said Fredrickson next to her. She heard Jones murmur assent, too, but Trepalli was conspicuously silent. Or maybe he was too far to hear her. Bert grunted. He already knew about the cattle prod.

The cultivated field gave way to low poplar bushes and fallen branches, and Kate slowed to watch where she put her feet. She pulled the flashlight out of its clip on her web belt and hung on to it. Made of metal and its foot-long length filled with heavy batteries, it made a good weapon if she should need one.

Her goal was to make it through the trees and into the next field as quickly as she could. If Kendrick had made it through, she would see him and call to the others. If he tried to remain hidden in the trees, she would call St. Ives and get him to send Fallon and Black as reinforcements.

The screen of trees was maybe thirty feet deep and consisted of a lot of fir and black spruce, growing close together. The whole area smelled faintly astringent, like a Christmas tree farm. After low branches whacked her a few times in the face, Kate took to putting her left arm up as protection. Her shoulder protested but she ignored the pain.

Despite being careful, she almost tripped a few times and had to slow even more. She sounded like an elephant trying to tiptoe on egg shells. She couldn't hear the others. Either they were much more graceful than she was, or the sighing of the wind through the trees covered up their noises.

"Over here!" Bert suddenly called and her head jerked up. He was ahead of her.

She flicked the flashlight on and swept the beam through the trees, picking her way through as quickly as she could. She caught a movement from the corner of her eye and glanced over her shoulder. Someone—probably Fredrickson—had turned his flashlight on, too.

As she emerged from the cover of the trees, the beam of her flashlight caught two figures running in yet another cultivated field. Fifty feet ahead, Kendrick—judging by his height, it had to be the veterinarian—was ahead, but Bert was catching up.

She broke into a run, glancing to her right, hoping to see her constables emerge from the trees, but so far, it was just her and Bert. The beam of her flashlight danced wildly as she ran to assist Bert without tripping over a clod of soil in her heavy boots.

Bert and Kendrick ran silently, desperately, with only Kate and the moon as witnesses. Kate's breath came in short gasps as she pushed herself to catch up. She spared a grateful thought for all those mornings on the treadmill, then pushed herself even harder. From behind, she heard shouts as Trepalli, Jones, and Fredrickson finally emerged from the trees.

She had seen Bert run like this once before, on a beach in Gimli as they both desperately raced to catch a killer.

They had been too late, then, but a fierce elation rose up in her now as she saw Bert give a final burst of speed and reach for the vet's shirt.

But Kendrick stopped suddenly and turned, and Kate saw a flash when something long and thin caught the moonlight as his arm arced down toward Bert.

Bert jerked and moved away with a shout but Kendrick followed, holding the cattle prod like a fencing foil against Bert's chest.

"No!" screamed Kate, putting on a burst of speed.

Kendrick looked up at her in alarm. Before he could bring the prod to bear on her, Kate reached him and, with the momentum of rage, swung the flashlight down on his forearm, breaking the bone and sending the vet to the ground, clutching his injured arm and screaming in agony.

CHAPTER 22

Fredrickson looked up from Bert's sprawled body. "He's not breathing."

Even in the faint moonlight, Kate could see the fear in his eyes. Without a word, she dropped to her knees next to Bert. Fredrickson had pulled him onto his back and now Bert just lay there, eyes closed. Still.

She pressed her fingers against his warm neck, feeling for a pulse. Nothing. With fingers made nimble by need, she unzipped his jacket and ripped open his uniform shirt to expose his chest. Even in the moonlight, they could all see the angry red mark left by the cattle prod over his heart.

He looked dead.

Without a word, she began chest compressions, going fast and deep, feeling his sternum sink two inches, then rebound after every compression.

The night air was cold, but not as cold as the blood rushing through her.

Dimly, she heard Trepalli calling for an ambulance and then sending Jones back to the farmhouse to guide the EMTs to their location.

Fredrickson knelt on the other side of Bert, ready to take over from her when she tired.

She counted out thirty compressions, then stopped to tilt Bert's head back and give four quick breaths. Then she resumed the compressions.

A hundred a minute, she remembered from her first aid course, and she despaired of being able to keep it up. Already her breath was coming fast and her arms were tiring. She stopped to give Bert four more quick breaths. Before she could return to the compressions, Fredrickson took over, pushing down on Bert's chest to urge his heart back to motion.

Her whole world telescoped to this moment, to this spot in the middle of a farmer's field, to this man.

One other thing she remembered from her first aid course. CPR in the field seldom helped people who'd had a heart attack.

But that's only because they usually have an underlying condition, she told herself desperately. Bert's heart stopped because it was electrocuted, not because it was sick.

They took turns applying CPR, turns breathing for Bert, turns guarding the vet, except for Kate. She refused to leave Bert's side. When she wasn't applying CPR, she checked for a pulse, and waited to give him breath.

She heard Trepalli on the phone, giving directions, but her focus remained on Bert's still, still form. Only the chest compressions gave him a semblance of life.

Oh, God.

Then the emergency medical techs were there with a stretcher, led back to the field by Jones. Trepalli talked to them, then they firmly pushed Kate away and took Bert off at a stumbling run with one of the EMTs straddling Bert on the stretcher to continue compressions and Fredrickson helping them carry it.

Only then did Kate surface to find herself standing shivering in the farmer's field, staring down at the prone figure of the vet. Her whole body hurt and her heart was beating so fast, it felt like it was going to burst out of her chest. Her back and armpits were covered with the sweat of exertion and now that she had stopped, she was cooling down in the cold night air.

"My arm's broken," said the vet. "You need to get me to the

hospital, too." Now that she heard him, really heard him, she had the feeling that he'd been saying the same thing for a while.

"Shut up," said Trepalli mildly. He was looking at Kate. "He's going to be all right," he said. "You know he is."

Kate nodded jerkily. But all she could see in her mind's eye was Bert's still face.

* * *

She kept Fredrickson with her and ordered Jones to drive Trepalli and Kendrick to the hospital. Before they left, she took Jones aside and told him to get Trepalli checked out, too, no matter how he objected.

Jones was surprised to learn that Trepalli had been on the receiving end of the cattle prod, too.

"Holy..." he said.

Kate knew what he was thinking, but Trepalli had only received one burst of the prod, and he was much younger than Bert.

Her mind shied away from the thought and she slapped Jones on the shoulder, maybe a little harder than necessary.

"Go," she said. "Don't waste time."

She was pretty sure Trepalli hadn't incurred any lasting damage, but she wasn't going to take a chance.

She and Fredrickson watched the red taillights of the patrol car disappear down the driveway.

"Ma'am?" said Fredrickson diffidently.

She looked up at him, noting distantly that six feet three inches was much too tall.

"Yes, Constable?"

"Are you sure you don't want to go to the hospital, too?" he asked.

She flinched and turned away. No, she didn't want to be at the hospital, sitting in the waiting room, waiting... Much better to be here, directing the search. Keeping busy.

As long as she didn't go to the hospital, Bert could still be alive.

They started with the house and had only gone through the top and main floors when they heard cars pull up in front.

St. Ives had sent Carlos Black and Terry Fallon to help them in the search, but she was surprised to see McKell enter the house behind the constables. His gaze immediately went to her and swept her from head to toe. He frowned.

Fredrickson headed for the basement while she sent Fallon and Black to search the clinic, handing them the set of keys she had found hanging by the back door.

"If none of these fit," she said," break down the door."

They nodded silently and left through the back door, flashlights in hand.

Once they were alone, McKell took her by the arm and pulled her over to a kitchen chair where he forced her to sit down.

"You look shocky," he said grimly. "Let me take you to the hospital."

She shook her head.

"Not yet. We have to finish up here."

"You've got three able-bodied constables here. They're perfectly capable of conducting a search. Come on, I'll take you in."

She shook her head again, more vigorously, and then stopped when she realized she might be losing control. She took a deep breath and lifted her gaze to his.

"I can't," she said softly. "I can't. What if he's dead?"

Her voice trailed off as her throat squeezed shut on the words and she had to look away from the compassion in her DC's eyes. He placed a hand on her shoulder and squeezed it gently. They stayed that way for long seconds, giving and taking comfort.

Then Fredrickson's voice floated up from the basement.

"Got it!"

* * *

Kendrick had hidden the tank in the storm cellar, behind bags of last year's potatoes. As near as Kate could tell, it wasn't damaged, but she would ask Charlotte's beau, Josh, to check it out.

She left Fredrickson in charge at the vet's house and grounds, and reluctantly agreed to go to the hospital with McKell, but only after they took the tank back to the detachment and locked it up in one of the three empty cells at the back of the detachment.

While McKell took the tank to the back, she filled St. Ives in on what had happened.

St. Ives led the way to the break room where he waved her to the couch and poured her a coffee. Then he sat in the hard-back chair opposite her and listened in silence, his gray eyes intent on hers.

It took a moment, but then she realized that he had done to her exactly what she and Samantha had done to McKell—made sure he was seated and safe, while not making a big deal out of it.

St. Ives had thick, black hair starting to go gray and while she knew him to be in his mid-forties, he had the kind of classical good looks that would just make him more attractive as he aged. And he knew it. She didn't know how his wife could stand him, sometimes, but as a cop, Kate had nothing to complain about. And it was useful having someone who spoke French on strength. He and his family had emigrated from France when he was five, and to this day, he spoke with a faint Parisian accent.

Just as she was finishing, McKell walked into the break room, his phone in hand.

"That was Trepalli," he said with a smile. "The doc thinks Bert is going to be all right."

Kate stood up, handed St. Ives her coffee, and walked out into the night-shrouded parking lot before her constables could see her cry.

* * *

Trepalli met them in the hospital lobby. It was almost two in the morning, and he still looked as fresh as he'd done at the beginning of the evening, except for the hint of a shadow on his cheeks. He still had his uniform jacket on, though it was unzipped, and she couldn't see his cap anywhere.

"Did you get yourself checked out?" asked McKell as soon as they were close enough.

"Yes, sir." Trepalli slid a glance over to Kate. "I'm fine. Heartbeat is normal. They want me to go see my doctor and arrange for more tests, just to be sure."

Kate nodded. Good.

"Did you call Amanda?" continued McKell, and guilt suddenly surged through Kate.

Amanda. Holy cow. She hadn't given her niece a single thought all night.

But Trepalli only nodded again.

"Yes. I told her I was fine and that Bert would be fine, too." Again, the sliding glance at Kate. "She says opening night was a success."

In spite of everything, Kate smiled. Of course it had been a success.

"The girl has skills," she agreed. "Call her back and ask her to come pick you up. I want you to go home."

He hesitated, then nodded.

"Will do, ma'am."

"What about Kendrick?" she asked, knowing she was delaying asking about Bert, but every time she thought of him, the tears welled up in her eyes. She had to regain control of herself.

"Clean break of the radius," said Trepalli, turning and leading the way through the empty lobby of the hospital to the emergency room.

The Mendenhall hospital was small by big-city standards, but its emergency room was well equipped and staffed. As Trepalli approached, a nurse at the desk on the other side of sliding glass doors pressed a button to let them in.

Trepalli led the way around the nursing station toward a series of curtained cubicles. Someone was moaning in one of them, but Kate didn't think it was Kendrick. Trepalli stopped at the nearest one and called softly.

"Jones."

The curtain opened to reveal Brendan Jones. Beyond him, lying propped up on pillows on a bed with wheels, was James Kendrick. He stared up at the ceiling, seemingly oblivious to the new arrivals. His eyes were bloodshot and his mouth tight with pain. His right arm and elbow were encased in plaster and rested on his chest on a small plastic sheet. His arm was supported by pillows.

Jones stepped out of the cubicle and closed the curtain behind him. He led them away from the examination rooms and stopped by the nursing station, where he could still keep an eye on the cubicle.

"It's a clean break and should heal well," he said without preamble. "The doc is worried about him and wants to keep him overnight."

"For a broken arm?" frowned Kate. She didn't want to leave the vet in the hospital. She wanted him in her cells where they could keep an eye on him.

"Suicide watch," said Jones.

"Crap," said McKell.

"So I'd better get back," said Jones. Kate placed a hand on his arm to stop him.

"I want someone with him at all times," she said.

He nodded. "Yes, ma'am."

"In the morning, bring him back to the detachment. We need to question him."

"Yes, ma'am," he said again, and headed back to the vet's cubicle.

At that very moment, Kate couldn't have cared less if Kendrick committed suicide. But he wouldn't do it on her watch, and he wouldn't do it before she got a statement out of him. They had him for theft of the semen, insurance fraud, and assault on a peace officer, but they still had very little on him for the murder. They had to get him to admit it.

He'd be an idiot to admit it.

"Where's Bert?" she finally asked.

Trepalli stepped forward.

"He was here half an hour ago, but I think they were preparing to move him. Let me check with the nurse." He went over to the nursing station and spoke to the older woman sitting behind the plastic barrier. After a moment, he returned.

"He's been moved to intensive care," he said, clearly trying to keep his voice even.

Kate's mind went blank. Then she blinked and remembered to breathe.

"Why? I thought he was all right." Dimly, she was proud of the fact that she had managed to keep her voice calm.

Trepalli shook his head, clearly miserable. "I don't know, ma'am," he admitted. "And if the nurse knows, she's not telling me."

Well, Kate knew where the intensive care unit was. Without a word, she turned on her heel and headed out of the emergency room. As the doors slid open to let her through, she realized suddenly that her stomach was upset. It was the smells, the constant lingering smells of antiseptic, medicine, and pain.

The intensive care unit was on the second floor, just past the surgical unit. Kate took the stairs instead of the elevator, welcoming the chance to move. She heard steps behind her as she ran up and glanced over her shoulder. McKell and Trepalli were both following her up.

She emerged at the top of the stairs and stood for a moment looking down the wide, dimly-lit hallway. The walls were still the washed-out cantaloupe they had been the last time she'd been here, a year ago. She walked over to the nursing station that stood at the junction of three hallways. The intensive care unit was straight ahead. There was no one at the nursing station, though two computers were on and a task light lit up some papers on a clipboard.

Up ahead, three doors lined one side of the hallway, with a window in the wall next to each door. Across the hall was one door with a sign on it that read "Staff only."

"Which room?" asked Trepalli softly. Something about the dim lighting, the empty desk, the darkened office beyond the desk—all of it seemed designed to keep noise down.

At that moment, the door closest to the desk opened and a woman stepped out, gently closing the door behind her. She looked up, caught sight of them, and started violently.

She was dressed in pink scrubs, with a stethoscope hanging around her neck, the business end tucked inside her chest pocket. Her hair was pulled pack in a thick, blonde ponytail that swung as she walked toward them.

Only as she approached did Kate see how young she was. Holy cow. She didn't look old enough to have graduated from high school.

She stopped when she was close enough to speak without raising her voice.

"I take it you're here for Mr. Langdon?"

Kate nodded jerkily. "Why was he moved to intensive care?" she asked. "We were told he was going to be all right."

The nurse cocked her head as Kate spoke, then smiled.

"He's only here because we have the best monitoring equipment, and we have the room," she said reassuringly. "No one is in intensive care tonight, so we offered to take him and keep an eye on his readings."

A wave of relief threatened to engulf Kate and she struggled against the debilitating feeling. Her whole body began to tremble and Trepalli placed a hand on her elbow, surreptitiously supporting her. McKell stepped closer to her, not touching but ready.

The nurse studied Kate for a long moment, then nodded to herself.

"He's sleeping now," she said, "and I don't want him disturbed, but you can sit with him for a while if you'd like. As long as you promise not to wake him."

Kate nodded, still trying to recover herself, and followed the nurse to Bert's room.

CHAPTER 23

Kate sat by Bert's side for hours, watching his chest move up and down. The only equipment on him was a clip on his finger to check his blood oxygen level, and electrodes pasted to his chest, arms, and legs. Next to her, a machine on a stand recorded his heart's electrical activity in reassuring, regular hills and valleys.

She watched him unwaveringly as the slow minutes ticked by, willing him to wake up and talk to her. Praying that he wouldn't wake up while she was there.

His face was covered in red and gray stubble and she had to resist the urge to stroke his cheeks. She didn't dare. Didn't dare take his hand.

At around three thirty, a man in jeans and a white shirt with the sleeves rolled up to his elbows walked into the room. He stopped in surprise when he saw her, then took in her uniform and nodded. He was about forty, Kate guessed, with graying brown hair that was receding in a pronounced widow's peak. She couldn't really tell what color his eyes were in the dim light, but they were light. Maybe gray or pale blue. He carried an electronic notebook in one hand.

"Chief Williams?" he asked softly.

Kate glanced at Bert to see if the sound had disturbed him, then nodded at the man.

"Dr. Whymark." He proceeded to study the display next to Kate, then tapped something out on his notebook. Then he pulled out a small flashlight and, to Kate's alarm, flicked it on, aiming it at Bert's cheeks, neck, and chest. Moments later, he turned the flashlight off.

"His color is good," he told Kate reassuringly. "And the readings look normal. But we're still going to send him to Winnipeg in the morning."

Well, it was already morning. Kate glanced at Bert's face again, but he slept on, oblivious. She nodded the doctor toward the door and followed him outside, closing the door behind her. The hallway remained empty, like something out of a movie. She wouldn't have been surprised to see a zombie shambling down the hallway.

Snap out of it, she told herself firmly, and turned to the doctor.

"What kind of tests?" she asked him.

He hesitated a moment and for the first time, Kate realized that, really, they had accorded her a great courtesy. After all, she had no right to question the doctor. No right to be here. No right to stay by Bert's side.

She wasn't family. She was nothing but a friend.

Her heart tried to flip over in her chest and she placed a hand over it. If the doctor noticed, he gave no sign.

"We need to understand why his heart stopped," he said quietly. "He is a strong, fit man. Yes, he's in his fifties, but that isn't reason enough for his heart to stop, even under the shock. There may be an underlying, undiagnosed condition."

Kate took a deep, steadying breath, ignoring the faint smell of old coffee and disinfectant. She wasn't shocked by the doctor's words. After all, she had suspected as much.

"What else?" she asked, steeling herself. "Is there brain damage?"

There. She'd said the words out loud. Did Bert sustain brain damage as they performed CPR on him? Did they fail to give him enough oxygen to keep his brain going?

The doctor shrugged.

"I spoke to the EMTs who brought him in," he said. "They were able to shock his heart back in the ambulance. According to them, you were on hand when he was attacked and were able to start CPR right away. Is that right?"

She nodded jerkily.

"Then I wouldn't worry," he said. "He was never really without oxygen. But Winnipeg will run tests."

She nodded.

"When are you transferring him?"

"Grace Hospital is holding a bed for him," said the doctor. "After breakfast, we're shipping him out."

All right, then.

The doctor left and Kate returned to the room and stood looking down at Bert. She tried to consider what she needed to do next but her thoughts were sluggish. Not enough sleep over the past few days. That, and a lot of stress, meant she wasn't at her best. She needed to get some sleep.

She made her way to the nursing station and asked the young nurse to find out where Kendrick had been placed, then made her way to the third floor. She didn't have to check the room numbers. Jones was sitting in a straight wooden chair by the open door of a room. A Styrofoam cup sat on the floor by his chair. The nursing station was at the far end of the hallway, a dark shadow with sharp pools of light from the lamps. She couldn't see anyone there.

The last time she had been in this hospital, she had prevented someone from killing McKell. She shook her head slightly. Maybe Bert was right. Maybe this policing stuff was just too dangerous.

Jones was leaning forward, elbows on his knees, studying his phone. He jumped up when he saw her emerge from the stairwell. He glanced inside the room quickly before joining her down the hallway.

"How is he?" she asked softly.

"Sleeping," said Jones. "I've cuffed his good hand to the bed rail, just to be on the safe side."

"Bet you the staff weren't happy about that," said Kate with a smile.

Jones gave her a lopsided smile. He looked a little ragged around the edges, but with him, that didn't necessarily mean anything.

"They were not," he agreed. "But they would be even more unhappy if he managed to hurt himself."

Kate nodded. She had no problem with ensuring the prisoner was secure.

"How's DC Langdon?" asked Jones.

Kate told him what the doctor had told her, then told him she was going home, but she would check in with St. Ives first.

"Try to get some rest, ma'am," said Jones.

She nodded, and chose not to wonder why he was suggesting it. She had no doubt she looked a little rough around the edges, too.

As she stood outside the hospital, waiting for one of the constables to pick her up, she called John Stendel, Winnipeg's chief of police and Bert's boss. She had delayed calling him until she had more information. As the phone rang at the other end, she glanced at her watch. Just past four o'clock in the morning. She wondered if he was in his own bed or in that of one of his pretty little things. The man acted like he was twenty-five instead of fifty-five.

Still. He was a good cop.

"Stendel," said a gruff voice suddenly in her ear.

"John, this is Kate Williams," she said. "We've arrested Dr. Kendrick, but Bert was hurt." To her dismay, her voice tightened up on the words. She coughed.

Stendel was quiet for a second.

"Tell me," he said finally.

So she did. When she was done, he told her he'd go to Grace Hospital to check up on Bert in the morning. And he promised he'd keep her posted on his condition.

"What about the vet?" he asked. "It's our warrant. We need to take him into custody."

In the old days, Kate would have bristled, but now she just nodded. In the distance, she saw a patrol car turn down the road leading to the hospital.

"Yes," she agreed. "But he attacked one of my constables." She told him about the attack on Trepalli. "So I reserve the right to question him. Send someone to fetch him after lunch. If I haven't gotten anything out of him by then, I never will."

Again the pause. Then Stendal sighed.

"He's pretty strong, Kate," he said gently. "He'll be okay."

Kate nodded again but couldn't speak. She hung up just as Fredrickson pulled up to the entrance.

CHAPTER 24

She crawled into bed at four forty-five and slept like the dead until eight thirty. By nine thirty she had showered, changed into her uniform, and stopped at Tim Horton's for a coffee run. Because she still felt thoroughly miserable, she splurged on a dozen donuts for the crew. It was going to be a hard day.

As she waited at the counter to pay, she suddenly remembered the last time she had been here. James Kendrick had been in line behind her and they had had a pleasant conversation before she headed out to Winnipeg. Had that meeting truly been accidental? Or had Kendrick arranged it to try and build some kind of bond with her? To try and find out what she knew or suspected?

Her eyes still felt gritty in spite of the drops she had put in them before leaving home. But as she walked to her Edge, balancing the trays of coffee and the box with the donuts, she decided that, all things considered, last night could have turned out much worse. Bert was still alive. Trepalli had not been hurt permanently. They had arrested the vet for theft, fraud, and assault, and hopefully, in the next few hours, they would add a charge of murder.

She took a deep breath of the cool morning air with its hint of sweet hay and damp soil. The sky remained cloudless, promising some real warmth by afternoon.

She got behind the wheel and pulled out into the sparse Saturday morning traffic.

* * *

Jim O'Hara looked up from the duty desk computer as she walked in. It was like seeing a monolith look up.

At six feet three, O'Hara towered over most of the other constables; Charlotte had to special order his uniforms because he was so broad-shouldered that the regular fit... well, didn't. He was a quiet man who felt no need to fill the silences with useless talk. Kate knew he made a lot of people uncomfortable, but she always found him restful to be around.

He nodded a greeting at her and she smiled back. She set her coffee cup on the counter by the log book. She'd left the other cups in the break room, knowing that O'Hara preferred to bring his own coffee from home.

"Donuts in the break room," she informed him.

His eyebrows rose and he smiled. He had gray eyes surrounded by charcoal lashes and he kept his dark hair short. He was only thirty-one, but the deep grooves on either side of his mouth made him look older.

Unmarried, still. Not surprising, maybe, as he spent a lot of his free time with his elderly father who lived in a long-term care facility in Winnipeg.

He watched her pull open the tab on the plastic lid of her coffee cup and take a sip. When she set the cup down again, she looked up at him.

"All right. Report."

"The search of Dr. Kendrick's property gave us a bunch of bills that haven't been paid, plus a warning letter from the bank about being in arrears on his mortgage. We've brought his laptop in, but I think Winnipeg is going to have to go through it. Nobody here has the expertise."

Kate nodded. She certainly didn't.

"Where's the vet?" she asked.

O'Hara nodded toward the cells.

"Jones brought him in before shift change. I'm checking on him every few minutes."

"Any problems overnight?" she asked him.

O'Hara knew what she was asking.

"No, ma'am. At least none that Jones reported."

All right, then. She glanced around the duty room. After all the busy-ness of the past week, it was weird to see the place so deserted. But it was Saturday, after all. Some people actually had lives.

"The constables are on patrol?" she asked. "Everything quiet?"

"So far. When do you want to do the interview?" asked O'Hara.

She didn't really want to interview the vet. She didn't have the stomach for it, not after seeing Bert lying in the field, not breathing. She had thought she would be furious with the vet. Instead, all she felt was weary.

"Give me half an hour," she said. "I have to work my way up to it."

He grinned.

"DC McKell asked me to call him when you came in. I think he wants to watch."

Kate nodded. Fine. Maybe McKell could help her with the interview. She might need all the help she could get.

"There is one more thing," said O'Hara as she turned away. "Kendrick is refusing to take painkillers."

Kate considered that for a moment. "What kind of painkillers?"

O'Hara glanced down at his notebook.

"The hospital gave him T-3s." He pulled out the drawer under the counter to show her the plastic amber bottle. "I'm keeping them here. He refuses to take them. He won't take Advil or regular Tylenol, either." He hesitated. "Jones said he could hear him moaning from the pain all night."

Huh. As she headed for her office, she considered what that might mean. Maybe Kendrick had had bad experiences with painkillers before? Maybe he was a recovering addict and didn't dare take anything that might trigger a recurrence?

Maybe he felt he deserved the pain?

She had decided to go through her email while she drank her coffee, but she ended up staring out the window, her thoughts alighting here and there, unable to settle on anything.

The sound of footsteps on the linoleum floor brought her out of herself. She turned away from the window to find McKell standing in her doorway. He wore jeans and running shoes, and a crisp white shirt under a gray sweater. He carried a bulging white plastic bag in one hand. His blue eyes were clear and he was freshly shaven.

"You probably went to the gym, too, didn't you?" asked Kate, disgruntled. He couldn't have slept much longer than she had. He had some nerve looking so fresh.

McKell just laughed and raised the bag.

"I brought Kendrick a change of clothes. If we let him have a shower, he might feel more inclined to cooperate."

Kate didn't feel *inclined* to be charitable, but McKell was right. No matter what he had done, it was her duty—their duty—to treat him with respect.

She unclenched her jaw.

"Fine. I'll get one of the constables to supervise."

"I can do it," said McKell. "No need to pull anyone off patrol."

"He's got a cast," Kate reminded him.

"And I've got a plastic bag," he said.

Half an hour later, James Kendrick emerged from the cell block with his hair still wet but slicked back, and wearing a clean pair of jeans and a blue denim shirt.

His eyes looked gray in the morning light and were bloodshot. He hadn't shaved, of course, and his stubble was all gray. He stood in the middle of the duty room, holding his good hand by his side as if he didn't know what to do with it. His broken arm was in a sling. McKell walked in behind him.

Kate had been standing by the duty desk, reading the log book. Now she looked up, aware that O'Hara had swiveled on his stool to face the vet.

"Dr. Kendrick," said Kate. "Would you like a coffee before we get started?" He'd already had breakfast at the hospital. "We also have donuts."

He looked at her dully, and if she hadn't known about his refusal to take drugs, she would have wondered.

"Coffee would be nice," said Kendrick, his voice rough as if he hadn't used it in a while.

Kate nodded and glanced at O'Hara, who got up without a word and went to the break room. Kate led the way through the ident room to the back, aware that Kendrick was only a few feet behind her. Aware that he might make a break for it, or attack her, or any number of other impulsive moves that she couldn't anticipate.

But... Something in his movements, in the slump of his shoulders, in the haggardness of his face told her that James Kendrick was spent.

She opened the door to the interview room and turned on the light, then stepped aside to let the vet by. He walked into the room and went to the chair he had occupied yesterday morning.

O'Hara arrived with a mug of station coffee and set it in front of the vet, along with a sugar packet, creamer and a plastic stir stick, then left the room without a word. Kate closed the door, knowing that McKell would be standing in the ident room, watching through the glass. Maybe O'Hara would be, too, if the phone wasn't too busy.

She tried not to stare at the steaming liquid in the vet's cup. It would be very easy for him to toss the contents at her, but there would be no point. He knew it was over.

She sat down across from him and turned the recorder on.

"Mendenhall Chief of Police Kate Williams interviewing Dr. James Kendrick," she recited, and added the time and date. Then she looked up at the vet.

"Before we get started, Dr. Kendrick, it's my understanding that you've refused painkillers for your broken arm. Would you like one now?"

Kendrick shook his head.

"No. I'm fine."

He wasn't fine and she could see it in the grooves on either side of his mouth. But she couldn't force the man.

"Dr. Kendrick, you were informed last night of the charges against you, which include theft exceeding five thousand dollars, fraud exceeding five thousand dollars, and aggravated assault against a peace officer. Do you understand these charges?"

As she spoke, Kendrick closed his eyes as if to shut her out. Now he opened them again and looked at her.

"I understand," he said hoarsely.

She nodded.

"You were also informed that you have the right to counsel. If you do not have a lawyer, we will provide you with the phone number for a lawyer referral service. Would you like to retain or consult with a lawyer now?" she asked.

He shook his head.

"For the recording, please," she said, nodding at the machine.

"No," he said. "I don't want a lawyer."

Kate hesitated.

"Are you sure, Dr. Kendrick?" she asked softly. "You have the right to legal representation. Everything you say can be used in court as evidence."

Kendrick shrugged and then, remembering, repeated, "I don't want a lawyer."

"All right," she said finally. She leaned back against her chair and clasped her hands on the table in front of her. She wasn't prepared for this, hadn't taken the time to work out a strategy with McKell. Maybe she was the wrong person to be conducting the interview. Maybe she was emotionally compromised. She examined her emotional balance and her motives and decided that it was too late. She was committed now.

Kendrick took a sip of coffee, then kept his left hand wrapped around the mug. The arm in the cast rested on the table in front of him. She knew from bitter experience that it hurt to have it hang down without support, even with the sling. He studied the top of the table as if his fate were written there.

Kate sighed deeply and decided to just plunge ahead.

"Dr. Kendrick," she started, then stopped. He looked up at her, his eyes serious. For a crazy moment, she wanted to ask him what the hell happened. But she couldn't. Not right away, anyway.

"How long have you been a veterinarian in Mendenhall?" she asked.

He blinked as if surprised by the question.

"A little over fifteen years," he said.

"In that time," she continued, "have you ever had to deal with the police?"

He paused, looking at her. Then he shook his head.

"For the recording, please."

"No," he said. "I haven't."

"That's what our records show," she agreed. "Can you tell me about last night?"

He took another sip of coffee and watched her over the cup. There was something in his eyes that she couldn't quite read. Despair? Anger?

Resignation.

"I think we'll have to start further back than that," he said softly.

Kate nodded. He could go as far back as he wanted. "I'm listening."

He sighed and seemed to deflate. He shook his head almost ruefully.

"It started with the wedding."

Kate blinked at him. What was he talking about?

He looked up at her.

"My daughter's wedding," he added. "My wife and I divorced almost sixteen years ago when my girls were eight and ten. Pamela took the girls back to Ontario to be near her family, and I rarely got to see them. But last year, my eldest got married."

Kate nodded encouragingly, though she couldn't see where he was going with this.

"It's the father's job to walk his daughter down the aisle," said Kendrick, "and I did. And it's a father's job to pay for the wedding," he added. "And I did."

Kate was starting to see a glimmer of light.

"Tell me about it," she said softly.

"You have no idea," said Kendrick grimly. "The country club. The flowers, the catering, the wedding favors." Kate had no idea what wedding favors were. "The goddammed dress alone was almost eight thousand dollars."

Holy cow.

"Eight thousand dollars?" she asked, trying to keep her voice even.

He nodded in agreement.

"I was already having problems with the practice. I had a second mortgage on the property. I couldn't afford that kind of insanity. I should have said no, of course. Should have made her keep it simple, more affordable."

Kate nodded but kept silent.

He shrugged.

"I know. Why didn't I, right?" He sighed. "She's my baby. I haven't been around much for her and her sister these past years. And…" He looked down again as a tide of red crept up his cheeks. "And I let them believe I was doing well for myself. They thought I could afford it."

She could see it. A dad wanting his baby's special day to be perfect. Sinking deeper and deeper into debt as the wedding plans unfurled.

"After that," he continued, "I could never seem to get on top of the bills. The debts just seemed to snowball."

Kate nodded sympathetically.

"What did you do?" she prompted.

He clasped his broken arm closer to his chest as if to protect it. "I had to let staff go. Cut back on extras." He shook his head. "Nothing seemed to help."

Misplaced pride, thought Kate. Why not sell the practice?

"Tell me about the bull semen," she said.

He rubbed his face with his good hand. It sounded like he was rubbing sandpaper.

"It seemed like a neat solution," he admitted. "I persuaded Johann to order the expensive semen. A little over fifty thousand dollars' worth. I would pretend it got stolen. Johann's insurance would cover his loss. There would have been no negative effects to him or his farm."

"What were you planning to do with the semen?" asked Kate softly. She had an idea, of course, but she needed to hear him say it.

Kendrick's smile was twisted.

"You meet all kinds of people in my line of work," he said. "I knew a guy in North Dakota who would pay me thirty thousand for the semen. All I had to do was wait until the investigation died down and then take the tank to him." He sighed deeply. "It would have solved all my problems. Or most of them, anyway."

"How does that work?" she asked. "Isn't there a question of…" What the heck did they call it? "Provenance?" she finished lamely.

He shook his head. "The value is in the calves. They would come from good bulls, which would translate to good sales. He didn't want a certificate."

Kate studied him. From his point of view, it probably had looked like a solution to his problem. She considered her options for a moment. She had to be careful here. She didn't want to step on Winnipeg's toes, but she didn't want to waste this opportunity, either.

"So Johann bought the semen," she said, trying to guide the conversation back to where she wanted to go.

He glanced away from her.

"That's right."

"Did Ernst know his brother was buying the semen?"

Kendrick hesitated, then shook his head.

"No, he didn't." His face was red again, and he didn't meet her gaze.

Kate waited. Finally, Kendrick looked up at her, clearly expecting another question.

She kept her face neutral.

"Tell me what Ernst said when he found out."

Kendrick sighed and looked up at the ceiling of the tiny room.

"He was furious. Accused me of taking advantage of Johann's dementia."

Kate nodded encouragingly.

"Tell me about Johann's dementia," she said.

The vet was silent for so long that she thought he wouldn't answer. Then he looked at her. She could see the pain of his injury etched in the lines of his face and considered offering him painkillers again, but she didn't want to interrupt the flow. Instead she waited. James Kendrick was an intelligent man. He knew where this interview was going.

"It had been getting worse over the past year," he said finally. "Johann Mulvahill was a fine, fine man, but he was making increasingly irrational decisions, then forgetting he had done it. It was really hard to watch the dementia taking him."

Yeah, sure, thought Kate cynically. It was hard to watch until the dementia suited his needs.

"Tell me about going to see Johann at the hospital," she said, jotting a few words down on her pad so he wouldn't see the anger in her eyes.

When she looked up, she found him staring back at her with such despair in his eyes that she almost felt sympathy for him. Was he going to try to lie now?

"Dr. Kendrick?" she prodded.

He nodded and looked away from her.

"He borrowed another patient's phone and called me when he was in the hospital. He asked me to come and see him. He said he was confused about the whole semen purchase."

He stopped again and Kate waited. She hoped he wouldn't see on her face the judgment she was feeling. Maybe he did, because he looked away. Then his shoulders squared and he looked back at her.

"So I went to see him."

All right, then.

"When did you go see Johann Mulvahill at Grace General Hospital?"

Let there be no doubt about what she was asking him.

"Tuesday afternoon," he said softly.

"Around what time?" she asked.

He frowned, clearly trying to remember. Then he shrugged.

"After three. Before five."

"Tell me about your visit."

Kendrick pushed the coffee mug away from him as if he couldn't stand to look at it anymore, and for the first time, Kate became aware of the smell of the coffee, of the generic soap they kept in the cell block shower, of the shampoo she had used that morning. Her stomach regretted the coffee she had drunk before the interview.

"He wanted to know about the semen. Why I had pushed him to buy it."

She waited. And waited.

"He was going to ruin everything," he whispered, and Kate hoped the recorder had captured it.

Kate closed her eyes briefly and thought about the old man in his hospital room, suffering from dementia but with enough acumen left to wonder what was going on. Kendrick must have worried that he would call his brother. That his whole, carefully constructed scheme would start to unravel.

"And then what happened?" she asked, opening her eyes to look at him.

He held her gaze and she saw regret and horror in his eyes before he closed them.

"I didn't mean to, but God help me, I strangled him."

* * *

To her surprise, McKell, Trepalli, and Samantha were standing in the ident room when she and Kendrick walked out of the interview room. The vet looked at them, then his gaze landed on Trepalli, who stared back at him impassively, arms crossed over his chest. The vet looked like he wanted to say something, then he shook his head and turned away.

Kate led him back to the duty room, where O'Hara escorted him back to the cells. Once he was secured, she went into the break room where the other three had gathered. Trepalli sat on the love seat, nursing a coffee, while McKell lounged against the counter. The smell of burnt coffee permeated the room.

Everyone was in their civvy clothes except for her. Samantha had swollen, red eyes, a runny nose, and kept a tissue in her hand. She stood away from the other two and kept her arms crossed over her chest as if to keep her hands tucked away.

Kate studied her from head to foot, noting the haphazard way the woman's dark hair had been pulled back into an untidy ponytail, the scarf around her neck, the sweater under her jacket.

"You look like death warmed over," she told her acting DC.

"And I feel worse," admitted Samantha. Her voice sounded rough, completing the picture of someone suffering from the flu.

Kate opened her mouth to ask why she was even here, but McKell jumped in.

"Chief Stendel called a little while ago," he told her. "I guess he tried you on your cell but you were otherwise occupied."

Kate held her breath and felt her shoulders tense in preparation for the blow.

"He wanted to let you know that Bert looks good and seems perfectly normal. He's undergoing the tests today and will probably be discharged from the hospital tomorrow."

She nodded, but couldn't bring herself to speak. He was safe. At least for now. Until the doctors figured out why his heart had stopped.

"Also," continued McKell, "Stendel said he was sending a couple of officers to pick up Kendrick after lunch." He smiled a little smugly. "Should I call him back and tell him we've wrapped up the case for him?"

Even Samantha grinned at McKell's evident satisfaction. Kate could hear O'Hara answering a phone call in the duty room and glanced out the window as a battered green Subaru pulled into the parking lot and parked in one of the visitor spots. A moment later, a young woman got out and headed for the detachment door.

"All right," said Kate. "Call him. Tell him we'll email him a transcript of the interview as soon as possible." She would call Charlotte in to transcribe it today. She didn't want to wait until Monday. "I'll get O'Hara to make sure Kendrick is ready for transport and get the paperwork ready."

Trepalli spoke up. "I could come with you if you wanted to take Kendrick in yourself."

Kate shook her head.

"I'm not going to Winnipeg," she said calmly. "And I'm not sending anyone else, either. Since we've done everything else for them, they can come and pick up Dr. Kendrick. But we're hanging on to the tank." It was evidence in the theft, which was their case. She ignored the frown on Trepalli's face. It wasn't her refusal to take Kendrick in that bothered him. It was her refusal to go to Winnipeg and see Bert.

But she couldn't. What would be the point?

"Now," she said, turning to Samantha. "Why aren't you home in bed?"

"I was," said Samantha. "But one of the folks I was trying to talk to yesterday finally got back to me this morning."

Kate nodded. Samantha had obtained a copy of the resumes for Mark Pinkley and Jason Cromarty, the two Porter Security guards who had been on duty when the break-ins and vandalism had taken place at the Riverview construction site. She'd been able to contact Pinkley's previous employers—there were only two previous ones, despite his age. He was clearly a long-term man. None of his previous employers had raised any red flags.

But Cromarty's employment record was a different matter. For a young man, he seemed to have had an awful lot of jobs, all of them in the security field.

"What did you find out?" she asked Samantha.

Samantha fished in her jacket pocket and pulled out her notebook. She flipped to the right page and stared reading, pausing occasionally to wipe her dripping nose.

When she was done, all three of them looked at her, their eyes wide. Trepalli finally expressed what they were all feeling.

"Son of a bitch," he said.

CHAPTER 25

"You still don't have anything on him," argued McKell.

Trepalli and Samantha had left fifteen minutes earlier and McKell had followed Kate into her office, where he now sat across from her, being the voice of reason.

She looked past him at the window. The tops of the maple trees across the street were a cloud of pale green. She should open the window, let some fresh air in. Instead she sighed and turned back to McKell.

"I know. All we have is circumstantial evidence."

It was *compelling* circumstantial evidence, but circumstantial nevertheless.

She shook her head at Cromarty's sheer brazenness.

"The man stood there and looked me in the eye, and complained about how his neighbors teased him about the thefts and the vandalism."

McKell grinned at her.

"He definitely has a set, I'll give him that, but we can't prove anything."

"Yet," said Kate. "I can't prove anything *yet*."

The evidence was mounting up. Samantha's contact had been the owner of the last security company Cromarty had worked for, in Edmonton. Cromarty had resigned after a building the security company had been guarding was torched. The building was a project owned by yet another numbered company. Kate was willing to bet that some of the officers of that company would be the same as those in 128444, Inc.

It was all coming together now. They just needed a little more time.

Her cell phone rang suddenly and she jumped as it vibrated against her thigh. As she fished it out, McKell stood up.

"I'll see you later," he said softly and left with a wave.

Kate looked down at her screen. Trepalli.

"Hello, Marco," said Kate. "What's up?"

"Chief, I'm at Riverview," he said, and before Kate's eyebrows could even rise, he hurried on. "Did you know that Cromarty's place is for sale?"

* * *

He was right. Cromarty's place had a big realty sign hanging from the balcony.

Trepalli had parked his 1965 silver Mustang across the way and up a few houses and Kate pulled up behind him, wondering if he was actually trying to be discreet in that thing. She needn't have worried. There were no cars parked in front of Cromarty's place. He was off duty and it was Saturday. The man was out.

Trepalli unfolded himself from the driver's seat and walked over to join her. Kate noticed a couple of kids playing outside a few houses away. They were eyeing the Mustang with interest.

"Nobody home that I can tell," said Trepalli. He'd put a black fleece jacket over top of his long-sleeved blue tee-shirt, but now he unzipped it. There was no wind between the small houses and the sun beat down in a promise of heat later on in the day.

"We can't be sure until we ring the bell," said Kate and promptly set out for Cromarty's house, Trepalli trailing behind her. She didn't want to talk to Cromarty yet, but she wanted an excuse to look around his place.

She rang the doorbell and stepped away from the door. A recycling bin stood by the door and she peeked inside while Trepalli wandered over to the fence and peered over. Only a few cans and bottles rested at the bottom of the bin. Kate joined Trepalli at the gate and studied the tiny backyard. On either side were other tiny backyards, all separated by white picket fences.

All these units bordered on the green belt. Trails crisscrossed the green belt, allowing people to walk their dogs or take a short cut to the main road and the grocery store on it. These were the choice lots, with the added privacy of trees at the back and tall fences. The backyard next to Cromarty's was filled with planters and flower boxes, all with fresh green shoots poking their heads out of the soil.

She spared a thought for her own flower boxes and backyard. There hadn't been any time to give landscaping a thought over these past few months. Maybe she could persuade Amanda to help her with at least the flower boxes. After all, the girl had copious amounts of free time.

She was still smiling to herself when Trepalli poked her with his elbow and she followed his gaze.

There, leaning against the back wall of the house, was a mountain bike. It had fat tires covered in dried mud.

She studied the back fence and sure enough, there was a gate in it.

"That's how he did it," muttered Trepalli. He nodded toward the woods. "All he had to do was park his work car somewhere out of sight, take one of the trails to his back fence, get on his bike, and cycle to the construction site."

Cromarty could easily have walked to the site, of course, but that would have increased his chances of being seen and recognized.

A door opened next to them and they both started. A woman came out of the house next door and jumped when she saw them staring at her. She was middle-aged, with a bit of extra weight on her that she carried well. Her curly blonde hair was up in a loose bun and Kate only saw the gray when the woman stepped down into the sunlight.

"Hi," she said. "Can I help you?" She studied Kate's uniform for a moment, but her gaze lingered longest on Trepalli. The boy still had it.

"We're looking for Mr. Cromarty," said Kate with a smile.

"Is it to do with the fire?" asked the woman, shaking her head. "What a terrible thing that was, wasn't it?"

"Yes, ma'am," agreed Kate. "Mr. Cromarty?"

"Oh, he's away right now," said the woman.

"Away?" asked Kate.

"Red Deer, I think," said the woman. "Looking for a place to live."

Kate's eyebrows rose. "He's moving away from Mendenhall?"

"That's right," said the woman. She shook her head. "I think the fire really shook him since it happened on his watch. As if it was his fault." She sighed. "Anyway, he'll be back in a week to move out. He's already got a job in Red Deer."

"That was fast," said Kate. "Another security company?"

The woman nodded. "I think so. He didn't tell me the name."

"That's okay," said Kate. "We'll catch up with him when he gets back."

The woman locked her door and turned to walk toward the parking lot. When she was far enough away, Kate took out her phone and took a few pictures of the backyard, the back gate, and the mountain bike, with a close up of the tires. They couldn't go inside his yard, but she could certainly document what was in it.

As they walked back to their vehicles, Kate could smell bread baking and her stomach rumbled in response. She hadn't had lunch. And now that she considered it, she realized she hadn't had breakfast, either. No wonder she was starving.

The kids who had gathered around Trepalli's Mustang scattered at their approach.

"So, where's Amanda today?" asked Kate. She hadn't seen the girl since Thursday night's friends and family gathering.

Trepalli glanced at her. "She's over at the house, getting ready for tonight."

"What's on the menu?" asked Kate, stopping by the Edge.

"Pork chops in milk with steamed vegetables and a house salad, or vegetarian lasagna with Caesar salad. For desert, a choice of spumoni ice cream or tres leches."

Kate slid a glance over at him and he grinned.

"Three-milk cake. With any luck, there'll be leftovers."

She smiled. It was hard to believe that, only a few short hours ago, he had been attacked with a cattle prod. Youth certainly had its advantages.

"Tell her I'll drop in to see her later," she told him as he headed for his car. Trepalli stopped and turned back to her. He seemed to hesitate. Then he walked back to her, glancing around to make sure he wouldn't be overheard.

"We all know he's the ass responsible for the thefts and the fire," he said. "How do we prove it?"

Kate patted him on the arm. "We don't need to. We gather all the evidence we can and turn it over to the RCMP. They've got the resources to deal with it all—the thefts, the vandalism, the arson, and the insurance fraud."

She saw the struggle on his face and understood how he felt. She hated the thought of turning the case over to the RCMP but the crimes committed were transprovincial. At least, she suspected they were. Mendenhall didn't have the kind of resources needed to connect all the dots and gather all the evidence from the cases in Alberta, Saskatchewan, Ontario, and Manitoba.

And who knew how many others there would be, once they started digging.

"He assaulted you," Trepalli pointed out. "And now he's running."

"Let him run," said Kate. "There's nowhere he can go that we can't find him."

"He's only part of the story, though," said Trepalli, leaning down a little. "He doesn't do this for kicks. He does it for money."

Kate nodded. That would be the trickier part. Proving that he was on 128444, Inc.'s payroll. Unless the Mounties could find a direct financial correlation, it would be almost impossible to prove that the arson had been ordered by the company.

She sighed.

"We'll do what we can, Marco," she said with determination.

That was all they could do.

He looked back at Cromarty's house and his lips tightened. Finally he nodded.

"All right," he said. "I'm around if you need me." Then he got into his Mustang and left, much to the admiration of the small group of kids who emerged from between the houses to watch him.

Kate got in the Edge and pulled out. The warm sun had lured

more people out of doors. Kids played on the grassy common areas and a few teenagers hung out by one the houses. Maybe they were trying to figure out what they could do for fun now that the apartment building had burned down.

Such a curmudgeon. Who needed a judge and jury when she was around?

Without deciding to, she turned down Mr. McClusky's road and drove to the erstwhile construction site. To her surprise, half a dozen men—make that five men and one woman—were working on the site.

She pulled to a stop when she recognized Elijah Rudger, the foreman. He looked around and waved at her as she got out.

"Afternoon, Chief Williams," he said with a smile.

"Hello, Mr. Rudger," said Kate. "Are you rebuilding?"

He laughed. "Dear God, no," he said. "Remediating. We have to haul all the burned bits away, salvage what we can of the infrastructure, and fill in the hole."

The breeze from the river seemed to flow right up the cliff and past the open space that used to be that monstrosity of a building. It was a nice counterpoint to the warm sun.

Kate watched the crew in the pit hauling up burnt sheet of wood. The whole place stank of wet, burnt wood.

"That can't be cheap," she muttered. Was she wrong? If 128444, Inc. was all about profit, there was no way they would remediate the site if they didn't need to.

"No choice," said Rudger with a smile. "The judgment came down on Friday. Even if the building hadn't burnt down, the company would have had to tear it down and remediate. They decided to do it right away while the crew was still available."

Well, well, well. Wasn't that a happy coincidence for the company? Now that the building had burned down, they could claim it on their insurance. There was no guarantee that insurance would have covered the costs of taking the building down, especially if the company was deemed to be in the wrong.

Yet another thing to add to the list of circumstantial evidence.

She studied Rudger's smiling face.

"You certainly seem to be cheerful for a man who's about to be out of a job."

He shrugged.

"Another few days here, then I get to go home. And I will never have to deal with these buggers again."

Kate grinned at the heartfelt sentiment.

"Take care of yourself, Mr. Rudger. I'm sorry this job turned into such a headache for you."

"Thanks," he said. He nodded at the pit. "I blame the security company for not doing a better job. Especially for family."

Kate, who had turned away, turned back to Rudger.

"Excuse me?"

He nodded. "Yeah, I was surprised, too. I was in Winnipeg yesterday. The insurance company wanted to talk to me. When I was done, I went over to Mr. Hodgson's to collect our final paychecks. It was dinnertime and Hodgson was in the backyard having a barbecue. While I waited for him, I saw one of the guards we've been dealing with sitting with a beer in the yard."

Kate blinked up at him.

"Do you remember his name?"

He shook his head.

"I didn't, but when I left, I asked one of Hodgson's kids who was playing in the front yard. Turns out the guy's name is Cromarty and he's Hodgson's cousin."

CHAPTER 26

Kate finished typing and sat back, rereading her report. She had crammed everything they knew about 128444, Inc. and Jason Cromarty, Porter Security, the vandalism and thefts, the insurance companies—everything she could think of—into the ten-page document. She would sit on it until tomorrow to make sure she hadn't forgotten anything, and then she'd contact the RCMP liaison officer in Winnipeg.

With any luck, the Mounties would be able to take Mendenhall's work and parlay it into convictions for Cromarty and 12844, Inc.

She glanced at the clock in the bottom right hand of her monitor. Almost three. If she wanted a bit of a visit with Amanda, she had to go now before the girl got too busy. She debated going home to change into her civvies but decided against it. Amanda was used to the uniform, and Kate wanted as much time with her as possible.

O'Hara was on the phone when she left and he gave her a small nod of acknowledgment. She hadn't seen any of the constables on shift today. According to O'Hara, they'd been busy dealing with reports of a stolen car, cows getting out of a pasture and onto the highway, and a small accident at a nearby farm involving a tractor and a lost tourist. Typical Saturday.

As she got into the Edge, she realized that her hands were shaking, and remembered that she still hadn't eaten. She rolled down the windows to let the accumulated heat escape and pulled out of her parking spot. Maybe Amanda would have leftovers from yesterday.

There were a lot of cyclists out, competing for road space with automobiles. She made a mental note to ask O'Hara to put a reminder on their website for motorists to pay attention to the presence of cyclists, and for cyclists to obey the rules of the road. She sighed. Every year, they had a few accidents, some more serious than others. Maybe she would ask the radio station to put out the reminder as a public service announcement.

The firefighters had pulled the fire engine out of the fire hall and were washing it, a favorite pastime when it was sunny and warm. A few of the firefighters saw her and waved. She waved back.

By the time she turned down Amanda and Trepalli's street, she had reached the conclusion that Mendenhall had had a population boom over the winter. She didn't remember so many kids around before. They were everywhere—playing hopscotch on the sidewalks, riding their bikes or skateboards, playing tag on their lawns. It was reassuring to see them all outside on a beautiful day.

Take that, technology, she thought.

Trepalli was just coming out of the house when Kate parked behind Amanda's green Tercel.

"Beating a strategic retreat?" asked Kate, walking up to him.

He grinned.

"No ma'am. Grocery run." He waved a piece of paper at the house behind him. "She's in the kitchen."

"Of course, she is," agreed Kate. She let Trepalli go and made her way to the back of the house. As she climbed the back stairs to the deck, she glanced at the table she had been seated at on Thursday night when James Kendrick had flirted with her so clumsily, and Bert had accused her of being unprofessional.

The outrage rose up again, only to be tempered by the memory of him unconscious and being carried away by an ambulance.

The back door suddenly opened and Amanda stepped out, squinting into the sunshine.

"Hi, Aunt Kate!" Amanda shaded her eyes with a hand over her brow, and frowned. "You look like you could use a good meal and twelve hours of sleep."

Kate rolled her eyes and hugged her niece.

"Nice to see you, too," she said. "How did it go last night?"

Amanda beamed at her and led her to the nearest table, pushing Kate into a seat.

"It was great! Like a dinner party. They all loved the food. A few people made reservations based on the food, but I could only take them in two months!"

Kate smiled at her niece's enthusiasm. "Everybody's heard about your cooking, Pumpkin. You're a hit."

Amanda smiled happily, but her eyes looked worried.

"I can't do anything about the sleep," she said, studying Kate's face, "but I can feed you. When's the last time you ate?"

When Kate admitted that she hadn't eaten anything yet today, Amanda tsked and told Kate to stay where she was while she fixed her a plate. Kate leaned against the metal chair back and thanked the gods for nieces who liked to cook. She folded her hands over her belly, allowing the sun to warm the back of her head and shoulders. She was almost asleep when Amanda came back out with a steaming plate.

"It won't be as good as it was yesterday, of course," she apologized, "but at least it'll fill you up."

Kate looked down at the plate. Chicken Kiev, if she didn't miss her bet. Green beans with lemon and almonds. Roasted potatoes.

Her mouth flooded with saliva and she gratefully accepted the knife and fork her niece handed her. As she set about eating, Amanda went back inside to return a moment later with a napkin and a glass of sparkling, orange-flavored water.

Kate applied herself to her meal and only looked up when it was finished.

"Thank you," she said, a little embarrassed at how she had wolfed the food down. Amanda grinned.

"You need a minder, Aunt Kate," she teased. "I happen to know that Bert would love the job."

A sigh escaped before Kate could keep it in. She looked at her niece and shrugged.

"That ship has sailed, Amanda. I wish people would accept it."

Amanda crossed one leg over the other and swung her foot. She wore cropped blue pants, an old, white, cotton shirt that hung over the pants, and a pair of loafers with no socks. She still somehow managed to look casually elegant.

"We can't accept it because we can all see what's right in front of our noses," said Amanda sharply. "You and Bert love each other. He clearly wants to be with you, so the question is, why don't you want to be with him?"

How had they descended so quickly into such a personal discussion? Kate didn't talk about her feelings easily and it felt bloody awkward discussing them with her niece, but at the same time, Amanda was in a unique position to understand.

In the background, she could hear the shrieks and laughter of children playing. Kate took a deep breath and plunged ahead.

"Last fall, after the attack on McKell, Bert broke up with me." She saw the look of shock on Amanda's face but didn't stop. "He was mad at me and afraid for me. He didn't like the risks I took for my job." She shrugged. "I think he was hoping I'd agree to either quit or tone down what I do. But that wasn't going to happen."

Amanda nodded.

"That was fear talking," she said. "If he'd been thinking clearly, he would have known better."

"He followed me to Montreal, if you'll remember."

Amanda nodded. The girl had returned home after breaking it off with Trepalli, citing exactly the same reasons Bert had cited to Kate. Amanda hadn't wanted to be with a man who could be injured or killed every time he was on the job.

"He apologized and asked me to marry him."

Amanda's eyes widened.

"You said no?"

"I said no."

"Why?"

Kate hesitated, reluctant to put the reason into words. But she'd probably never get a chance like this again.

"Because he was right. I'm not ready to retire and my job is unpredictable. Mendenhall is a small town, but in under two years, we've had two shootings and a murder, and an attempted murder on McKell."

Amanda remained silent, looking down at her swinging foot, her lips pursed. Kate took a drink of the sparkling water. Finally, Amanda looked up.

"So, you're doing this for Bert?" There was a strange look in her eye.

Kate shrugged.

"Mostly." She cocked her head and studied her niece. "How did you come to terms with Marco's job?" she asked. "I know that was the reason you broke it off. You didn't want to be with a cop."

Amanda nodded.

"That's true. When I realized—I mean, truly *realized*—what the job was and how risky it was, I ran. All I could think was, what if something happened to him?"

Kate waited. Then Amanda smiled gently at her.

"While I was back home, I realized something else. Yes, he might get hurt on the job. Even killed. But that can happen to anyone. Life doesn't come with guarantees, Aunt Kate, not for any of us. You know that. I decided that, come what may, I was going to spend as much of my life with Marco Trepalli as I could."

They were silent for a moment, studying each other across the gulf of thirty years. Finally, Kate sighed.

"I guess the difference here is that I can live without Bert."

Amanda shook her head.

"Aunt Kate, the real question is, do you *want* to?"

CHAPTER 27

D id she want to?

Kate spent the night tossing and turning, running her conversation with Amanda through her mind.

Did she *want* to live without Bert?

How could she not know? She was a grown woman with a lifetime of experience behind her. She had always known her own mind. Why was it so difficult now to figure out what she wanted?

It was as she was showering that the answer came to her. It was because Bert had moved on, despite what everyone thought. Charlotte had seen it last weekend, when she saw Bert at the play with another woman. Bert was dating again. And the way he had spoken to her at Amanda's party... those weren't the words of a man who was still in love. He had questioned her judgment. Her professionalism.

He had moved on.

She shut the water off and slid open the shower curtain, only then realizing that she was crying.

* * *

On Monday morning, she got up early, determined to get herself back on track. The day had dawned overcast and as she got dressed, it started to rain. She pulled a clean uniform out of her closet and put a plastic bag over it before running out the door and to the gym.

She was there at her normal time—though she had missed quite a few times last week—but she worked out alone. McKell never showed up.

Disappointed and a little worried, she finished her workout and left. Maybe McKell had overdone it last week. Sure, he looked good, but was he fully recovered? Had she and Samantha pushed him too hard?

Mendenhall came to life as she took the Tim Hortons' drive-through and stocked up on coffee. No donuts today. New leaf, healthy living and all that. She made a face at herself in the rearview mirror and drove to the detachment.

Shift change had already occurred and her constables were already on patrol. O'Hara looked up as she walked by the duty desk window.

"Good morning, O'Hara," said Kate. She set the coffee tray on the duty counter by the log book.

"Ma'am." He nodded in greeting.

"Anything of note overnight?"

He shook his head.

Sunday nights were always quiet.

She hesitated a moment, then asked, "Any word on DC Langdon?"

O'Hara turned those cool, gray eyes on her.

"St. Ives said the DC was discharged from Grace Hospital yesterday."

Kate nodded as if her question had been casual curiosity.

"Good," she said crisply. "I'll be in the shower. Save me a coffee."

"DC Paterson called in sick," said O'Hara. "Flu."

Kate nodded. Yes, Samantha Paterson definitely had the flu.

By the time she came out of the locker room, freshly showered, hair tucked up and uniform on, Charlotte had arrived and Holmes was standing by her desk, looking over her shoulder at her monitor. They both looked around as Kate walked into the duty room.

"Morning, Chief," said Charlotte with a smile. Today she wore a pair of black pants and a green cotton vee-necked sweater. Kate automatically looked at the woman's feet, but Charlotte had wisely chosen to wear closed shoes today.

"Chief," said Holmes in greeting. His startlingly dark brows were drawn in a frown as he turned back to the monitor and pointed something out to Charlotte. He wasn't a very big man, only about five feet eight inches tall, but he had large hands.

Kate considered asking what the problem was, then decided against it. They'd tell her if they needed her. She walked over to O'Hara and asked him to put something up on the website about spring and bicyclists being out and about.

"You know the drill," she said, grabbing her coffee out of the tray. It smelled wonderful. "And maybe ask the radio station to put up a public service announcement?"

He nodded and set to work, and Kate headed into her office. She wanted to read over her report again before sending it on to the RCMP.

She was engrossed in the report when she became aware that someone was standing in her doorway. Startled, she looked up.

Bert leaned against the doorjamb, arms crossed over his chest, a serious look on his face.

Kate examined him carefully, but he looked healthy. Still too thin, maybe, but none the worse for almost dying.

For actually having died.

She swallowed hard.

"You look good for a dead guy," she said.

He didn't say anything, just looked at her. He wore jeans and a rain jacket over a cream-colored sweater that complemented his ruddy complexion.

"What's the matter?" she asked, suddenly worried. His brown, copper penny eyes seemed to bore into her. She stood up. "Bert, what's the matter?"

He finally straightened and came into her office, closing the door behind him. He never took his eyes off her. In the dismal light of the rainy day, the gray in his red hair seemed much more prominent than usual.

"You never came to see me," he said quietly. "I want to know what that means."

For a moment, Kate's mind went blank. Then confusion filled her.

"What it means?" she asked. "I kept tabs on how you were doing. We all did."

His expression didn't change.

"I was told you were with me at Mendenhall hospital."

She blushed. She could feel the tide rising in her cheeks and cursed her fair coloring.

"Of course I was," she said calmly. "Until we knew you would be all right."

He remained silent and an alarm went off in her.

"You *are* all right, aren't you?"

He remained impassive for a moment longer, then shrugged.

"Turns out I may have a heart condition that no one knew about. Something about a thickening of the heart muscle's walls." He took a deep breath. "That's what caused my heart to stop when he got me with the cattle prod."

Kate just stared at him, unable to absorb what he was saying. Finally she looked down at the top of her desk. She could feel her blood slowing down in her veins and was sure her own heart was about to stop.

"What does that mean, exactly?" she asked, looking up at him.

He shrugged again.

"Nobody knows for sure. They've run tests but the best they can tell me is to keep living my life as if I didn't know about the condition. I could die tomorrow, or I could die in thirty years."

Kate's mouth was suddenly dry and she couldn't speak.

He could die tomorrow.

He had already died.

"How does your girlfriend feel about this?" she finally croaked out.

He stared at her for a moment, a puzzled expression on his face.

"My girlfriend?"

"Yes," said Kate, suddenly impatient. "Your girlfriend. Your new fling. Whatever."

Bert's eyebrows rose and he stepped closer to the desk, directly in front of her. Only the expanse of the desk separated them now. She could smell the cedar undertones of his new aftershave and felt herself getting annoyed all over again. Had his girlfriend given him the aftershave?

"I don't know what you're talking about," said Bert, spreading his arms.

For Pete's sake. What kind of game was he playing?

"Charlotte saw you at the play last weekend," she said shortly.

Bert blinked, then a broad smile replaced his look of confusion.

Just what the hell did he think was so funny?

"That was Annabel, my cousin from Revelstoke," he said. "She was in town for work. Katherine Adele Williams, are you *jealous*?"

For the second time, she blushed. Then she shrugged.

"Don't be silly, Bert," she said gently. "I have nothing to be jealous of. You and I aren't together anymore."

Suddenly he reached across the desk, placed a hand on either side of her face, and pulled her into a kiss. Her hands found the desk to keep from toppling into him. She became intensely aware of the heat of his body, the roughness of his hands on her face, the firmness of his lips on hers. By the time he finished kissing her, she was breathless and flustered. Before she could say anything, he released her and stood back, spearing her with his gaze.

"Kate, I don't know what's going to happen to me, or how much time I have left. All I know is that whatever time I have left, I want to spend with you. Now I want to know how you feel."

Still flustered by the kiss, Kate suddenly wished they were anywhere else but her office. She took a deep breath, reminding herself of all her arguments against continuing the relationship, but when she finally spoke, she was surprised by what came out of her mouth.

"You have some nerve questioning my judgment."

Bert blinked in confusion.

"What?"

"At Amanda's party. You accused me of compromising the investigation."

This time, he blushed.

"Oh, that," he muttered. "I saw that damned vet touching you. I think I may have lost perspective."

She stared at him. In spite of everything, she felt a smile tugging at her lips. "Why, Bertram Russell Langdon, were you *jealous*?"

His face turned brick red and he shrugged.

"Unappealing, I know, but at least we can be unappealing together."

She laughed and he grinned shamefacedly at her.

"Now will you please come over here so I can give you a proper kiss?" he asked plaintively.

In the two seconds it took her to round the desk and ease into his arms, she decided that yes, she was willing to take whatever life gave her—one day or thirty years. She would take what she could get, and so would Bert.

When they finally came up for air, Kate became aware of voices raised in laughter in the duty room. She disentangled herself from Bert and rearranged her hair and clothing before opening the door. There was nothing she could do about the color in her cheeks, however.

She emerged from her office, with Bert right behind her, to find Rob McKell standing fresh and crisp in his uniform in the middle of the duty room, surrounded by Charlotte, O'Hara, and Holmes. They all looked around as Kate and Bert approached.

Kate looked McKell up and down and raised an eyebrow questioningly.

He shrugged self-deprecatingly.

"Paterson told me she wouldn't be coming in for a few days, so it seemed like the right time to come back." He suddenly turned serious. "If that's all right, of course."

Kate struggled to keep from grinning and pasted a stern expression on her face.

"Do you think you can remember what the job is, or do I have to retrain you?"

Holmes and Charlotte laughed outright and even O'Hara grinned before turning away to answer the phone.

As she smiled at her DC, Kate felt Bert standing behind her, ready for whatever came next.

THE END

ABOUT THE AUTHOR

Marcelle Dubé writes mystery, science fiction, fantasy and contemporary fiction. She grew up near Montreal and. after trying out a number of different provinces (not to mention Belgium), she settled in the Yukon, where people outnumber carnivores, but not by much.

Her short stories have appeared in magazines and award-winning anthologies. Her novels include *Ghosts of Morocco, Shelter* and the Mendenhall Mysteries series.

To find out more about her, visit:
www.marcellemdube.com

NOVELS BY THE AUTHOR

Mendenhall Mysteries series:

The Shoeless Kid
The Tuxedoed Man
The Weeping Woman
The Untethered Woman
The Forsaken Man

Backli's Ford
Ghosts of Morocco
Jilimar
Kirwan's Son
Obeah
On Her Trail
Shelter